> **"I'm a Rakan v...**
> **for a living. I'm no...**
> **afraid of Ee...**

"You look about as scary as a warm bowl of honey," he said. "And don't even get me started on your mouth."

"What about my mouth?" I asked.

"It's a two-hundred-dollars-an-hour mouth, not a tell-me-all-your-secrets-or-I'll-kill-you mouth."

I smiled slowly. "Win our bet, and I'll let you have my mouth for free."

"Agreed. But get ready, cookie, because I want your mouth all over me."

Gena Showalter features alien huntress Mia Snow in her acclaimed novel AWAKEN ME DARKLY

BOOKS BY GENA SHOWALTER

Awaken Me Darkly

Enslave Me Sweetly

Savor Me Slowly

Seduce the Darkness

Ecstasy in Darkness

Dark Taste of Rapture

Deep Kiss of Winter

Last Kiss Goodnight

Black and Blue

ENSLAVE ME
SWEETLY

GENA SHOWALTER

POCKET BOOKS

New York   London   Toronto   Sydney   New Delhi

Pocket Books
A Division of Simon & Schuster, Inc.
1230 Avenue of the Americas
New York, NY 10020

This book is a work of fiction. Any references to historical events, real people, or real places are used fictitiously. Other names, characters, places, and events are products of the author's imagination, and any resemblance to actual events or places or persons, living or dead, is entirely coincidental.

This Pocket Books paperback edition October 2013

POCKET and colophon are registered trademarks of Simon & Schuster, Inc.

For information about special discounts for bulk purchases, please contact Simon & Schuster Special Sales at 1-866-506-1949 or business@simonandschuster.com.

The Simon & Schuster Speakers Bureau can bring authors to your live event. For more information or to book an event contact the Simon & Schuster Speakers Bureau at 1-866-248-3049 or visit our website at www.simonspeakers.com.

Manufactured in the United States of America

10 9 8 7 6 5 4 3 2 1

ISBN 978-1-4767-5300-3
ISBN 978-1-4165-2298-0 (ebook)

To Jill Monroe, who said, "If you're going to name her Eden, you might as well let her smell like Paradise."

To Sheila Fields, who said, "She's a killer. So what. Nothing wrong with enjoying a job well done."

To P. C. Cast, who said, "Someone should write a book about a man with a forked penis."

People often ask me where I get my ideas. Well, I blame the lovely ladies mentioned above. Without them, this book would have been about a depressed assassin who smells like sterile air cleaner when she happens upon a man with a normal penis. Thanks, ladies.

ENSLAVE ME
SWEETLY

CHAPTER

1

As I lay in the rafters of the Old West Cattle Co., surrounded by dust, shadows, and the smell of stale hay, anticipation raced through me. I cradled an A-7 pyre-rifle in my hands, the barrel aimed at a steep angle. Below me, several halogens hung strategically from the walls, giving me the visibility I needed, but at the same time shielding me from view. No one wanted to stare up at those harsh lights.

To be honest, I didn't like staring down at them.

The warehouse boasted no furniture for my target to hide behind. Only people (human and alien), dirty floors, and weapons. Right now, a crowd of other-worlders teased and taunted two naked, whimpering females banded to the far wall. The bastards who weren't participating were watching, waiting their turn. My anticipation for the kill increased, and I gripped my gun tighter. The tormentors were having such a lovely time, but *my* fun would come when I broke up the party with a few rounds of deadly fire.

See, I'm paid by the government to destroy other-worlders so vile, so disgusting, they can't take a chance alien rights advocates will get involved in the case. I'm not AIR, Alien Investigation and Removal. I'm worse.

Just a little longer, Eden. Information first. Kill second. EenLi (my target) and his compadres were abducting humans and shipping them off-planet to sell as slaves. I needed to know where they were storing the human "cargo" before deportation. More than that, I needed to know how they were hopping from one planet to another.

Oh, I knew they were using interworld portals—the same portals they'd used to invade our planet. I just didn't know where or how to find these portals.

I should have known exactly where they were. I'm an alien. A Rakan. A golden one, some humans call us, because our hair, skin, and eyes are embedded with diamond-flecked gold. But I was conceived here and raised by a human. The portals are as much a mystery to me as they are to every other Earth-born.

One of the women screamed, slicing into my thoughts. A man was pinching and twisting her nipples, laughing at the pain and panic he inflicted. My finger twitched on the trigger. *Hold. Hold.*

Tonight I'm going to prove I'm as capable as any

man—as any human. Over the years I've been delegated the easy marks, the ones requiring no more skill than a blind man in a virtual game. Since my father is also my boss, he's the reason for my lack of hard-core cases. I know he hopes to protect me, but I'm long past the need.

My success tonight is critical. I took this case against his wishes, and I would not fail.

I had my target in sight: EenLi Kati, a.k.a. John Wayne and Wayne Johnson. He was a thirty-something Mec, average height, with eerie, narrow white eyes. We didn't know a lot about Mecs, only that they had some control over the weather and preferred hot, dry climates.

Like every Mec, EenLi possessed opalescent skin that glowed different colors with different emotions. He was the leader of this elusive group, and right now his skin glowed bright red. The bastard was pissed.

Dressed like a desperado from the past—hat, boots, and spurs—he stood in a shadowed corner, arguing fiercely with another Mec known as Mris-ste. The latter wore boots and spurs, but had opted not to wear a hat. Who did they think they were fooling? Cowboys. Please.

They spoke in their native tongue—a halting, guttural rhetoric of clipped syllables and high-pitched timbres. Languages were one of my specialties, and I'd mastered this one years ago. As I listened, I managed to pick up words like *bodies*, *profit*, and *underground*.

Technically my assignment is to eliminate EenLi. However, I'm going to do Mris-ste for free. A bonus, if you will. At the thought, my lips curled into a half smile. The two men had been working together for over a year. No telling how many males and females they'd raped. No telling how many people they'd enslaved.

I drew in a measured breath, then slowly and calmly released every molecule of air. Sharp, spiky splinters from the old wooden rafters dug past my shirt and into my belly, but that wasn't the worst of my discomfort. The air was stifling and hot, and it didn't help that I wore military fatigues and a face mask. The heat wave blasting through New Dallas had yet to dissipate—probably because of the Mecs. Sweat pooled between my shoulder blades and ran down my back.

I yearned to spirit-walk just then, to force my consciousness out of my body so I could leave my body behind and walk unnoticed, *invisible*, below. Like a ghost. A phantom. I had killed many of my targets like that, but I only did so when my body was totally and completely protected. Otherwise, I was left physically vulnerable because I couldn't do my job and guard my body at the same time.

Just then EenLi's cell unit erupted in a series of beeps, and he barked an irritated "What?" into the receiver. I couldn't hear the voice on the other end, but whatever was said caused the otherworlder's spine to stiffen and his fingers to clench into fists.

One heartbeat of time passed. Two.

As he continued to listen, he removed his hat and swirled the gray felt between his fingers. Give the man a pony and ask him to shout "Yee haw." That's all the scene lacked. By the time he returned his hat to his shiny, bald head, his skin pulsed so brightly red, I wanted to shade my eyes.

Finally, he replaced the unit in his back pocket. Then, growling low in his throat, he shoved Mris-ste, propelling the hatless Mec backward. The latter man's long, dark hair (obviously a wig) danced around his shoulders.

"Tell me you moved the tainted cattle from the Pit," EenLi shouted. "Tell me you have not screwed this up yet again."

The pit. The pit. I rolled the phrase through my mind. An image quickly clicked into place, and I frowned. The Pit was a local bar known for its criminal patrons, druggies and whores who bought their way into oblivion. Could that be the place under discussion?

"Well, I—they have been moved," the other man offered, righting himself. "I am not so stupid that I would leave the sick in cells with the healthy."

Cells . . . I'd followed EenLi inside the bar just two days ago, but he had never left the main area. Had never even gone to the bathroom. I hadn't noticed any doorways leading to other rooms. The cells could be hidden. Or underground. Very, very interesting.

"Do you want to know who just called me, Mris-ste? Pablo. He found two of our cattle dead in their cells. They'd obviously been sick, and you left them there."

"I . . . I . . ." Mris-ste's opalescent skin began to pulse with blue. Even without the distinctive shading, the alien would have reeked of fear.

"How many died in the move?" EenLi demanded.

"Three," came the shaky reply.

This enraged EenLi further. His scowl turned black. "We were to deliver twelve. Not seven. You idiot!"

"I am sorry."

"Your sorry doesn't bring my cattle back to life. If one more is lost, just one more, I will sell your worthless hide to make up the difference."

Mris-ste shook off the threat with a nervous laugh. "We will not lose any more. This I swear. I gave the sick to Rose. She will care for them until they are well."

I knew Rose. Sahara Rose, human. Twenty-six years old. Blond hair. Blue eyes. I'd trailed her for a few days after taking this case. She was a known alien sympathizer and had spent many nights in EenLi's bed. I knew where she lived, what kind of car she drove, and what brand of vaginal lubricant she secretly used whenever her lover visited. And, of course, I now knew she was hiding some of the missing humans.

"There is no time to find more cattle," EenLi said. "The portal opens in one day."

The portals weren't always open? I'd always assumed aliens traveled through whenever they wanted. *Tell me where they are . . . tell me where they are . . .*

He didn't.

EenLi soon changed the subject, and the two men actually began discussing how to dress the female slaves. Information I didn't need.

It was time.

I preferred close kills to shots fired over a long distance. Nothing wrong with enjoying the fruits of my labor up close and personal. Sauntering into the middle of all those men, however, significantly decreased my odds of success. I'd stay here.

My anticipation renewed as I closed one eye, my face mask and powered autoscope narrowing my field of vision. Still locked on target? Check. Disposable silencer in place? Check.

I knew I had one chance to nail him. Just one. Because the moment I fired, everyone below me would whip into action, aiming and firing their own weapons straight at *me*.

EenLi began to pace in front of Mris-ste as he expounded on the merits of stiletto heels and *kristales*, jewel stones brought over from Mecca. I kept my barrel still. My pyre-rifle produced heat-sensitive fire bullets, and those would follow him straight into hell.

One. He moved away from Mris-ste.

Two. He turned, facing Mris-ste.

Three. He stepped into my line of fire, and I squeezed the trigger.

A whiz. A scream. The big, bad Mec went down like a depressurized hovercraft, his hat rolling off his head like tumbleweed. Only it was the wrong Mec. This one had thick brown hair. I stilled. No. *No!* My fire bullet had slammed into Mris-ste. Not EenLi.

When had EenLi given him the hat? When the hell had EenLi given him the hat? I'd watched them. Once I'd locked on target, I hadn't lost my focus.

Shock bubbled inside me as the men below cursed and shouted, scrambling for their guns. Bullets and blue fire launched in my direction, raining like deadly hail. Remaining calm, focused, I dropped my rifle and grabbed the thick wire beside me, already anchored to a sturdy beam. Then I jumped. I kept one hand clasped to the metal handle that allowed my downward slide, and used the other to whip out the pyre-gun strapped to my waist, dialed to kill.

I started firing.

As I descended, a bullet cut into my left forearm. I didn't stop, didn't even slow down. The determination rushing through my veins muted the fiery sensation of being shot to a sharp sting. Oh, I knew I would feel it later—in full force.

I wished I had time to doctor up. The longer the slug remained inside my body, the more damage it would do to me. Earth metals act as a deadly poison to me. To all of my kind. But the mission came first.

I had to finish this. Fast. Maintaining my inner balance, I continued shooting, not taking time to aim, but simply allowing a continuous stream of fire to discharge; the blue beams of molten heat spewing from my gun lit up the warehouse like a nuclear war.

The moment my feet hit the ground, I released the wire and reached for my other gun. With both of my hands armed, I scanned from left to right, taking in every detail.

EenLi was gone. Gone! He must have hit the door running the second Mris-ste fell. I couldn't chase him down, not pinned in by gunfire like I was. That meant . . .

I'd failed.

My shock grew, almost freezing me in place, but I kept firing. Kept moving. Bile rose in my throat. I'd truly failed. I'd missed my target and allowed him to stroll from the building as happy as he pleased.

I failed echoed continuously through my mind.

I shook my head in disbelief. All I could do now was get the two women and myself out of here alive.

No, I thought in the next instant. I was taking down any man who'd been stupid enough to stay. My gaze scanned the area again. Five aliens remained inside the warehouse, their bullets and fire spraying all around me. Calculating the distance between them and the chained women, I started running forward.

Right at them. I cringed when another bullet struck me. Twenty feet. Not much, but enough to risk what I was about to do.

I dropped one of my weapons and reached for a mini grenade in my side pouch. In one fluid motion, I pulled the firing pin with my teeth, tossed it, and dove to the ground.

Boom!

The impact threw me backward, slamming me into a wall. Air shoved from my lungs. When I was able to breathe, dirt and ash bypassed my mask and filled my nostrils. Instinctively, I covered my face with my hands as fiery wood chips rained. Then, several minutes passed in silence. No return fire. No screams or moans.

When I looked up, all five Mecs were strewn across the ground, lifeless. The human women were bloody and bruised, but alive. They were— No, I realized then. Only one of them was alive. The blonde. The other, the one with curling red hair, had been caught in the crossfire and stared out at the charred warehouse through lifeless eyes.

My eyelids squeezed shut, and I let my head sink into my hands again. The atmosphere was thick, hot, and laden with smoke. I needed to drag in a deep breath, to fill my lungs with oxygen, but didn't dare.

There was no help for it, no other choice; I had to call my father. With shaky hands, I tugged out my cell unit and said, "Boss," taking comfort in the sound of the automatic dial.

I trusted this man with my life. He was the one who had found me as a small child, alone and lost on the streets after my parents died. I don't know why he'd taken me in, and I couldn't ask him. He stiffened every time I brought up that horrible night. But he'd raised me, loved me, and trained me to be an assassin just like himself.

And I had just let him down.

He answered after two rings. "What happened?" were the first words he spoke, his raspy voice upbeat. He clearly expected me to give him the usual "all went well" report. Over and over he'd advised me not to take this case. When he'd realized he couldn't talk me out of it, he'd followed me here "just in case I needed him."

Most important information first. "The target is on the run. I've got one human casualty, another wounded." My self-disgust rang loud and clear in my tone.

"How in the hell," Michael, my father, said haltingly, "did that happen?"

"I don't know. I had him locked. I fired, and the next thing I knew, he'd switched places with his partner."

"How?"

"I don't know," I repeated.

"Damn it, Eden F." He only called me that when he was mad, or seriously worried. "I told you not to take this case. I told you to leave it alone."

"I'm sorry," I said on a ragged breath. And I was. Because of my failure, a human slaver was even now roaming free. Worse, he knew he was being hunted. He'd be more careful now. I'd just screwed the entire operation. "I think some of the slaves are in cells inside the Pit. It's a bar on the east side of town." I opened my mouth to tell him the rest, but my mind went blank. A thick fog covered my thoughts. I blinked, shook my head and beckoned them back. "Some are with a human, Sahara Rose."

"I'll put a man on it. You bring the survivor to me. Damn it," he snarled again and disconnected.

Silence greeted me. And in the silence, I noticed that the throbbing in my arm had increased. I looked down. Though my vision was clouding, I studied the gaping, oozing wound. The bullet had done more damage than I'd thought. I was losing blood fast. Too fast.

Fighting past the pain and weakness, I pushed to my feet. My knees wobbled, and my bones liquefied, and neither showed any sign of improving. Even my stomach battled a sharp pain. I stumbled over to the woman. She flinched as I reached out and cut her free. Then she sank to the splinter-sharp ground and sobbed, her dirty hair covering her naked shoulders. I tried not to think about the other one, the one who wouldn't go home this night or any other.

The crossbow strapped to my back suddenly weighed me down like a concrete block, and the ache in my stomach intensified. It was becoming harder and harder to breathe.

A wave of dizziness assaulted me, heavy and strangely seductive . . . lulling me to the ground beside the woman. When our arms touched, she uttered a terrified gasp and hastily scooted away. Her movements were so jerky, she flung dirt onto my legs. I wanted to comfort her, but my mouth refused to form the right words.

What the hell was wrong with my stomach? Slowly, so slowly, I lifted my shirt. There, just below my ribs, was another bloody, gaping wound. When had I received that? I hadn't even felt the bullet go in. Wait. Yes, I had. When I'd run with the mini-grenade. Damn.

I set aside my cell unit and reached inside my pouch, withdrawing a thin silver Extractor. Bracing myself for what I was about to do, I bit my bottom lip, centered all of my strength, and jabbed the damn thing into my stomach wound. Instantly the metal-sensitive prongs elongated and probed for the bullet. A scream ripped from me.

How much time passed before the small, round tip was removed, I didn't know. I only knew desperation, pain. And fear. I wasn't ready to die. Not here. Not now. I laughed humorlessly. Not as a failure.

Concentrate. I had to concentrate. Though I craved a moment's rest, a single moment to close my eyes, I repeated the entire process, shoving the now bloody device into my forearm. When I pulled out the last bullet, my shoulders sagged in relief. Distantly, I heard the woman crying.

Quickly losing energy, I found the syringe in my pouch and injected myself in the heart with pure molybdenum to slow the spread of copper or brass or whatever the bullets were made of. Searing pain erupted. I screamed again, long and loud, until my vocal cords cracked.

The now-empty syringe fell from my suddenly limp fingers. I hurt everywhere, but a comforting lethargy was already working through me. A minute, maybe less, and I'd be out.

I reached blindly for my cell unit, my fingers somehow closing around it. "Boss," I said. The word emerged so weak and broken, I experienced a moment's surprise when the phone began to automatically dial.

He answered on the fifth ring this time. "What?"

"I'm hit."

"It just gets better every time you call," he said, his sarcasm heavy. I caught the thick undercurrent of concern, however. "Can you make it to the safe house?"

"I'll . . ." A murky web of darkness wove through my mind, blackening my eyesight, paralyzing my muscles. "Try."

Oblivion seized me in its demanding grip.

CHAPTER
2

I was floating.

No, not floating, I realized a second later. Strong male arms cradled me tightly, securely. The scent of pine and man wafted to my nostrils, and male strength radiated all around me. Someone was carrying me. Who? Why? A thick, smoky cloud blanketed and scattered my thoughts, keeping the answers just beyond my grasp.

"Is she going to make it?" someone asked. I recognized the broken, concerned voice. Michael, my boss. My father.

"Don't know," a second man said. I didn't recognize his voice at all. The timbre was deeper, more raw than any I'd ever heard before. So distant, so uncaring. "She's lost a lot of blood."

Both voices seemed to drift from a dream, surreal and remote. Which man held me? My father or the stranger? Probably the stranger. My rescuer emitted a kind of heat far different from any I'd ever encountered before. His warmth seeped into me, as soothing and gentle as a lullaby.

"We need to cut these clothes off her," the stranger said. "Get her out of the mask so she can breathe."

"Wait till we get her in the car." Michael's tone broke further, was more hurried. He always freaked when I was injured. Even the smallest scratch undid him.

Minutes passed. Maybe hours. I didn't know, didn't care. Time had long since become immeasurable. All I had was the solid embrace of my rescuer, but even that was soon denied me as my body was eased to the cool ground. Hands tugged and ripped my clothing, causing my wounds to throb. I gasped as air kissed my bare skin. In the next instant, the mask was jerked from my face.

Someone sucked in a breath, and it wasn't me. Then . . . silence.

"Shit," the stranger exhaled, his tone laced with . . . awe?

Fingers coasted gently over my cheekbone, then through my hair, comforting and soft. Sleep . . . I'd sleep a little longer.

I'd missed EenLi. I'd failed.

Over and over, those words echoed in my mind. I'd missed EenLi. I'd failed.

His smug face drifted into my thoughts, shimmering just beyond my consciousness. I reached for a pyre-gun, but managed to grab cool, soft sheets instead. The events in the warehouse flashed, playing out like an old video. The gunshots. The blood. The blinding pain. Is that why I felt so empty and hollow, like a nocturnal phantom whisking from cloud to cloud?

EenLi's image wavered, then disappeared. I raced after him, but my limbs were suspended in motion, and I remained in place. He laughed. The sound taunted me.

You're a failure, Eden. A failure. I'd had one job. Just one. And he had walked away from me without a single scratch.

When aliens first arrived almost a hundred years ago, humans had tried to destroy them all. They almost destroyed themselves instead, or so I've been told. To survive, a sort of peace was reached between the different races on the condition that agents be allowed to kill predatory otherworlders. My target had been predatory, no doubt about it. I should have destroyed him, but I'd let him get away.

Failure, failure. Failure. The word rang in my head and jarred me awake. My eyelids popped open. A gasp lodged in my throat. Deep breath in. Deep breath out.

I lay still for several moments, trying to calm my racing heartbeat. Shadows enveloped me. No, wait.

Small streams of moonlight danced from the window, revealing a lacy canopy and high, vaulted ceiling. Where was I? I struggled to turn my head, to scan the rest of my surroundings, but my muscles refused to obey, keeping me in the same chin-up position. Using all of my energy, I tried again.

Still nothing.

What was going on? Why couldn't I move? Sparks of panic lit inside me but were quickly extinguished by confusion. I heard the beep-beep of . . . something. Smelled the sharp tang of antiseptic. On a wave of relief, my shoulders sagged into the softness of the mattress beneath me. A hospital. I must be in a hospital.

Relaxed now, I licked my lips, realizing my mouth felt dry and cottony. Thirsty. I was so thirsty. My tongue flicked out, moistening my parched lips. "Thirsty," I croaked out.

No one was there. No one could hear me.

"Thirsty," I gasped again.

Perhaps a heartbeat later, a man stood beside my bed. I couldn't make out his features, only that he was tall and muscular. A drugging warmth radiated from him and slid along my body. I wanted to turn toward him, sink into him. Inside him. I shivered.

"Where's Michael?" I asked.

"Sleeping. Finally. Here," he said, his deep, raw voice familiar to me. He held a cup and straw to me.

I drank deeply, the cool, sweet liquid flowing down my throat. Never had anything tasted so wondrous.

"That's enough," he said and tugged the straw from my mouth. "Sleep now."

A direct order. His tone left no room for argument. Usually I didn't respond well to that type of "do what I say or suffer the consequences" command. This time, however, I was too tired to argue.

I closed my eyes. The last thought to drift through my mind was, *I'll instruct that man on how best to speak to me tomorrow.*

"Wake up."

The strong, determined voice prodded at me relentlessly.

"Wake up."

A callused hand shook me, working in sync with the voice. Evil. They were both evil and deserved to die a horrible death.

"Wake up, sweetie."

I attempted to roll over and bury my head in my pillow, but my sore, tired limbs resisted. That caught my attention in a way nothing else could have. I jerked at my arm. Nothing. I kicked out my leg. Nothing. Panic rushed through me, and I struggled to open my eyes.

"That's my girl," the man said, relief heavy in his tone.

Stark white light pounded into the room, its unwelcome fists leaving nothing untouched. Too bright, I thought, squinting, still struggling. But slowly, very slowly, my eyes adjusted. My gaze locked on the

glowing restraints that bound me, on the plain white
T-shirt I wore and the white silk sheet that covered my
lower half. Then I narrowed my gaze on my uninvited
guest. Michael Black. My boss. My adopted father.

The panic dissipated completely, leaving me weak,
and I settled back into the auto-adjust mattress, my
spine stiff with anger.

Every line of Michael's handsome face was etched
with concern, from his piercing hazel eyes to his
broad, unsmiling mouth. His graying hair, usually
styled perfectly, fell in disarray around his temples,
and his expensive suit possessed more wrinkles than
a Genesi.

"Why am I banded?" I asked, my vocal cords
hoarse. Bands were stronger than handcuffs and could
not be removed without severing an appendage. They
bonded to alien skin, locking the prisoner in place.

"You were thrashing uncontrollably, which kept
opening your wounds."

"Unband me. Now." I gave the order, making
sure there were no emotions in my tone. I would not
show weakness. Not to this man who seemed to have
no weaknesses himself. But Michael knew me better
than anyone, and he knew I didn't like the feeling of
helplessness. I never had. Besides, I doubted I had the
strength to move upon threat of death, so the bonds
were unnecessary.

He did as I requested, pressing an ID button and
causing the lasers to unwind from my skin. He settled

back into the plush azure chair beside the bed. "How are you feeling?"

"Good," I said, surprised that I meant it. Except for a sense of weakness, fragility, and the dull ache in my side, I remained mostly unscathed. "Thirsty, though. Will you get me some sugar water?"

A cup was perched on the nightstand, and he handed it to me. I downed the cool, sweet contents and closed my eyes in surrender. Sugar acts as a revitalizing agent for my kind. Though there aren't many Rakans left, the ones that are here are probably responsible for consuming three-fourths of the earth's annual sugar crop.

"That copper really worked you over," he said.

"It always does." I scanned the room. Thick crimson and navy carpet adorned the floor, and several imperial gold floor lamps climbed toward the arched ceiling. There were three open windows, the holographic shade turned off. The walls boasted bronze stucco and ornately carved, gilded mirrors. Obviously, this was not a hospital. Even my coverlet shouted wealth. Soft emerald velvet and white silk sheets surrounded my skin in a delicious cocoon.

"Where am I?" I asked.

"My house."

That told me nothing. The man owned estates all over the world. "Which one?"

"New Mexico. Closest one to New Dallas."

"You redecorated since I was last here."

He nodded.

I arched a brow. "Would you care to tell me why I'm here instead of a hospital?" There were special hospitals specifically designed for agents like me: paid killers, as well as alien. I'd been a patient numerous times.

"One, you were delirious and I didn't want anyone to hear the things that you were saying. You were moaning and groaning about your failure with EenLi. I want everyone to think you let him go on purpose. Two, I didn't want your name on record as having received gunshot wounds. And three, I didn't want anyone else brought in on this case."

Though I was glad, I sighed deeply. I would have liked him to be able to sit back and simply bask in my success, no interference required. "Playing my protector again, Michael?"

He shrugged, but glanced away. "Actually, *my* boss thinks this situation works out for the best. EenLi used to work as an agent, and he—"

"What?" I blinked. Surely I had misheard.

"EenLi used to work as an agent. For me, specifically."

I tried not to gape. "Why am I just now hearing about this?"

He shrugged again, the action stiffer, more clipped. "He was supposed to be an in-and-out job. I tell you what you need to know, and that was something you didn't need to know."

"A target's training *is* a need to know. He probably knew he was being watched the entire time."

"I doubt that," he said. "He was an okay agent. Good at finding people, which is why we kept him on, but not much else. He was too emotional, had too many vices. I guess that's why he decided to make more money selling slaves. End of story."

I closed my eyes for a brief moment. "So why is your boss glad he escaped?"

"The government now wants to know where those portals are, and they think EenLi will lead the way." Michael leaned back in his chair, watching me. "They've decided they don't want him dead until they know."

"I followed him for weeks. He never revealed a single portal's location."

"Orders are orders. He lives until he divulges how he's planet-traveling."

What if EenLi never gave the information they wanted? Did that mean the murdering criminal would get to live a long, happy life? I didn't voice my questions, though. Michael knew how I felt about law breakers. My gaze traveled the length of my T-shirt-and-sheet–clad body. I looked thinner. "How long have I been here?"

"Thirteen days, six hours, forty-eight minutes." He propped his expensive Italian loafers on the cherry wood nightstand. "I had everything you needed brought here."

"Even a doctor?" That would have totally defeated the purpose of keeping me here, out of the government's watchful eye.

"No," he said hesitantly.

I arched a brow. "Who patched me up?"

"Lucius Adaire."

"That tells me nothing. Who is he?"

"A man. A human."

My curiosity grew about this Lucius Adaire, and I studied Michael. Just the mention of this mystery man had caused the easy line of his posture to stiffen and a glimpse of uneasiness to enter his eyes.

Michael had seen the worst life had to offer—he'd even caused some of it—so he rarely became uneasy. Why now?

"Tell me about him," I prompted.

"In a minute," he said. He picked a piece of invisible lint off his pants. "You remember anything else about that night in the warehouse?"

The job came first, always. I didn't try to return to the conversation on my mysterious doctor. I centered my thoughts and replayed every minute I'd spent in that warehouse through my head. Then I leveled my gaze at Michael. "EenLi said a portal was going to open in a day. That day has already passed, of course, but that means the portals aren't always open, that he can only send his cattle, as he calls them, through on certain days."

"What opens them?"

"He never said."

Michael scowled. "Damn, we can't seem to catch a break. After I picked you up, I sent a group of men to the Pit. It was empty, top and bottom. There were cells underneath, but no one was in them."

My stomach knotted, and I scrubbed a hand down my face. "Was there evidence of recent use?"

"Makeshift toilets that hadn't been emptied. Manacles with dried blood—which we analyzed and cross-referenced with the victims' blood types. Every drop had an exact match."

"What about Sahara Rose?"

"Gone, her house abandoned. She packed in a hurry, that much was obvious."

"Wonderful," I muttered, almost afraid to ask my next question. But I had to. I needed all the facts. "What about the human woman at the warehouse? The survivor?"

Leaning back, he rested his hands behind his head and gazed up at the ceiling. His lips pressed tightly together as a long, protracted silence enveloped us. "You don't want to know," he said softly.

I pushed out a breath and shook my head in disgust—disgust with myself. With EenLi. "She's dead, isn't she?"

Michael nodded, his expression apologetic. "I'm sorry, sweetie. Her wounds were too extensive. She died before we got there."

I bit the inside of my cheek and fought back a razor-sharp crest of regret. "What was her name?"

"Don't torture yourself this way. You did what you could."

"What was her name?" I insisted.

"Amy," he supplied, reluctance heavy in his tone. "Amy Evens."

Amy Evens. She'd been young, probably no more than twenty-five, with pretty blond hair and wide blue eyes. Like every young woman, she'd probably dreamed of love and a happily ever after, yet she'd been raped, abused, and had died alone.

My disgust and hate for EenLi grew in intensity, but most of all, my disgust for myself grew. I was to protect the innocent; that was part of my job. I closed my eyes, hoping to block the images hovering there, images of both women alive and chained to the wall, neither knowing Death had knocked on her door. I'd failed in every way there was to fail. I had failed to kill my target; I hadn't even managed to save one human life.

These wounds of mine . . . I deserved every one of them and more. A resolution to make it right solidified within me. "What do we do now?" I asked, once again facing Michael.

"My guess is EenLi's still in New Dallas, putting together another crew. I want you to go there, find him, find those damn portals, and finish your job."

A moment passed before his words sunk deep enough inside me that I was able to respond. Shocked, I said, "You're letting me have another shot?"

"You know his MO better than anyone. You know his habits; you've studied him. Plus, I know you. You'll want a chance to fix this, and I love you enough that I want to give it to you."

"I—" I pressed my lips together. The fact that Michael trusted me enough to right my wrongs propelled a thrill of pride and happiness through me, and I had trouble finding the words to express my gratitude. I guess I'd assumed his protective instincts would surface, and he would command me to stay behind.

I truly loved this man.

"Do you think any of your agents are secretly working with EenLi?" I asked. "That would explain how EenLi knew to trade places with Mris-ste."

"I already have a man on it, so don't worry about it."

I nodded. "Thank you for giving me another chance," I said, allowing all of my appreciation to seep through my voice. "I know I don't deserve it. I'm not going to let you down."

"Don't thank me yet," he said wryly. "You'll be working with a partner."

What? "Absolutely not." Shock quickly replaced all of my happiness, and I jolted upright, winced, and glared over at him. "I work alone. Always."

"Not this time," he said, resolute. Final.

"I'm perfectly capable of finding the portals and killing EenLi on my own." I *needed* to do it on my own. I couldn't allow someone else to fix the mess I had created.

He crossed his arms over his chest and stared over at me. "Then why isn't he dead?"

That was entirely beside the point—even though he was right. "I will not work with one of your agents."

"Yes," he said calmly, assuredly, "you will. Lucius," he called without removing his gaze from me. "Come meet your new partner."

As if the man had been standing behind the entrance, guarding it, the thick metal doors instantly slid open. He strode stealthily inside, not emitting a single noise: not the swish of clothing, the plod of footsteps, or the rhythm of breath. He was as human as Michael, but where my boss was lean, this man was solid muscle. Where Michael was average height, this man was tall. Where Michael was aging, this man was all vitality.

He stopped at the foot of my bed. The scent of pine soap and sheer maleness wafted from him. He wasn't near enough to touch, but I could feel the warmth of his skin, beckoning me, lulling me. That warmth, that scent . . . I recognized them. A moment passed, and I sucked in a breath.

He was the one who had carried me. *He* was the one who had given me sugar water last night. *He* was the one who had stripped away my clothing. My stomach knotted at the thought of his hands on me, undressing me, seeing my naked flesh. A shiver of awareness fired down my spine.

His lips were soft and lush, as pink as flower petals. The rest of his features, however, were granite hard, boasting deliciously rough planes and harsh angles. Cheekbones carved from stone. A nose sculpted from steel. Black eyebrows slashed over his eyes, eyes so blue they could only have been created from ice chips, regarding the world with an I've-seen-it-all acerbity. Right now those eyes bore down at me, into me.

He wore a tight black T-shirt, the same inky color as his chopped hair and form-fitting jeans. Simply standing there, he exuded a masculine intensity that shouted, *I'll fuck you or kill you—take your pick.*

I suddenly felt vulnerable. Exposed. It didn't matter that I was covered by clothes and a sheet. I was lying in a bed; I was injured. And he knew what I looked like naked. More than that, I was not operating at full strength and probably resembled a sick tabby kitten, mussed and disheveled.

I forced a cool facade, hoping I exuded regal composure. I didn't know this man, and I didn't want him seeing me as anything less than controlled.

"Have you ever killed anyone, Sparkie?" I asked, hoping to put him on the defensive. He'd take over if I let him.

Not a glimmer of emotion lit his features. He remained in place, silent, unconcerned. Distant.

With a conscious effort, I tore my gaze from him and attempted to ignore his very existence. "I don't need or want a partner," I told Michael.

"Tough," he said, his expression hard.

"I work alone," I said again, my tone colder than ever before. I was surprised liquid nitrogen didn't spray from my mouth.

"Not anymore," he replied again.

"I will not—"

"Your protests will change nothing, sweetie. I want you to work with Lucius, and so you will. That's an order."

"He'll get in my way."

"He knows what he's doing."

"I doubt that. Men like him are all brawn and no brain. How can I do my job if I have to watch his back too?"

The man finally deigned to speak.

"Listen, *cookie*," he said, his voice rough, low, as if his vocal cords had once been damaged. "The day I need you to save my ass is the day I'll find myself a new job. Maybe cloning flowers. Maybe walking robotic dogs. I'll decide when the time comes. Until then, you take care of yourself, and I'll take care of you."

With that, he exited the room as quickly and silently as he'd entered.

The moment the door clicked shut, I pinned Michael with a fierce stare. "Did he just call me 'cookie'?"

Michael's lips twitched, and amusement turned his hazel eyes to a bright, vivid green. "You deserved it after that 'all brawn and no brain' crack."

"How can you expect me to work with that man?"

The twitching became a full-blown smile. "Consider it penance for your sins."

I didn't let his amusement soften me, though I did love to see him happy. "I'll tell you one more time, Michael. I don't need a partner." *Let me do this,* I silently beseeched.

Something deep and dark flashed across his features. "You'll work with him, or you'll work for another agency. Understand?"

He meant it. Michael never threatened. Only promised. And with it put like that, I couldn't refuse. I nodded stiffly. My hands fisted at my sides, but resolve slowly moved through me. "Can he do anything besides look pretty?" And tough.

"I guess you'll just have to wait and find out."

"That's comforting, Michael. Very comforting." I knew Michael, knew when he was turning stubborn. Anything I learned about Lucius, I'd have to learn on my own.

He sighed. "If you're on edge with him, you're less likely to make mistakes with him."

How wonderful to hand out little gems of wisdom at a time like this. Thanks. For nothing. "Any other bits of ingenious ramblings you want to toss my way before I kick you out and get some rest?"

"Yeah." He chuckled. He always liked when I reverted to my old spoiled-princess ways. "I want you operating at full capacity in three days. Otherwise, I'll let Lucius have the mission."

He left me alone then. With his parting words, he had sealed my fate. I'd be back in fighting shape within *two* days and not a moment more. Whether it was feminine pride or simple arrogance, I would not let Lucius find any satisfaction in taking what was mine.

I still had something to prove. More now than ever.

I would not be a failure. Not again.

"'Cookie,' my ass," I muttered.

CHAPTER
3

Later that night I forced myself out of bed. My muscles screamed in protest, but I managed to stay upright. The white T-shirt I wore hit my knees, leaving the rest of my golden legs bare. Darkness and moonlight mingled together, offering a hazy cocoon. Only silence touched the air. The rest of the house slept peacefully.

My movements slow and halting, I maneuvered down the mahogany staircase and into Michael's office. I loved this room, with its intricately carved desk, the high shelves filled with real books—not the holobooks sold in stores—and the fresh scent of leather. I traced my fingertip over the world globe, over the maps of the universe lining the walls. Over the chessboard. Michael and I had spent many nights in this room, talking and laughing. Strategizing.

No time for reminiscing, girl. Get to work. I plopped

into the plush chair behind the desk. After bypassing his ID scans and voice-activated computer—just like he'd taught me—I searched for a file on Lucius Adaire.

All information had been permanently deleted. I wasn't surprised. Michael didn't want me to know about Lucius, so of course he'd removed every piece of information. Smart man, my father.

Frustrated and overtaxed, I slipped back inside my room. I needed a few hours sleep before morning arrived. Just before I reached the four-poster bed, however, I stilled. I was not alone. I sensed heat, smelled pine.

My eyes narrowed on my uninvited guest. Looking casual and unconcerned, Lucius lounged in the padded chair beside the bed. I scowled over at him.

"Find anything?" he asked smugly, as if he knew what I'd been doing.

I didn't bother answering him. I climbed onto the bed, the mattress adjusting to my weight, and closed my eyes, though I remained alert. The covers were warm and soft, a soothing caress against my skin.

"What do you think you're doing?" he demanded.

"Sleeping. You're welcome to stay and watch like the pervert I'm sure you are."

"I don't think so. Get up." Leaning toward me, he reached out and shook my shoulders none too gently. "Get dressed. We train."

A man of few words. How quaint. "You want to

pretend to be my physical therapist and give me a massage, I'll let you touch my shoulders. Other than that, keep your hands to yourself. Got it?"

"Not a morning person?"

"I'll let you know in the morning. For now, I'm resting. Get out."

"Are you always this bitchy?"

I didn't take time to find my calm center. I simply came up swinging, jerking myself into a sitting position and letting my fist fly. I nailed him in the jaw. His chin didn't even turn, but I winced on impact. His bones were more solid than steel, and I wasn't at optimum strength.

Had he had enough time to stop me completely? Probably. Had he had enough time to move away? Most assuredly. My movements were slower than usual, my reflexes dulled.

A glimmer of humor lit his eyes, making the blue appear almost purple. "Get your ass out of bed. In the shape you're in, otherworlders will eliminate *you*, not the other way around. I'll meet you in the basement gym in half an hour."

"Get out of my room."

"Half an hour," he said. "Don't be late."

When I heard the doors close, I forced myself out of bed. I felt sorer now than I had been five minutes ago. I blamed Lucius, of course. But damn if I didn't look forward to training with him. I loved a challenge. In my current state, I probably couldn't beat him. I could do a lot of damage, though, I thought, grinning.

I saturated my wounds with a cyanoacrylate adhesive—a superglue for injuries—and took a lingering shower, luxuriating in the steaming, rose-scented liquid. Most people had to bathe with dry enzyme and glyceride spray. Michael could afford water, thank God. Showering was almost a hobby of mine.

I'd been told Raka was a planet with more water than land. Perhaps bathing was something all Rakans enjoyed. If my parents had survived their night of terror, I could have asked them. Would have given anything to ask them. A pang of remorse hit me, just as it always did when I thought of my parents. I missed them terribly.

When I climbed out of the tub, I felt more limber, less awkward. I glanced at the wall clock. Three forty-five. I couldn't help but smile. Thirty-*three* minutes had passed since Lucius had ordered me to be in the gym. I imagined him pacing, waiting impatiently for me.

Reaching up, and experiencing only a slight twinge in my side, I secured the length of my gold hair from my face and rummaged through a dresser filled with clothes. In all of his homes, Michael kept a room and wardrobe just for me. I donned a red sports bra and matching spandex shorts.

My stomach growled. I'd had nothing more substantial than sugar water in days. As I entered the kitchen, the smooth, marble tile was cold against my bare feet. Real coffee, not the synthetic blend, simmered in the silver pot sitting on the platinum countertop, saturating the air with a thick, caffeinated aroma. I wrinkled my nose in distaste. How anyone could drink that crap, I didn't know.

With the press of a few buttons, a turkey sandwich slid onto the counter hatch. I sprinkled it with sugar and managed to eat half before my stomach protested.

Forty-nine minutes had passed.

I finally sauntered my way into the basement gym. I was grinning.

Lucius was there, pounding away at the punching bag, looking sexy as hell. How annoying. With his irritating personality, he should be ugly. Hideous. His bronzed skin stretched taut over muscles and sinew. Several scars laced his ribcage. Sweat glistened and traced small rivulets down his bare chest and back, catching in the waist of his black shorts. He didn't spare me a glance.

I spent the next two hours stretching on the mat and centering my energy, forcing my body past the barriers my injuries had set. At times, I found myself unsteady and shaky. A good shaky, though. The kind that let me know I was alive. I'm sure Lucius would have preferred I made use of the weights, maybe the virtual boxing ring.

Usually, I did train in the ring. I didn't want to go

that route today. Instead, I pranced off the mat and to the bar across the far wall. I stretched one leg up, glancing over at Lucius. I nearly gasped when I realized he was watching me, his eyes heated and intense.

My gaze slitted on him. "Enjoying yourself?"

"Let's practice," he barked. "If you think you can handle me."

"I've been handling men like you for years, Sparkie."

A muscle ticked in his temple. "Let's get a few things straight, *cookie*. You don't like me and I don't like you. You don't want a partner, and I sure as hell don't need one—especially an arrogant female otherworlder with no talent that I can see."

"Then why did you agree to work with me?" I ground out.

"A paycheck is a paycheck, baby, and your daddy is paying out the ass to have me here."

"We're paid by the government, *baby*. Get your facts straight."

His lips pursed, and he cut off his next words.

"At least you got the better end of the deal," I muttered.

"How's that?" He arched a brow. "You failed your last mission, and I've succeeded every damn time."

I worked my jaw in irritation. Like I really needed a reminder of my failure. Like it wasn't front and center in my mind, even in my dreams. "In all my years as an agent, that's my only failure. One I plan to rectify."

"You've succeeded at easy cases, sugar. That's nothing to be proud of."

Bastard. "Have you even made a single kill?"

"If you have to ask, you're not a good judge of character."

Cold, hard death gleamed in his eyes, speaking of innumerable kills. My hands clenched at my sides. "I've made kills, too. Many, in fact."

"I'm curious," he said. "How did you eliminate those targets of yours? Annoy them to death?"

Scowling, I closed the distance between us until we were nose to nose. Our breath mingled, and I could feel the vibration of his strength. I could not seem to hold my usual cool facade with this man. I responded to him whether I wanted to or not. "Why annoy them when I can use my knife—when I can take a human like you, cut you up, and sauté you for breakfast?"

He studied me for a long, silent moment, his eyes raking over my curves with heated intent. "That's one glorious ego you've got there."

"I've earned it. You, however, have probably never—"

"That's enough, children," Michael said, suddenly filling the doorway.

We both spun around and faced him. With a feigned nonchalance, he leaned against the thick wooden frame. He held a cup of steaming coffee in one hand and an unlit cigar with the other. "I leave you two alone for a few hours and you turn on each other. Work together on this or find yourselves new jobs." He shook his head and gave me his complete attention. "I meant to give you more time, but something's come up." Now he turned to Lucius. "Finish your training, then explain to Eden what I want done today."

With that, he left us alone.

"Explain now," I said, glaring at Lucius. I wanted to run after Michael, but that would have amused my *partner*, I'm sure.

"Anyone ever tell you if you're nice to a man, he's more likely to be nice to you?"

"Please explain what Michael wants done," I said, the words ripped from my throat.

"Not until after we train," he said, drawing out each syllable with relish. He eyed my injured side. "You, cookie, are in desperate need of it."

I had to swallow back a rush of curses. How did he keep getting the upper hand? "I'm ready when you are," I said through gritted teeth. As a Rakan, I didn't have special, instinctive fighting skills. As a trained assassin, I *did*. I would not be the easy mark he obviously considered me. Injured or not.

He claimed his place on the large blue mat in the center of the gym.

Gathering my energy, centering at last, I placed myself just inches away from him. My strength was not at the level I wanted it, but for now it would have to do. I considered my battle strategy. Focus. Keep my thoughts clear. Don't allow an emotional reaction.

"I won't go easy on you," he said. "I don't care that you're a woman, and I don't care that you're injured."

I'd trained with holograms more fierce and lethal than this man, so his warning didn't frighten me in the least. "You plan to take me down all by your little self?" I laughed. "Good luck, Sparkie."

Uttering a low growl, he sprang at me.

In one fluid motion, I leaned to the side, effectively avoiding impact. He whizzed past me and tripped on his own feet. "Tsk, tsk, tsk. You let your anger get the better of you."

Pivoting, he advanced on me. I kicked him in the stomach, but that didn't slow him. He reached me all too soon and grabbed me by the shoulders. This time I couldn't evade him; he moved too quickly. He tossed me down, and I hit the mat with a smack. I winced at the sharp ache in my side but quickly leapt to my feet. And just like that, before I could drag in a breath, he was on me again, shoving me down, his hands wrapping around my throat to choke me.

"You're too slow," he said.

I knew that. The slower I moved, the more time my opponent had to consider his next action. I broke Lucius's hold with a quick thrust to his elbow. Not enough strength to break his arm into two pieces, but enough to hurt. Then I kicked him in the chest, sending him stumbling backward. When he regained his momentum, he launched at me. Twisting, I sprang up and sidestepped. Gave another fluid twist. Kick.

Contact.

My foot slammed into his midsection, knocking the air from his lungs. As he doubled over, trying to suck in air, I lunged, elbow raised. With one downward slice, I connected with his cheekbone.

He howled.

I grinned. "Still too slow?"

"Not a bad move," he said, rubbing his cheek. After a moment of staggering, he stood to his full height. "Let's see what else you've got." He went low, spinning on his heels, at the same time performing a booted strike. Anticipating such a move, I jumped.

Not far enough away, however.

The heel of his boot ground into my calf. My knees knocked together, buckled, and I propelled onto my face. Cool foam met hot flesh. I lost my cockiness.

He jumped on me, his chest pinning my face to the floor. His warm breath fanned my ear, my cheek. Everywhere his skin touched mine acted as a live wire, singeing me, making me ache—not in pain, but in lust. I had trouble drawing in a breath, but when I did, I inhaled the savageness of his scent. The wildness.

"What should you do in this position?" he said calmly.

I should place one palm against my cheek, then extend my other arm and roll over. But his long, thick fingers were surprisingly gentle as they slid down my arms, and I remained in place, doing nothing. His touch wasn't like that of an enemy, but like that of a lover.

An unwanted wave of need and desire crested inside me, growing hotter, hotter still. It didn't help that he had an erection. Thick. Hard. Hot.

He didn't want *me*, I knew. Not really. Men were simply turned on by physical contact. And we'd definitely gotten physical.

Knowing he would have desired any woman under him failed to diminish my own lust as it should have. Dark, dangerous fantasies sprang to life. Naked bodies, moans of surrender . . . Without thought, I arched my butt toward him, seeking more of his heat, craving deeper contact.

And that's when a fragrant cloud of cinnamon and honey surrounded us. The moment I smelled it, my cheeks burned a bright red and I fought frantically for release. If Lucius knew anything about Rakans, he'd know we only emitted that scent when desperately aroused.

"Let me go," I shouted. I couldn't have erected a calm, cool mask if my life depended on it. "Let me go right now." I extended my arm as I should have done earlier and tried to roll over.

He pressed me down with more of his weight, keeping me immobile.

"What's wrong with you?" he barked. "Be still,

woman. And when the hell did you put on that perfume?"

He didn't know.

I immediately relaxed. It was one thing to desire him, but quite another for him to know about it. He seemed like the type of man who would use that against me, mock me.

"Get off me," I said more calmly.

"What are you going to do if I don't?" he asked. "I've got you pinned, and you know what? There's not a damn thing you can do about it. So it looks like you've got yourself a bit of a problem."

"You think so?" I replied, nearly breathless. I had to get him off me before I did something stupid. Like whimper . . . or spread my legs.

"I do," he said confidently. There was a pause, then, "Was I too rough?" he asked gruffly.

I forced myself not to struggle. "I happen to like it rough."

"Liar." His voice was now low and husky. Full of sexual energy. "I think you like it slow and tender."

My God, if he kept talking to me like that, I was going to rip off his shorts and demand he take me right here. "Damn you. Don't you want to teach me a lesson?"

"Maybe next time." He paused. "When a man has you pinned like this, the best thing you can do is bite his arm and use the distraction to twist yourself around." Before I could take his advice, he jumped off me and stood to his feet.

Feeling strangely bereft, I wrenched to my back and kicked, swiping his feet out from under him. Down, down he tumbled. I laughed when he hit. "To do something like that?" I asked him.

His laughter mingled with mine, the sound of it raw and genuine. He didn't move to rise, but remained in place. "Good move."

"Thank you."

When our amusement died, he anchored one of his arms behind his neck and frowned. "I want that bastard EenLi killed. Not because it's our assignment, but because he deserves to die."

I glanced over at his profile; it was as harsh and savage a view as full frontal. "You make it sound personal."

"Every mission is personal, but I'm sure Michael told you EenLi used to work here."

"He did."

"When he left, he killed several agents. Agents who were my friends." Lucius turned to face me, the glint in his eyes feral, hard. "If at any time I think you're holding me back, I swear I'll kill you myself."

My eyes narrowed. "I'm only going to say this once." I held up one finger, just in case he needed a visual. "I'll speak slowly so you understand. If *you* hold me back, I'll send you crying back to your mommy— cut up like a Christmas ham."

Another flash of amusement played at the corners of his lips. "Good with knives, are you?"

"Very," I said with utter confidence.

"Fair enough. Warning received." Quick as a snap, he rolled on top of me and pinned my shoulders to the mat with his knees.

I brought my legs up behind him and wrapped my ankles around his neck. My thigh muscles ached when I jerked him backward. Down he went, up I went. The moment his back hit, I used the momentum to pull myself the rest of the way up and planted my elbow in his stomach.

His breath whooshed out. "That's the second time you've elbowed me," he panted.

"Has EenLi showed up anymore?" I asked, pushing to my feet. Just for fun, I dropped and thrust my elbow into his lungs.

"Damn it!" When he caught his breath, Lucius said, "A few more times in New Dallas. We think he murdered a human female."

"That's not his usual MO. EenLi abducts, rapes, and tortures. He rarely kills. There's no profit in a dead body."

"I know. I think he's desperate and made a mistake." Lucius spun and lashed out, his foot slamming into my forearm. Into my wound.

I winced, but maintained my balance. My God, that hurt. He wanted me to cry "unfair," but I didn't give him the satisfaction. I leapt, whirling in the air, one fist cocked and ready. Contact. I nailed him in the temple.

His chin whipped to the side.

"It usually takes him months to round up the right slave candidates, since he only wants those that meet his buyers' specifications," I said. "Why act hastily now?"

"From what you told Michael," he said, dancing to the side when I came at him again, causing me to miss him, "some of his last shipment died from some sort of sickness. His buyers wouldn't have liked that. They asked for a certain number, I'm sure, so he has to supply that exact number. And don't forget, you killed his top man, so he's doing some of the dirty work himself now."

"Makes sense." Since the move had worked for me before, I went low, kicked out. My leg connected with his ankles. When he tumbled down, I jumped and pinned his shoulders with my knees, my crotch near his face.

He met my eyes, then purposefully slid his gaze downward. "Nice view."

I shivered and tried to halt the new flicker of awareness sparking within me. Short, inky locks of hair spiked over his forehead, giving him a just-roused-from-bed appearance. "Look, I'm not like other women you know. I'm tougher than you think. I've done things and been places most people only fear."

"You're still a woman," he said, as if that explained every secret of the universe. "And you're a Rakan, the most peaceful race ever to slink their way onto this planet."

Slink? I should break his nose for that. "I'm a Rakan woman who kills people for a living. I'm not afraid of you, and I'm not afraid of EenLi. I *will* kill him."

An unreadable emotion glimmered in his eyes, and I wondered what he was feeling. Admiration? I wished. Doubt? Most likely.

"Why do you choose to kill otherworlders when you yourself are an otherworlder? Isn't that like killing your own brother?"

"My reasons are my own and no business of yours."

"I've read your file," he said. "No reason is mentioned."

Stunned, I blinked. Michael had the nerve to delete Lucius's file so I would have to learn about him on my own, but he left my file for the man to peruse at his leisure? Fury seared me, and lightning snapped along my tongue. "Like my reasoning, my file is my business and mine alone."

He remained unperturbed. "I'll be honest. You're a contradiction, and I haven't figured you out yet. By killing otherworlders, you protect humans," he said, "but humans hunt your people for their golden skin."

"I'm as much an earthling as you are. I was born here, raised here. The fact that I'm Rakan . . ." I gave a stiff shrug. "You're human. Would you kill a human if you had to?"

"Absolutely," he said. His eyebrows arched. "Would you?"

"Absolutely," I replied. "You, in particular. Some people, no matter their race or gender, are bad and need to be destroyed. That's the only way peace will be reached."

Those full lips of his curved sensuously, and I had the sudden, unwelcome urge to lean down and nibble them.

"You want to know what Michael plans for us today or what?" he asked.

I nodded and fought a rise of color in my cheeks because I'd forgotten Michael's dictate so easily. Stupid lust. I didn't like this man. Remember?

"Last night one of our agents caught Sahara Rose. She's being held in New Dallas," he said, not bothering to try and move me off him. "Michael wants us to fly there and question her, get whatever information we can."

I nearly jumped to my feet in excitement and anticipation, but managed to remain where I was. "When do we leave?"

"Two hours." He clasped his hands over my thighs and squeezed. Not enough to hurt, but enough to get my attention. "I want to question her alone, which means you need to stay here."

I laughed. I just couldn't help myself. "You're kidding me, right?"

"There's no way you'll get answers out of her. You look about as scary as a bowl of warm honey."

"Looks do not determine ability," I ground out,

losing all traces of humor. I'd heard similar words my entire life. As a teenager, my spoiled, pampered self had loved that kind of statement. As an adult, and in light of my recent failure, I hated—*hated!*—hearing such a thing.

"And don't even get me started on your mouth," he continued.

"What about my mouth?" I asked slowly.

"It's a two-hundred-dollars-an-hour mouth, not a tell-me-all-your-secrets-or-I'll-kill-you mouth."

"You know what?" I said. Oh, this was going to be fun. He obviously had no idea what he was about to encounter with his interrogation. "I'm willing to make a bet with you. I'll give you ten minutes to get a single answer out of Sahara Rose. A single answer." I'd followed the woman for days. I knew her. Lucius, with his towering build and hard-ass I-don't-give-a-shit edge, would intimidate her into absolute silence.

Wicked intent gleamed in his expression. "And when I *do* get an answer out of her?" he asked, both brows raised.

"I'll let you have my mouth for free."

He didn't hesitate. "Agreed."

"Don't you want to know what I get if you fail?"

"I don't plan to fail."

"You still have to offer me something I want."

Now he hesitated. "What?" he asked suspiciously.

"When your ten minutes are up, I want you to step aside and shut the hell up. I'll get the information we need. Afterward, you're going to get on your knees and praise my ability."

His lips stretched to a full, anticipatory grin. "Agreed. But get ready, cookie." He lifted up, getting so close I felt the warmth of his breath on my face. "I want your mouth all over me."

CHAPTER
4

I want your mouth all over me.

I tried not to think about Lucius's parting words as I luxuriated in the softness and decadence of Michael's private ITS—Ionic Transport System—a jet that ran on vibrations of subparticle strings of energy rather than gasoline. Complete with four laser cannons and retractable wings. I tried not to imagine my mouth devouring Lucius's hard, muscled body, his moans of pleasure in my ears, his hands gripping my hair, the taste of him teasing my tongue.

Unfortunately, I thought of little else and spent nearly every moment of the flight to New Dallas lost in a sensual haze. The cloying scent of honey still wafted from me—and there wasn't a damn thing I could do about it. At least Lucius hadn't mentioned my "perfume" again. I might die of acute mortification if he did—I could even picture the headline of my obituary:

"Alien Assassin Survives Antique Gunshot, Laser, Knife Wounds, Poison, and Explosion, Only to Succumb to the Stupid-ass Comment of a Human Male."

I pushed out a breath and settled deeper into the plush leather seat. The private, luxury ITS offered a smooth ride, a lavish sapphire couch and a gilded table. If it weren't for the panoramic view of white clouds and blue sky, I might have convinced myself I lounged at home, reflecting on the success of my last mission.

Instead, here I was. A failure. Partnered. Lusting after a human.

Rakans were sensual by nature. Creatures of peace, pleasure, and decadence—qualities I'd battled for many years, and thought I had conquered. Or rather, killed, along with all of my victims.

I sighed. I hadn't set out to become an assassin. I asked to train with Michael and his agents simply to spend more time with my father. To impress him. He respected his men, and I'd wanted that respect for myself. Wanted to be more than his spoiled, pampered, *lazy* daughter—something he'd been teased about often. He'd never complained, had actually taken pleasure in indulging me, but I had begun to notice the difference between his men and me.

Reluctantly Michael agreed to let me participate. Throughout training, I was pushed as hard as the men. I fought, I hunted, I learned the intricacies of weapons. Afterward, I watched my male counterparts leave and return from assignments while I remained behind. I heard them discuss the atrocities being committed by their targets, and I felt their pride at protecting those weaker than themselves.

Becoming an agent soon became my real goal. As the days passed, it was less about Michael and more about *me*. What I could do to help.

Finally Michael allowed me a chance to prove myself. That first kill had been less difficult than I'd expected. Less difficult than everyone expected. That's when I realized the destruction of evil was a sensual dance and my means of keeping the peace. Killing *was* my nature.

Lucius stretched out his long, thick legs, eating my personal space. He sat across from me, no part of our bodies touching. Still, I felt the heat of him, and I didn't like it. I didn't like him, period. He upset my inner balance. An inner balance I desperately needed. Distraction was as much an enemy as any one of my targets.

I *knew* that. I did. Yet here I was, consumed by a man who made me ache in ways that had nothing to do with physical injuries.

I stole a quick glance at him, my gaze locking on his lips. Though pink and lush, they somehow appeared hard just then. Abrasive. Just like the rest of him. But I didn't think they'd be hard when kissing a woman. No, they'd be tender and silky. Hot. Perfect. Utterly perfect.

A man who looked like he did, comprised of razors and nails, muscle and sinew, belonged in wars. Not on top of a woman, giving untold pleasure. And yet I'd be willing to bet he excelled at both. Not that I would ever find out firsthand.

Shifting to the side, I allowed myself to take in the rest of him. The change in his appearance still surprised me. The man had somehow transformed himself before leaving New Mexico. After our *innocent* tussle in Michael's basement gym, we'd gone our separate ways to shower and change clothes. Lucius had emerged with his dark hair bleached completely white, his left eyebrow pierced, and the base of his throat sporting a skull tattoo. What sucked was that, despite the differences, he was still just as sexy as hell.

"Want to tell me what you're thinking about?" he asked casually.

My heart hammered at the sound of his voice. Like I was going to admit that little gem.

He hadn't said a word about the change, and neither had I. I could guess why he'd done it. Obviously he'd been to New Dallas before—under a different identity. *This* identity. He'd probably worked with the men we were meeting, and they knew him as this man.

Lucius continued to watch me, I noticed, his ice-blue gaze intent. At least his eye color hadn't changed. That sexy, electric blue should never be concealed.

"You might as well tell me," he said. "I'll get it out

of you sooner or later, and you'll be doing yourself a favor if it's sooner."

"I'm just imagining your failure with Sahara Rose," I lied.

His pierced black brow arched, raising the silver stud. "If the thought of my failure is what put that 'fuck-me-now' expression on your face, keep thinking about it. Please." The last word sounded foreign on his tongue, as if he'd never spoken it before.

I fought to keep my expression neutral, to keep from scowling or moaning. With his words, he placed his pleasure-giving image right back in the gutter of my fantasies.

"Must you be so crude?" I ground out.

"We kill people for a living, cookie, and you're balking at my language?"

We might both be killers, but we were different on so many levels. I worked for peace, for the good of the people. He worked for money. My allegiance would never waver. His probably shifted with the wind.

"Oh, wait," he added. "You're a princess, a spoiled little rich girl. And don't try to deny it. I've heard stories about your teenage years. Crying and pouting when you didn't get what you wanted. 'I asked for a blue dress, Daddy, not green,'" he mimicked in a high voice. "Boohoo." He rolled his eyes. "Of course you're balking at my language. Girls like you can't be happy, no matter their circumstances."

My eyes narrowed. I was *not* that girl anymore.

I hadn't been for a long, long time. When I began my agent training, I'd even stopped calling Michael "Daddy." I'd called him what every other agent called him. "Too bad there isn't a price on your head," I muttered. "You're one target I'd take great joy in destroying."

"Who says there isn't a price on my head?"

My brows arched. "Is there?"

He shrugged. "You're the hotshot tracker. You tell me."

Our gazes clashed and held. Some invisible force refused to release me from its grip as I studied him. His features were as granite-hard and unreadable as ever. Nothing about his expression or body language betrayed his thoughts.

"Okay. Maybe there's more than one," I said. "You're not the kind of guy who knows how to play nice. Most likely, you have enemies in every city, country, and hellhole you've ever entered."

The moment I spoke the word "play," his eyes dropped to my lips. The word actually hung between us like a living, breathing thing. Was he imagining naked, sweaty bodies? Drugging kisses and pleasure?

I glared at him, silently commanding him to look away. He didn't. In fact, his stare became more intently focused on my mouth. Such intense scrutiny unnerved me, but I was used to controlling my actions. My body would obey the will of my mind, not my lust. I wanted to squirm and turn away, but

I forbade myself even an inch of movement. For my job, I'd often sat in one place for hours, surveying my prey, not giving away my location by a single breath.

I decided to challenge him by turning his own question against him. "What are *you* thinking about?"

He arched his pierced brow again. "Do you want the honest answer or the same shit you gave me when I asked?" He didn't give me time to reply, but finished with, "I'll give you the honest answer." He leaned forward, his mouth twisting upward, his eyes darkening. "I'm thinking how hot and wet and eager your lips will be when I win our bet."

Breathe. Just breathe. "You don't even like me."

"I don't have to like you to want you."

How like a man. Thankfully the landing gear moaned as it disengaged, saving me from slicing that smug grin off his face with the three-pronged razor strapped to my ankle. Never mind that I didn't like him and wanted him myself.

The self-driving ITS glided smoothly into its programmed location, a private airstrip in New Dallas. Lucius and I hustled outside. A step behind him, I found myself watching the way his butt moved. Nice. Damn him.

The sun glared directly overhead, causing midday heat to wrap around me. My gold skin burned easily, more easily than a human's. When possible, I wore long-sleeved shirts (with accessible slits for weapon handling) and tight black pants (also with accessible slits). I slid my dark sunglasses into place. Because I belonged to a hunted race, I also shoved my golden hair under a black ball cap.

A fine sheen of sweat formed, and a dirt-laden breeze kicked up. I hurried into the air-conditioned backseat of a bullet- and laserproof vintage Hummer. Two of Michael's employees waited in the front. Both were physically fit humans in their mid-thirties. I recognized them and nodded. Ren, the muscled brute in the passenger seat, had asked me out on numerous occasions. I'd always turned him down. His wandering eye irritated me.

"Thanks for the ride," I said.

"No problem, baby," Ren said, giving me a welcoming smile. "Anything for you." As he spoke, he sent me a wink. He even skimmed his gaze over my body, and I wouldn't have doubted if he mentally willed my legs apart.

Any reply I offered would have encouraged him. I knew that from experience. So I kept my mouth closed.

The easy atmosphere changed when Lucius entered the vehicle and folded his big frame beside me. Ren avoided looking directly at him, but his lips pressed together in disdain. The driver, Marko, whipped around, facing us. His olive complexion and dark eyes were rosy with . . . fury?

"You guys have met before, I take it," I muttered.

"He broke my fucking nose," Marko snarled.

Lucius remained unperturbed. "I'll break it again if you don't turn your ass around and get us where we need to be."

There was a sizzling pause, a suspended moment between the escalating tension where I was one hundred percent confident the three men were going to kill each other. Wait. Let me rephrase. I was one hundred percent confident Lucius would kill Marko and Ren. I doubted anyone or anything could hurt Lucius Adaire.

And wasn't that a funny realization? When I'd first met the man, I'd accused him of being all brawn and no brains, too pretty to actually fight. He'd proven himself capable during our training session. I'd give him that much.

I adjusted the sunglasses on my nose. Obviously, Lucius had served time in the military. Special forces, black ops maybe. Perhaps he'd even worked for AIR at one time. He moved silently, fluidly, with the patent stillness of a predator. He didn't balk at the thought of violence; he embraced it.

I still didn't want him as my partner, though. How could I prove myself? How could I prove my worth and my capabilities with this tough man at my side? Despite his threats to let me die if I got in his way, he just might jump in front of me if gunshots erupted. Agents were protectors by nature, and he wouldn't be able to help himself.

"I'm not paid by the hour, ladies, so let's get this job done," Lucius added.

I watched as Marko's flush turned ruddy, his eyes narrowed to dark slits. He slowly turned away from us. His back and shoulders were stiff, and an aura of fury radiated from him. Ren was slower to turn around. He glanced from Lucius to me, from me to Lucius. He'd never seen me with another agent before, so undoubtedly he wondered what the hell I was doing with this one. I offered no explanation, and switched my attention to the window.

Trees were dry and yellow from lack of water. Tumbleweeds rolled up the fenced enclosure and along the runway, and men rushed to remove them. Seconds later our coordinates were programmed into the car and we were speeding down winding back roads. No one spoke. In the silence, my awareness of Lucius became electric, a spark begging to burst into flame. The hard length of his thigh pressed against the firmness of mine. Where our clothes met, my nerve endings sizzled. He smelled good. Too good. Like soap and man and a hint of Michael's woodsy cigars.

To preserve my sanity, I forced my mind from such dangerous territory and concentrated on the coming confrontation with Sahara Rose. Such a gentle, fragile creature, and that fragility made her a weak link in EenLi's chain. I'd always wondered why the slaver had used the girl. Stupidity? Or desire? The latter was most likely the answer. Desire could make the sanest of people do foolish things. Wasn't I becoming proof of that?

Soon the Hummer eased to a stop in front of an old, dilapidated farmhouse on the verge of collapse. Appearances were often deceiving, and I knew this was one of those times. Inside, those splintery walls were solid and impenetrable. Trip wires and land mines littered the surrounding property. Computers and other equipment protected the "home" from invasion—as well as keeping prisoners inside.

"Ten minutes," I reminded Lucius as I jumped outside. I didn't want anyone opening my door and helping me out. Femininity and delicacy were two things I didn't want to project right now. I slammed the door closed with more force than necessary. "I'll be watching the clock."

The heat hit me instantly, once again wrapping around me like a thick blanket. Bright rays of sunlight baked everything in their path. The barren ground. The twigs and rocks. Lucius strode to my side, his long, muscled legs making short work of the distance. He radiated heat of his own, but it left a far different feeling inside me than the sun did.

"Don't be surprised," he said briskly, "when I win after only five."

I secretly smiled. So cocky, yet so doomed for failure. I hadn't had this much fun in years. If ever. But I gave no outward reaction to his words. Instead I turned and marched forward. He stayed close to my side.

There was no one waiting for us at the door.

Instead, guards and agents abounded inside, a few watching our every move as we passed the rickety-looking threshold. Since we would never have made it to the porch without clearance, we didn't have to endure retinal scans or fingerprint IDs. Besides, we were expected. And since Michael Black controlled this little building as well as everything and everyone inside it—and he wasn't here—I guess that made me the boss for now.

My shoulders straightened at the thought.

The chipped front door closed automatically. My hands remained close to the knives strapped to my thighs. A habit, really. Immediately, I took stock of my new surroundings. Eleven men manned the first room. Two were stationed at the computer terminal in back; three were seated on the only couch, cleaning and testing weapons. The rest of the men were relaxing and talking over coffee.

Cool air welcomed me in an open embrace. Relieved, I tugged off my cap, and my hair tumbled down my back. I hated wearing hats because they retained heat, but I also didn't like hair in my face. The gold locks restricted my vision—and a good assassin needed to see everything around her. I should have cut it off long ago, but it reminded me of my mother—the only reminder I had, really—so I never had. I reached up and tugged my hair into a ponytail.

"Take Lucius to the prisoner," I said to no one in particular.

A short, stocky bull of a human immediately stepped up to my—growl—partner. "This way," he said, not meeting Lucius's eyes.

Lucius made to follow him, but I stopped him with a hand on his forearm. He paused, leveling an expressionless glance at me. "Leave your weapons with me," I said quietly.

He laughed. Actually laughed, a booming sound that filled the room. But when he spoke, his voice was as quiet as mine had been. "Not a chance."

"Did you hear what happened to that AIR agent Dallas Gutierrez when another agent took a weapon into an interrogation?"

His smile remained, softening the harsh planes of his features. "I can handle myself. Besides, I wouldn't do you the favor of getting myself killed before I claim my prize." With that, he shook off my hold and strode away. At least he hadn't called me "cookie" in front of the men.

I turned to Ren, who had followed us inside. "Where can I observe?"

A muscle ticked in his jaw, but he replied helpfully, "I'll show you."

He ushered me down a well-lit, narrow hallway that slanted down, taking us underground. With every step, the temperature became damper, cooler. The walls were plain, a little dirty, but there were no visible cameras or sensors. Still, both were there, I knew, watching our every move. I knew how Michael operated, and the man left nothing to chance. Even though security cameras were illegal without a proper license—which Michael didn't have because he didn't want anyone knowing his business—I knew they were here.

"What's with you and Adaire?" Ren asked, breaking the silence.

I didn't spare him a glance. "What business is it of yours?"

"Lucius Adaire is a killer."

I had to smile at that one. "So am I. So are you, for that matter."

"No, I mean a vicious killer. He'll kill anything. Women. Children. I'd watch my back if I were you."

I didn't allow myself to react to his words. "Well, you aren't me." I still wore my sunglasses, so I looked over them and leveled him with a pointed stare. "Besides that, I always watch my back—even while I'm with you."

The hallway finally ended. We stood in front of what looked like an average wall. Ren laid his hand against a corner section, and two panels opened. A disposable, computer-operated needle pricked his index finger, and a small sample of blood was taken.

When the computer recognized his DNA, the wall—consisting of two steel plates—split down the middle, admitting us. I didn't know if Ren had spoken the truth about Lucius. The two men weren't friends, so there was a very real possibility Ren had embellished his story. However, I didn't like to think of Lucius as a killer of innocents—the very innocents I strove so hard to protect.

"Come on," Ren grumbled, unhappy with the lack of reaction he'd gotten from me. He led me into a small room. One entire wall boasted a holoscreen that played out the happenings in the other room. I saw the small, plain blue room, the two wooden chairs. I sank into Observation's only chair, a padded stool, forcing Ren to stand beside me.

I watched as Lucius crossed his arms over his chest and glared down at a pale, trembling Sahara Rose— who wasn't speaking. She did whimper, though, but that didn't count. Her blue eyes were wide and watery, and she kept tugging on her light-colored hair.

Grinning, I glanced at the clock beside me.

Ten minutes, then I was going in.

CHAPTER
5

Five minutes down. Five minutes to go.

I almost hated for the ten minutes to end. Lucius was simply too entertaining. Screaming at Sahara Rose failed, so he tried cajoling. Intimidation through silence failed, so he switched to I'm-a-nice-man-and-you-can-tell-me-anything mode. Whenever he approached her, her trembling and sobbing increased, but she never spoke a word.

When at long last she began screaming hysterically, he turned his back to me. He reached up with one hand, looking as if he wanted to scratch his head. He flipped me off.

I laughed. Desperation clung to him, growing darker in his features, becoming heavier on his shoulders. The best thing, I had to admit, was that his antics kept my mind off EenLi and my own failure.

Another three minutes passed with no results.

Lucius tried to hide it, but I caught several pan-icked glances at his wristwatch. I had to choke back another round of laughter. I'd never been one to enjoy another's pain, but *please*. Watching this hard-assed man flounder ranked right up there with consuming an entire bowl of sugar-covered peaches—my biggest weakness.

I glanced at the digital clock next to the screen. Only one minute to go. Lucius began to pace franti-cally, begging—actually begging—Sahara Rose to utter a single word. His eyebrow ring glinted in the light.

"Please," he said, the word hard against his lips. "Please, just say your name. Curse at me. Anything. I'll pay you. However much you want."

She continued to tremble in her corner, lips pressed together, tears in her eyes. At least she'd stopped screaming.

"I'm begging you. Tell me your name. That's all you have to do. I'll leave, then. You'll never have to see me again."

Five . . . four . . . three . . . two . . .

One.

I resisted the urge to jump up and shout. Lucius burst forth with a stream of curses so foul and black Sahara Rose nearly seized. She did sink into a faint, her hair fanning out around her.

"He's going to kill her," Ren gasped. He whipped out his cell unit, and held the small black box to his lips. "We need backup—"

I grabbed the unit and tossed it to the ground. The sound of cracking plastic greeted my ears.

Ren's mouth gaped open, and he blinked at me in shock. "What the hell did you do that for? I need to protect the suspect. She's—"

"Fine," I said confidently. "She's fine. He won't hurt her."

"The hell he won't." Back and forth Ren paced, his agitation manifesting itself in the brisk way he moved. He jerked a hand through his hair. "He's in a rage. He won't be able to control himself."

"For God's sake, calm down, Ren. You're working yourself up over nothing. His anger is directed at me. Not Sahara Rose."

"You?" He ground to a halt. A gleam of confusion entered his eyes, as if I'd spoken a foreign language and he needed to translate the words. "I don't understand."

"Nor do you need to."

Gaze narrowing, Ren snatched at the gun holstered at his side. I quickly laid a hand on his wrist. "Lucius won't hurt me either," I said.

"How the hell do you know?"

I smiled sweetly. "Woman's intuition."

Lucius stormed from Sahara Rose's cell wearing an expression of utter violence. His eyes blazed bright blue, his cheeks glowed vivid red. His muscles were bunched and ready to spring into action. I laughed. Ren paled and blinked at me as if I were insane.

Maybe I was. Who else would laugh in the face of such a man's fury?

He deserved it, though. He'd been so confident of his success. And he'd failed. I had the chance to show him up, to beat him. I laughed again. How fun this was going to be.

I'm not sure how many seconds passed before Lucius stormed inside the observation room. Beside me, Ren froze in place. Lucius's gaze locked on mine. He braced his legs apart and fisted his hands at his sides.

I didn't even try to hide my amusement. "You lost," I said.

His eyes narrowed. "That doesn't mean you'll win."

"But it means you lost."

He popped his jaw, but didn't respond.

"I'm going to enjoy this," I said. "A lot." I unbuttoned the first three buttons of my shirt, causing the material to gape and reveal the lacy edges of my bra. Both men watched me, Ren with fascination—it didn't take much to douse his fear, did it?—and Lucius with fire. Lusty fire or black, angry fire? I wondered, as I pulled out my ponytail and combed my fingers through my hair. I licked my lips.

"I'll be back in five minutes," I said.

His eyes narrowed further, mere slits that completely blocked the color of his irises. "That confident?"

"Oh, yes. If you'll excuse me, Ren. Agent *Luscious*," I said, nodding to Lucius before I sauntered past him and out of the room. Had I forgotten to mention that Sahara Rose didn't like men? Oopsie. She might be EenLi's lover, but she found men sexually repulsive. Little Miss Sahara Rose liked her phallus strapped on and plastic. The more delicate and sexy the woman, the more susceptible Sahara Rose became.

Did I feel guilty or ashamed or even less of an agent for using my femininity as a weapon? Hell, no. Look at everything Lucius had tried. Look how sublimely he failed. A good agent uses whatever means necessary to win. Men could scoff at my methods if they so desired, but let's be honest. They'd do the same thing if they could. Men never hesitate to use their strengths, so why should women?

Two armed guards stood posted at Sahara Rose's door, which was adjacent to the room I'd been in. Their gazes seemed to devour me. I knew it wasn't my appeal as a woman that so entranced them. I'd learned long ago that humans were simply susceptible to anything gold.

I arched a brow insolently, and one of the men quickly punched the code that opened the door. I swept inside without a word. There were two chairs. No bed. No table. A large, black screen comprised the far wall; that was it. This wasn't a room meant for comfort, but for intimidation. Michael hoped that the more uncomfortable the room, the less time the suspect would want to spend inside it.

I crouched beside the unconscious Sahara Rose,

growing angry with Lucius. He hadn't even attempted to catch her. I sighed. Her body was splayed across the floor in the exact position she'd landed in her faint. She'd fallen backward, but at least she hadn't cracked open her skull.

She was a young girl with too-pale skin and pretty, light-colored hair. A beautiful package, yes, but her looks were already fading and showing signs of wear. Stress could do that to humans—age them before their time.

Cradling her head in my hand, I gently brushed aside wisps of hair sticking to her temples. "Sahara Rose," I said softly. "Wake up for me, baby."

She moaned and murmured something unintelligible.

"Come on, sweetheart. Wake up."

Her eyelids fluttered open. When she realized where she was, absolute panic flooded her blue eyes. She struggled against my hold, but I held firm, keeping her in place. I might appear dainty because of my gold coloring and small bones, but my intense workouts kept me strong.

"I'm not going to hurt you," I whispered against her ear, letting my breath caress her cheek.

The moment I spoke, she stilled completely. Her desperate gaze sought me, and whatever she saw in my face made her relax. "That man. Is he—" She gulped, trembled.

"He's gone," I said, stroking her jawline. "After

the way he scared you, I sent him to clean the toilets. That's all men are good for, anyway."

"Thank you," she said, sinking deeper into my hold, clinging to me because I was the only lifeline she'd encountered.

"My pleasure, sweetheart. Can you sit?"

She bit her lip and nodded, then slowly eased to a sitting position. She wore a plain white top and matching drawstring pants. Both had been given to her courtesy of Michael. Because agents were nocturnal creatures who usually wore black, we always kept our prisoners in white.

"I want to go home," Sahara Rose said, her voice trembling.

"Soon, sweetheart," I promised, knowing it was a lie. This woman, no matter her reasons, no matter her sweetness, had aided a predatory alien. She would be punished in some way. That was the law. I experienced a twinge of guilt and regret, but brushed both aside. "First, I have some questions for you."

I pushed to my feet and looped my arm around her waist, helping her stand. I made sure my breasts mashed into her side. Just in case that didn't make her notice me as a female, I let my fingers slip under her shirt and latch onto her bare midriff. When she felt the heat of my palm, she sucked in a breath. Since my desire for Lucius had yet to dissipate, my honey scent wafted to her.

"To the chair," I told her. She gave me more of her

weight than necessary, and I helped her ease into the slatted seat. "Comfortable?"

Gazing up at me through her lashes, she nodded. "Yes. Thank you."

I grazed her cheeks with my knuckles and knelt in front of her, gently prying her knees apart to nestle my body between her thighs. Her eyes grew big, and she wet her lips. "I really need your help, sweetheart," I said. "Your life depends on it."

"I can't tell you what you want to know," she said, beseeching me with her gaze to understand.

"You can," I insisted. My fingers traced the waist of her pants, making her stomach clench. "You want to help me; you know you do."

"No, I can't," she said, but I could see the war raging inside her mind. EenLi had probably threatened her life or her family's life if she ever dared speak a word about his activities. But she didn't want to get in any more trouble.

"Please," I said, all feminine eagerness.

She gulped. "What do you need to know?" she asked hesitantly.

I played a look of reluctance across my face, as if I didn't want to involve her but had no choice. "I need to know about EenLi and his . . . cattle business."

Her lips compressed in fear, and she shook her head. "I can't. I don't know anything."

I spread my fingers over her thighs and ran them upward until I grasped her hips. Her mouth dropped open in surprise, but she didn't pull away. My eyelids dipped to half-mast, my lashes casting shadows over my cheekbones. I knew she caught a glimpse of my bra because when I glanced up at her, she flicked her eyes away guiltily. Her cheeks warmed to a rosy shade of pink.

Good. I had her attention, and she was responding to my femininity. "Sahara Rose," I said, pronouncing her name like it was my favorite food.

She gulped again. "Yes?"

"Please help me." I returned my hands to her waist, toying with the ties on her pants. "In return, I'll help you however I can. You'll never have to see EenLi again." That much was true, since I planned to kill the bastard. "Let's start with something little. Why don't you tell me why you helped EenLi in the first place? That's easy enough, isn't it?"

She bit her lip and nodded hesitantly. "I was living on the streets. He found me and took me in, made me his lover. He gave me money and food and a place to stay and he told me he would . . ."

Kill her if she betrayed or left him, I finished for her. "He trusted you enough to help with his cattle."

That war inside her continued to wage for several more minutes. Should she, shouldn't she? Should she risk angering EenLi, or risk believing in my aid? Finally, she sighed, and her shoulders sagged.

I knew then that victory was mine, and I fought to contain my grin.

"If I didn't help, *I* would have become cattle." Tears pricked her eyes, brimming over her lids. "He would have sold me, and I would have been taken to another planet."

Now we were getting somewhere. "Tell me about the ones who *are* taken off-planet."

"People give him orders," she said, taking my hands and linking our fingers. She was shaking, seeking comfort. "Like off a restaurant menu. Red hair, brown eyes, and so on."

"Who buys the slaves?"

"Humans. Otherworlders. Origins don't matter. Some of the buyers don't even live on Earth."

"Then how do they give EenLi their orders?"

She shrugged. "They come through the portals for a visit, I guess."

The muscles in my back jumped in anticipation of her next words. "Do you know where the portals are located?"

"No."

A wave of disappointment crashed through me. I reached up and brushed her hair aside. Her eyes closed, and she leaned into my touch.

"He never told me," she added. "His only job for me was to take care of the sick."

"If a human wanted to place an order, how would he do it?"

She pressed her lips together for a moment. "There's a man, Jonathan Parker. He's old money.

Oil, I think. He hosts parties at his house, and people tell him what they want. He tells EenLi."

I knew that the moment she spoke the name, every agent listening began searching our databases for Jonathan Parker. We'd have a printout of his entire history within minutes.

"Do you know the type of people EenLi is looking for now?"

She shook her head. "He never gives me those details."

"What about dates? When is a shipment due?"

"I don't know." She bit her bottom lip and gripped my hand. "Can I go home now?" A beseeching note layered her voice. "I never hurt anyone, I promise. I took care of them."

"I know you did. But you need to stay here a while longer in case we have any more questions. Besides that, you're safe from EenLi here," I added, squeezing her hand, "just like I promised." But more than that, if we ever decided to use her as bait, she'd be readily available.

Callous, I know, but innocent lives came before this one woman. Sometimes bad things had to be done to facilitate peace.

"I'll see that you're fed and moved to a comfortable room. All right?"

"Yes," she said reluctantly. "All right."

"You did real good, Sahara. I'm proud of you." Cupping her jaw, I inched upward and slowly brought my lips to hers. She immediately opened her mouth to deepen the kiss, but I kept it sweet, gentle, breathing in her scent and she mine. Feeling her softness, and she mine. She was a sad girl with a sad life, but she wasn't evil. "You'll tell me if you remember anything else, won't you?"

"Yes," she whispered.

I stood and stepped away, my fingers coasting over her jaw as I did. Giving her one last, lingering glance, I moved toward the door.

"Wait," she called. She too stood, the chair skidding behind her.

I didn't turn fully, but glanced over my shoulder. "Yes?"

"What's your name?" she asked.

"Eden Black." I paused. "Alien assassin. Don't worry. I *will* take care of EenLi."

Her "thank you" echoed in my ears as the door closed behind me.

CHAPTER
6

Blanketing my features to reveal nothing, I sauntered into the observation room. Lucius sat alone. Ren had probably bailed the moment I'd stepped out of Interrogation. Either that or Lucius had kicked him out, not wanting an audience for what was about to happen.

I remained in the open doorway, taking in the scene and allowing my anticipation to unfurl. Lucius occupied the only chair, his gaze clashed with mine, his legs splayed out in front of him, his arms locked behind his neck. Never had a man appeared more relaxed and at ease. He pushed a button on a remote he held, and the holoscreen went blank, blocking out Sahara's image.

"Close the door," he said in that rough, gravelly voice of his. I caught a hint of fury in the undertone.

Not so relaxed, after all.

A shiver trekked down my spine as I continued to stare over at the man, at my unwanted partner. I wanted to hear him say "Please," but knew there was a better chance of EenLi's head falling from the sky like manna.

I stepped inside, causing the double doors to slide closed automatically. Lucius tossed the remote on the floor. With every second that passed, something . . . murderous grew in his eyes, a gleam that belied his casual pose yet fit perfectly with his tone.

Feigning my own sense of nonchalance, I leaned one shoulder against the wall. "We're alone now, Sparkie. Was there something you wanted to say to me? Something you needed to do?"

His gaze slitted, blocking every hint of color from those ice-blue lasers. He remained very still.

"Tsk, tsk. You know that's not the required position." I showed no mercy.

He didn't get up.

"You lost."

"I know."

"Drop to your knees."

"Why don't you make this interesting," he gritted out, "and take off your pants?"

His words supplied an image of him kneeling between my naked legs. I stopped a shiver before it could form. My brows winged up. "You reneging?"

Very slowly, he eased to his feet, inching his big body higher and higher. I gave my cuticles my attention. I heard his teeth grind together, even thought I heard his jawbone crack. I flicked him an insouciant glance and patted my mouth to smother a fake yawn. That murderous gleam had branched from his eyes and now consumed his expression.

His black clothes rustled as he moved to his knees.

I studied my cuticles again, waiting, my breath suspended, the casual pretense the only thing keeping me from gaping.

"You did a . . . good job," he ground out. When the last word left his mouth, he sprang up. He wiped the dust from his knees, keeping his gaze locked with mine.

I hadn't thought he'd do it. What a puzzle he was. I could have nodded, said nothing, and saved him at least a hint of his stubborn pride. I could have . . . but I didn't. "Don't ever underestimate me again. You'll end up on your knees every time."

He ran his tongue over his teeth, but didn't reply.

"Next time, research your suspect before you interrogate her. That's where you went wrong."

His entire face bloomed red—in embarrassment, in renewed fury. Renewed? No. I doubted he'd ever lost the first batch of fury. He didn't like losing, but more importantly, he didn't like losing to me. A spoiled princess. Well, too damn bad. He'd gotten the best of me from the moment we'd met, so I intended to savor this victory.

"You were doomed to fail before you even stepped

foot into Interrogation. I tried to tell you, but you wouldn't listen. You refused to consider the possibility that I might know something you didn't. Well, guess what? I'd followed her for days. I knew her, knew everything about her. Your silly pride cost you this war."

"War?" He chuckled, the sound devoid of humor. "That was only a minor skirmish, cookie."

I rolled my eyes. "Big talk for a loser."

Lucius stalked a menacing step toward me. "You did good, all right. There. That's twice I've told you. I meant it then, I mean it now. But one day we'll have a reckoning, you and I."

I moved toward him, closing even more of the gap, a rush of adrenaline quickening the blood flow through my veins. "I do believe we will—if one of us doesn't kill the other first."

"I'm going to fuck you, Eden." He stepped closer. "Killing is optional. After."

My nostrils flared as I closed the remaining distance. I was excited, I admit it. Our noses touched, and my beaded nipples pushed into his chest. His breath fanned my lips, brushing every crevice. The scent of cinnamon and honey instantly enveloped us. Our heated exchange was playing havoc with my hormones. "You'll never have me."

Lucius never turned his attention from me. "Get a new goddamn perfume!" he shouted.

I blinked, felt a glimmer of satisfaction. "Why? Does this one bother you?"

He ran his tongue over teeth and flatly refused to answer. "Do you even give a shit about this case? Do you want to know what we have on Jonathan Parker or not?"

I stalked away from Lucius and to the door, opened it wide, and called for Ren. When he appeared, I said, "Make Sahara Rose comfortable. And be nice to her."

Ren flicked Lucius a nervous glance, then rushed off to do as he was told. I didn't turn around but remained braced at the entrance. "What do you know about Parker?" Feigning nonchalance, I rebound my hair.

"I'll tell you about him over lunch," he said, relish in his tone. He liked knowing something I didn't. He liked choosing when and where he'd tell me.

Since he'd gotten on his knees for me, I gave him this victory. Just barely. "I was just about to suggest that," I said with a faux casual shrug.

At my easy compliance, his lips dipped in a frown. He'd expected a fight, I know. "Let's get out of here. Too many ears."

"We'll need the keys to the Hummer."

"I pocketed them," he said, dangling the set from his fingers.

My hands tightened at my sides. I didn't like that he'd thought that far ahead and I hadn't. I strode from the room without a word, knowing he followed directly behind me. As we left the farmhouse, I had the last laugh, however. Several men whistled and waved good-bye to "Agent Luscious."

Lucius purchased half a dozen drive-thru burritos and tossed the sack into my lap. I held them without complaint as he drove for over an hour. Finally, he eased into a hidden thicket located in a richly treed patch of land—privately owned land that was well watered. He cut the locks off the gate and sneaked us inside.

Both of us, I noticed, continually checked the mirrors, making sure we weren't followed by anyone. The fewer who knew our business, the less chance there was of leaks.

He told the car to park, grabbed the sack, and said, "We'll eat now, then talk."

I caught the burrito he carelessly flung my way and ate what I could, but my appetite had yet to fully return. Plus, I preferred sweet, sugary foods. Always had. I often wondered what type of food grew on Raka, what I'd be eating if I was there.

It was sad that I didn't know much about my own people or my home planet. There simply weren't many Rakans left here to ask, hunted as we were. Michael once hired a Rakan tutor for me, but that had lasted less than six months. The man had taken a day off and never returned.

I knew the planet had two small suns, three large moons, and massive amounts of water. I knew there had never been a war, the crime rate was low, and the penalty for breaking any law was death. I knew the entire population was ruled by an iron-willed dictator and that many Rakans had left simply to escape him.

Is that why my parents had left? I so would have loved to ask them. To know them. They'd been taken from me so suddenly. Singing me to sleep one minute, lying in pools of their own blood the next. Murdered. Obliterated. I missed them more than I could ever say.

Leaning back in my seat, I waited patiently while Lucius consumed the thick, greasy wraps. He chewed slowly, sensually, like a man who savored every bite. I watched the way his mouth and throat moved in harmony, and unbidden images of him partaking of *me* invaded my mind. I forced my attention to the window.

Apparently, he didn't like my change of focus. "Let's take a walk," he said, throwing the last wrapper in the back seat with the others.

We exited on our respective sides. Lush, green trees filled the entire area, providing a luxurious shade. I stashed my hat and sunglasses on the car's dash. Fresh, vibrant air wrapped us in a welcome breeze. I'd traveled the world, many times, but I rarely experienced nature like this.

The tranquil area surprised me. "New Dallas has been under a dry spell since EenLi and his men arrived. How is this glen possible?"

"Michael keeps it well watered," Lucius said, reaching my side.

My eyes narrowed, and I experienced a spark of anger that Lucius knew something about my father that I didn't . . . until I recalled that Michael *had* told me about buying a patch of land in New Dallas. I'd forgotten. He owned so much land. Now, if I could just get him to tell me about Lucius.

"So what's your real name, O man of many identities? I seriously doubt it's Lucius."

"I have a lot of names," he answered vaguely.

We walked slowly, keeping pace beside each other, zigzagging through the thick trees and branches. Leaves and twigs snapped beneath our feet.

"I realize that," I said. "But I want to know your *real* name."

He glanced down at me. "I'll give you three guesses."

"We're alone, and there's no chance of anyone listening in on our conversation. You can tell me."

"Maybe I only tell women I've seen naked."

"Is your name Bastard?" I fluttered my lashes at him.

"Wrong." A hint of amusement laced his tone. "Only two guesses left."

Frowning, I stopped and stomped my foot. When I realized what I had done, my frown intensified. I hated when I reverted to my old princess ways. "That wasn't a true guess, so you can't count it."

"Too bad," he said, never slowing. "I am."

My frown became a scowl, and I jumped back into motion. "Forget it. Don't tell me."

"I wasn't going to. But now that I have your permission not to, I feel so much better," he said, sarcasm dripping from each word.

"You are such a jerk."

A teasing light sparkled in his eyes, softening his entire face. "My mother always told me women like mysterious men. If I tell you, I'll lose my mystery."

"You have a mother?" I hadn't meant the question to sound so shocked, but the words whipped out of my mouth before I could stop them.

"Yes, I had a mother. I didn't get much time with her, but she was very real. What, did you think I'd been spawned magically from fairy dust?"

"No. I thought you'd been spawned magically from the devil."

He laughed, the sound rich and husky and so inherently sensual my blood warmed.

"You read my file," I said, "so you saw that I'm Eden F. Black. Tell me your real name, and I'll tell you what the F. stands for." I frowned again when I realized I was skirting around the need to beg him for the information. Why the hell did I even care about his name? I wondered. The answer eluded me, but the fact remained that I *did* care. I had to know.

"That'd be a good bargain if I were even remotely interested in knowing your middle name."

My hands clenched at my sides as Lucius quickened his pace. He didn't dart a glance behind him to see if I followed. After a moment, I did. I was too curious to wait behind and play games. Besides, I didn't want him to know how much his lack of interest in my name bothered me.

When I caught up, he said, "You ready to talk business?"

"Always," I ground out.

"Jonathan Parker is old money, just like Sahara Rose said. I did a job here in New Dallas a few years ago. Jonathan's brother was abducting otherworlder children as well as human children, and forcing them to—perform with each other."

Our eyes met in a moment of unspoken understanding. Child pornography. I'd seen a lot of evil, but crimes committed against children always disgusted and infuriated me most. "You completed your job, I hope." We both knew I was asking him if he'd killed the brother.

"With relish," he said. "Slowly and painfully."

"Good." Very good.

"The point is, only a few people—very few people, at that—are allowed into Jonathan's life. We can capture him, but he won't talk under torture. His brother didn't. That means we have to gain his trust, get into his inner circle."

The catch in his tone warned me of impending ire on my part. I would have missed it, but I was extremely focused on everything about this man. "By we, you mean—"

"Me. I'm already in."

Of course. Every muscle in my body clenched.

"He knows me as Hunter Leonn," Lucius said, "the wealthy, pampered son of a dead Onadyn smuggler."

"Hunter," I said, playing the name across my tongue. "Cute. Nice irony. I also like the pampered part. You make a lovely spoiled little prince." I jerked a hand down my ponytail. "So you want me to sit back and watch you do the job, I guess."

"No." Moving his head left and right, he popped the bones in his neck. When he spoke again, he broke down the situation like I was a child. "I go in as Hunter. You'll go in after me as bait."

"Okay. So . . . who am I to become?"

"Yourself. You're a Rakan, a rarity. Your people have been hunted for their skin and are now nearly extinct. We can't change your identity. More than that, Michael is high-profile. Most believe he's a wealthy weapons dealer, and too many people know you as his daughter."

"I'm with you." Michael purposefully cultivated his image as a weapons dealer. After taking a job with the government, he'd needed a good cover, something that offered mass appeal to criminals and distanced him from his true identity. "Wait," I said after a moment's thought. "EenLi used to work for Michael. If I go in as myself, he'll suspect I'm an agent. He'll know Michael is protecting me."

"He won't know about me, however, and that's the important thing. From everything I've read on him, I think he'll find it amusing to steal Michael's precious agent."

"All right. I'm on board."

"Good. We're going to spread the word that Eden Black is moving to New Dallas. You're getting old, anyway, so you need a place of your own."

I sucked in a breath, the scent of sun, pine, and blooming flowers taunting me with their vibrant freshness. I glared up at him. A good motivation, yes, but not something I wanted to hear.

"Actually, we'll tell people you're moving out to escape a stalker. Does that suit your vanity?"

I punched his arm.

"You've acted as an otherworlder interpreter for Michael in the past," he said, rubbing the bruised muscle. "We'll find out which high-powered humans are in need of an otherworlder interpreter. As their employee, you'll have to attend parties and political functions, and that will put you in contact with Parker. And me. Your stalker." He eyed me up and down, lingering on my breasts. "Think you can handle it?"

A wave of awareness battled with a flood of irritation. I ignored his stupid question, already making a mental list of the things I needed to do. Rent an apartment here. Obtain a new wardrobe. Recondition my feet to high heels.

"I'll work my way back into Jonathan's circle," he said, "and mention that I met you, learned you were moving here, and followed. I'll let him know that I wanted you, pursued you, but you turned me down."

"That won't be difficult, since it's the truth."

"Shut up and listen." He glared at me. "You'll begin attending all the parties, and I'll play the love-sick fool."

I opened my mouth to offer another little gem: it was always best to stick to the truth, so we didn't get caught in a lie. He cut me off with, "You'll continue to rebuff me. Hard. I'll grow more desperate."

"I see where this is leading," I said. "After I turn you down, you'll place an order for me."

"That's right. Other men will probably want you too, if not Jonathan himself. Either way there *will* be an order placed for you, and you'll be taken. All you have to do is let them take you."

I nodded my head in approval. "I like it. How are we going to proceed after that?"

"I'll buy you, whatever the cost, then purchase us passage to another planet, where I will claim that I can keep you without worrying about legalities."

"And once we know how they're planet-hopping, we strike."

"Exactly. You're going to need new clothes," he said, giving me another intense perusal, a perusal that stripped away my clothes and devoured the naked body underneath. When his eyes reached my breasts, my nipples hardened. When they reached my stomach, my belly quivered. When they reached the apex of my thighs, a flood of warmth pooled there.

"I'd already thought of that," I said, my voice hoarse, dry. "I'm still known as Michael's spoiled, reclusive daughter. I know how to dress the part."

"Good. Because a sophisticated interpreter would not wear"—he gestured to my scuffed leather pants and hiking boots—"whatever it is you're wearing."

"Thank you for the fashion advice, Sparkie. I've always wanted a pierced, tattooed, bleached-out muscle boy to tell me how inept my fashion sense is."

His lips twitched. "Go to Michael. Tell him—"

"I know what to do." I arched a brow. "Can you say the same?"

"Yes. Smart-ass. Like I said, I'm going to renew my acquaintance with Jonathan. Give me three weeks before you show up. But no later, you hear me? Three weeks."

I batted my lashes at him and walked my fingers across his chest. "Why, Lucius Adaire, a.k.a. Hunter Leonn and Bastard Extraordinaire. I do believe you're going to miss me."

"No, baby doll, but you're going to miss me."

With no more warning than that, he jerked me into the hardness of his body, his lips instantly slanting over mine. His tongue thrust into my mouth, deep and probing. I moaned at the pleasure of it, at the heady flavor of him, and sank deeper into his embrace. I didn't protest, though I knew I should have. No, I tangled my tongue with his. I gripped his head and held him to me. I think I had wanted this since the first time I had seen him.

His arms felt like steel bands as they wrapped around me. His palms splayed out over my back and dipped lower . . . and lower . . . cupping my butt and pressing me into his erection. I spread my legs for better contact. Even through his clothing I could feel the long length of him, the thickness.

I'd never craved a man like I craved him. *You don't like him, remember?*

So what, my body responded. I'd have him and get him out of my system. Out of my mind.

The fragrance of honey and cinnamon seeped from me, surrounding us as surely as the trees, billowing sweetly in the wind. I didn't panic at the telltale sign this time. I welcomed it. The intoxicating scent blended with the pine soap scent of Lucius, creating a heady aphrodisiac.

With his hands still cupping me, he lifted me up. I wrapped my legs around his waist as he backed me up against a thick tree trunk. The bark bit past my shirt, but I didn't care.

"You've been driving me crazy, cookie." His voice whispered huskily along the column of my neck, making the nickname sound like an endearment.

I didn't comment. I was incapable of speech. All I could think about was stripping him naked and impaling myself on him. Riding him hard and fast. And often.

"It's that mouth of yours," he continued. He nipped at my jaw, ran his teeth along my earlobe. "I can't stop thinking about it. I hate it. I *should* hate it."

As I panted, I forced myself to find my voice. "Do you like my mouth better when it tells you to kiss me again?" I said rawly. "When it tells you to take off your clothes because I want to see you naked?"

He groaned.

My nipples pebbled, and I rubbed them against his chest, wishing we were already naked, wishing he was already inside me. It wasn't him I needed, I assured myself. Just sex. Only sex.

Instead of stripping me, he whipped away from me. My legs dropped to the ground. "Damn it," he growled, tangling a hand in his hair. "This isn't the time or place."

Several seconds passed before I found my equilibrium. When I did, his rejection nearly gouged me. More than his rejection, however, I resented his ability to stop what he'd started when I would have eagerly gone the rest of the way. Even though he was right. We both had jobs to do, and getting sexually involved right now was foolish.

My eyes narrowed as fury rained through my

blood, fury with myself for allowing him to distract me. "Touch me again, and Michael will have one less employee. Do you understand?"

Lucius remained silent for a long while, watching me, studying my face. Obviously, he didn't like my threat. Very deliberately, he reached out and palmed one of my breasts, tracing his fingertips around the nipple.

I didn't stop him, but I wouldn't back down or show weakness.

"Why?" he said, his eyes slitting to match mine. "You fear you'll die from pleasure?"

"No. You'll die. And not from pleasure. See, I'll take this knife," I patted the blade strapped next to his pride and joy, "and play a little pocket pool."

He disengaged from me completely and frowned. The lines around his mouth went taut, and a fire kindled in his usually arctic eyes. "That's the second threat you've made against my dick."

"Threat?" I laughed, the sound hollow. "Oh, no, Sparkie. It's a promise. And will be a pleasure."

"Just so long as you'll play with it, I guess I don't care what you do. But you'll have to be patient and wait until after the mission."

My hand twitched with the urge to blacken his eye. Maybe break his nose. "I usually don't have a temper," I said, "but you push me past every boundary."

"Two weeks," he said gutturally, as if I'd never spoken. "I want you back here in two weeks."

"You said three earlier."

"Two weeks," he repeated. "Or I'll hunt you down, and we'll finish this."

Threat or promise?

God help me, but I foolishly hoped the latter.

CHAPTER
7

Sharp, agonizing pain consumed me.

My body tensed against the assault it was even now enduring. Someone help me! I'd survived the extraction of copper bullets. I'd survived grenade blasts and C4 explosions. But this . . .

The pain was too sharp, too acute, spreading from one section of my body to another.

Fists clenched, eyes squeezed shut, I screamed, emitting a raspy sound more animal than human. My throat had already endured several similar screams in the past half-hour and now felt raw, aching.

If only my knives were nearby. My guns. Anything! But I was unarmed. I lay on a flat, white table, gripping the edges. I was vulnerable, exposed.

"I'm ready to do the other leg," the woman responsible for my torment said. The diabolical, evil devil incarnate herself: the esthetician.

"No," I gritted out. "Like hell you are." Years ago, I'd had this done every month. I'd worn nothing but designer clothes, had always looked expensive and sophisticated. What a lifetime ago that seemed. "Getting one leg waxed was bad enough. You're not touching my other leg."

"Big baby," she mumbled, gathering her supplies. Long blond hair cascaded down her shoulders, framing a delicate, elfin face. She was a wisp of a woman, just under five feet, with fragile bones and a tiny frame. Her angel face hid the beast inside.

I could snap her neck like a twig—and laugh joyously while doing so. Over the years I'd killed more people than I could count. Big baby? Me? I don't think so.

"Better be careful what you say to me, sweetheart," I warned. Before she could respond, however, I added darkly, "Just do it. Finish. And hurry."

My tormentor's rose-petal mouth twitched. If the bad guys learned about waxing, they'd be able to take torture to a whole new level.

"I expected more from you," she said with a chuckle, applying warm, oozing, sticky wax to my right leg.

In the wake of laser treatments and follicle-killing creams, waxing had become obsolete for humans long ago. Unfortunately, such treatments permanently damaged Rakan skin cells, forcing me to revert to these archaic practices.

As my tormentor jerked a strip of tape from my leg, quickly followed by another, and another, I pounded my fist against the table. I forced my thoughts elsewhere. Michael had already purchased and furnished an apartment for me in New Dallas, though I had yet to see it. I'd wondered, though—more often than I should have—if Lucius had sneaked inside and found the best escape routes and secured any weakened point of entry.

Most likely.

That man wouldn't leave anything to chance. But more than that, I doubted he trusted *me* to see to it. He was just like every other agent I knew, thinking women weren't as competent as men. I looked forward to proving them all wrong.

Most importantly, I looked forward to proving Lucius wrong.

Lucius . . . His picture formed in my mind. Cheekbones cut from glass. Aquiline nose. Piercing ice-blue eyes. Even in my mind, he regarded me with something akin to superiority. I seriously despised him. I desired him. I hated him. I craved him. My teeth bit into my bottom lip. I hadn't seen him in seven days. I missed him. Yes, I hated him.

With one kiss, he'd consumed my mind, my good intentions, my common sense. He'd taken my sanity and scorched me to the core, somehow branding his name into my every cell. Most days, I thought of nothing but him. I saw his face when I bathed. I heard his voice when I slept. I felt his heat when I walked.

In the whole of my life, I'd had two lovers. Neither of them had affected me so strongly. So deeply. And that Lucius did, a man I wanted out of my life at the earliest possible moment, irritated me. Yet I still wanted to see him again. I hungered for the sight of him. And my hunger had nothing to do with the case.

What was he doing right now? What was he thinking? Had I passed through his mind even once? *Stop it, Eden. Just stop.* Lucius's thoughts didn't matter. All that mattered was that he'd renewed his acquaintance with Jonathan Parker and that our plan ran smoothly.

"There," the esthetician said. "Your legs are finally done. That wasn't so bad, was it?"

"A knife wound *isn't so bad*," I grumbled and sat up. My gaze traveled the length of my legs, examining the supple, golden skin. "Being chained to a wall and awaiting my enemy's arrival *isn't so bad*."

She uttered a humorous snort. "You're acting just like a man. No, actually, most men would at least pretend to be tough."

"Go ahead. Laugh it up." I smiled darkly, leaning close. "But make sure you sleep with a weapon tonight."

Unperturbed, she returned my smile. "We haven't even done the bikini area yet."

I scowled.

Twenty minutes later, she laughingly waved me away. "I have never heard so much screaming."

I grabbed up my pants and tugged them on. Then—would the torture never end?—I strapped on a pair of high heels. My feet had grown used to boots. I stalked (okay, hobbled and stumbled) from the room. With the torturous waxing complete, I spent the rest of the day inside my room being fitted for a new wardrobe. My feet ached constantly. I didn't mind wearing dress suits and flowing gowns, as long as they hid my weapons. I would *not* go without protection for any reason. Ever. The shoes, though . . .

"Don't forget," I said to the seamstress, "to make room for my weapons."

She rolled her eyes and knelt at my side, sticking her pins in the ice blue material. "You want me to add a codpiece, too?"

I leveled an irritated stare at her. "Only if you can make it extra large." Did no one find me menacing? Damn it, my hands were stained with blood; I'd spent my life *killing* people.

"Funny," she said dryly. "I've worked for Michael for many years. I know the drill."

I at last found myself alone, but it didn't last. I didn't have time to change or sprawl across the bed before Michael knocked on the door.

"Enter."

The door slid open, and he entered hesitantly.

"Don't hurt me," he said, tiptoeing to the seat by the window and sinking into the plump gold cushions.

Laughing, I removed my shoes and tossed them on the floor with a thump. Relief! "I can't believe I used to do this stuff all the time. Fittings, waxings. High heels."

"I remember those days." He grinned fondly and leaned his head against the chair's edge. "So how are you feeling?"

I eased into the white velvet settee across from him. My dress puffed around me. The seamstress had given me orders to remove it and hang it the moment she left. I took a small bit of pleasure in disobeying. "I feel like the pampered princess I've always been accused of being."

He slid a long, thick cigar from his jacket pocket and placed the tip in his mouth. He didn't light it yet but savored the flavor as he studied me. "I meant, how are your injuries? I'm worried about you, sweetie."

"One hundred percent healed."

His brows winged up, and his eyes gleamed with doubt. "Not even a slight twinge of pain or weakness?"

"No," I said, total deadpan. I didn't feel guilty about lying to Michael about my lack of injury. I was *almost* one hundred percent. But I didn't want him to worry about me. Or worse, doubt me.

The cigar rolled between his fingers as he said, "Would you tell me if there were?"

"No."

Another grin lit his features. "That's what I thought. Stubborn girl. That's what you are, and that's what you've always been." His smile faded slightly. "You know, I never wanted you to be an agent."

"I know," I said, my tone soft.

"You came and asked me to let you train, and I . . ." He shrugged. "I just wanted you to learn how to protect yourself. Your kind is hunted. And my kind, well, you could have been abducted and used to get to me. I wanted you prepared. You proved stubborn, though, and wouldn't let me keep you behind the scenes."

I chuckled. "I remember how you had me play doctor to injured agents to show me exactly what kind of pain I was asking for. 'See the blood,' you said. 'See the pain in his eyes because that's what you'll get if you choose this line of work.'"

"But you never wavered." There was pride in his voice.

"No. I never wavered. I wanted you to see me as strong and capable. Like your men."

"I know."

"I love that you trust me now, that you've given me another chance. I don't think I can ever express just what that means to me."

Michael pushed to his feet and strode to the mini-bar. I insisted one be installed for my own personal use in every one of his homes. Sometimes it was the only way I could relax.

"You're my daughter," he said. "No matter what blood runs through your veins, you're my daughter and I love you."

"I love you, too." I knew he had a natural daughter. I also knew her mother kept her overseas, and Michael was rarely allowed to see her. I think I filled a void in his life.

Silence settled around us for several minutes before he said laughingly, "What kind of killers are we, having such a mush fest?" After clipping the end of his cigar, he claimed the nearest lighter and puffed. Smoke soon billowed around him. Cigarettes and cigars were illegal because they were air pollutants. But Michael lived in a world where he followed no rules but his own.

He poured a Scotch. "Want one?" he asked.

"Yes. Thank you."

He handed me the glass, and my fingers wrapped tightly around the cool container. He poured another. Sipping, I reveled in the way the smooth liquid warmed me and erased the twinges in my arm and side.

"Have you ever dealt with Jonathan Parker?" This was the first chance we'd had to talk business.

"From a distance."

"I'd like to see your files on him."

"Of course. They're in the study."

I didn't bother with shoes, but went barefoot. I took my drink with me. I'd never needed one more. I felt more on edge today than I had in a long time. Silently, we strode down the stairs, past Oriental vases, metal sculptures of gods and goddesses, and the trickling rock waterfall he'd had built into one of the walls. When the sealed door to the study sensed our presence, it opened automatically. The cleaning crew had already left, so we were alone and didn't need to worry about prying eyes.

"Sit," he said, indicating a dark brown leather recliner with a tilt of his head. "Relax."

I obeyed without hesitation, resting in the chair across from his desk. I breathed in the familiar scent of leather.

He padded to that desk, rested his cigar in an ashtray, and palmed a remote. He pressed a series of buttons, dimming the lights and causing a holoscreen to materialize over the far wall. A man's image flashed into focus. Human, thirty-something. Pale hair, a long aristocratic nose. Thin lips, but a handsome visage nevertheless. Arrogant brown eyes regarded the world with a nothing-can-hurt-me gleam.

Even with the warnings about the sun's dangerous rays, Jonny Boy obviously spent a lot of time outside. His skin was deeply tanned and lined more than it should have been. An aura of self-importance enveloped him.

I disliked him already.

"Does he like women or men?" I asked.

"He likes power."

"Typical."

"He's been married three times. The first wife died in a car accident." Michael pressed another button, and the image of a gorgeous young woman filled the screen. Black hair, green eyes. Flawless skin. "Her brand-new tires blew."

"Convenient for him."

"The second wife died in a car accident as well." Another young woman, this one with silvery white hair and big blue eyes, consumed the screen.

"Let me guess. Her brand-new tires blew?"

"No, her sensors gave out."

"What tragic accident befell his third wife?" I asked.

"Amazingly enough, she's still alive."

She wouldn't be for long, I thought. Not if Jonathan Parker had his way. I gazed up at the third wife's picture. Glossy red hair, sparkling brown eyes. A sultry vibe radiated from her.

"Obviously Parker likes his women young and pretty. Too bad they don't live long." I tapped my knee with one finger, smashing the puffed, satin dress. "There wouldn't happen to be a hit on him, would there?"

Michael's entire expression lit with amusement, easing the age lines around his mouth. "At this time, no, there isn't a hit on Parker."

"Too bad." I took another sip of my Scotch and savored the rich taste in my mouth for a long while. I wondered what type of persona Lucius—a.k.a. Hunter—had donned in order to immerse himself in Parker's world. Lucius wouldn't be tattooed. Nor would he be pierced. Most likely he'd have to wear a suit and tie, perhaps sport a pair of glasses. A sigh slipped from me as I set my glass on the small table beside me. No matter what persona he used, he would be—you guessed it—sexy as hell.

"Tell me about the man I'll be interpreting for."

"*Her* name is Claudia Chow, and she's a major player in the alien rights movement. Her dedication to otherworlder equality has made her the first human ambassador of alien goodwill." He grinned a guess-what-I've-done-now grin. "As of now she's on my payroll."

"Ambassador of alien goodwill?" I snorted. "What did you tell her about me?"

"Only that my daughter desired a change of scenery and needed a new job. I almost couldn't convince her to help me. However, the moment she learned her interpreter was a Rakan, she relented. I think she sees you as a new prize pet she'll get to parade around and show off."

"I can hardly wait," I said, my sarcasm heavy.

He pointed a finger at me. "Don't you dare kill her."

All innocence, I blinked over at him. "Give me

some credit. I do know how to use restraint when the situation warrants it."

A teasing light glowed in his eyes. "I thought so, too, until I saw you with Lucius. You're . . . different around him. Why is that?"

"That man—" My hands clenched. Michael was right. I *was* different with Lucius. More emotional. Lustful. On edge. Why? I didn't understand and couldn't answer Michael's question. "You trust him completely?"

"Of course." Slowly he frowned. "I never would have paired you with him otherwise." Michael lifted his cigar, rolling it between his fingers and causing smoke to waft around his hand. "This is a good plan the two of you have put together."

"Him. Not me." I crossed my arms. "I wish I could take credit." As soon as I spoke, I realized how true those words were and how great my bitterness. I might desire Lucius, but I resented him, too. This assignment should have belonged to me, and me alone. Not Lucius. Yet so far he was moving the pieces of the game on his own.

Was it wrong of me to feel that way? Yes. Did that matter? No.

Michael shook his head. "Sweetie, you've been injured. Don't be so hard on yourself. It's not a competition between you and Lucius."

Yes, it was. Sometimes I felt like I was in competition with the entire world. I wanted to be the best. Always. At everything.

"Go get some rest, Eden. We'll talk more tomorrow."

No point in arguing. I planned to go to bed as he'd suggested, I just didn't plan on resting. There was something I needed to do first. I pushed to my feet, closed the distance between us, and kissed his stubbled cheek.

"Good night," I told him.

He eyed me suspiciously, since he wasn't used to me obeying his orders. "Love you." I patted the cheek I'd kissed and strolled to the sanctity of my room. My feet sank into the rug as I skidded around a gold lamp and into my closet. I changed out of my dress and into a black shirt and a pair of black pants. I put on boots, not heels, and crawled atop the velvet green comforter.

Moonlight drizzled through the curtains, and the sounds of the night seeped from wall speakers, offering a lazy, almost sultry tune. Crickets hummed, and cars zoomed. I closed my eyes against the programmed noise.

I was going spirit-walking.

CHAPTER
8

Keeping my eyes closed, I internalized my focus to the deepest part of myself, gathering my energy there. Warmth soon churned inside my stomach, leaving the rest of my body cold. Determinedly I began to push that energy forward with mental hands, the weight of flesh separating from the etherealness of soul.

A cracking sound filled my ears. Slowly, so slowly, my spirit rose out of my body. Though the feat had become easier over the years, such a disconnection—for that was exactly what it was—required intense concentration and strength.

I'd wanted to visit Lucius so many times this past week, but had resisted. He'd called every night to give me a progress report, and every night I'd waited in anticipation of that call. Too much anticipation. By resisting seeing him, I had proved to myself that

I didn't *need* to see him. He wasn't a necessity. I had myself under control, and my defenses against him were well fortified. So what that I'd thought about him constantly today.

I took immense delight in the fact that he'd never know I had visited him.

We were located in different states, but that didn't matter. I'd find him. Usually I had to be within a mile or so of my target because I had to walk the actual distance to reach him. That had never been the case with Michael, who I could reach anywhere, anytime. After my kiss with Lucius, I knew it would not be the case with him either.

With my spirit freed completely, I became suspended in a place between reality and death, experiencing only an ephemeral lightness. I stood at the edge of the bed and stared down at my physical body. Even though I'd done this countless times before, I always experienced shock when I saw myself lying on the bed—there, but not really there.

The first time my spirit exited my body had been an accident. I'd been a little girl, only four years old, and had just discovered my parents' lifeless bodies sprawled in blood. In my bedroom. I'd run from them, run outside screaming for help. Michael had scooped me up and carried me back inside, to the nearest room. My parents' room. He'd placed me in their bed, said, "Stay here. Don't move. I'll take care of them," then raced away to do just that.

While I'd lain there, sobbing violently, I'd heard a cracking noise, like something breaking apart. At the time, I'd figured it was my heart. But the next thing I knew, I looked down and saw myself. I barely had time to rationalize what had happened before I floated to another room, to Michael.

He'd never known I was there, never known I watched him. He'd been in my bedroom, the bodies and blood gone—as if they'd never been there. Michael drank himself into oblivion that night, his hands shaking, what he'd seen almost too much for him to bear. Later, he told me the killer had been a man who'd intended to rob the house.

He also told me he'd killed the bastard for me.

I'd spirit-walked many times after that, each time beginning and ending of its own accord. My Rakan tutor had vaguely mentioned that some of our kind had this ability, but he himself hadn't, so he hadn't known how to teach me. Over the years, however, I'd honed the skill. I now controlled every aspect: when, where, how long.

I'd never told anyone. Not even Michael, though I loved him more than anyone else in the world. I wanted him to see me as human as possible, I guess, like a real daughter. I'd almost told him once, after he'd gifted me with the car I'd begged him to buy me. In the end, I hadn't wanted to spoil the moment.

Others—well, if people learned I left my body unprotected, unguarded, and vulnerable to attack, I'd fall prey to my enemies. The huntress would become the hunted.

With a sigh, I brought myself back to the task at hand. Right now my physical body was splayed out like the fairy-tale Sleeping Beauty. Utterly still, golden hair spilling around my shoulders and arms. If not for my shimmering gold skin, I could have easily passed for a human.

I closed my eyes and pictured Lucius. Pictured the hard planes and angles of his face, pictured the silkiness of his lips. The width and sinew of his chest. Soon a ghostly wind ruffled my hair. I lost the foundation under my feet. Tugged by an invisible cord, my spirit began to move. Faster. Faster. Lights whizzed past me, twinkling in and out of focus. Soon a mixture of voices—one a rough but cultured timbre, the other a smooth baritone—gained in volume.

I stopped suddenly, abruptly, and gasped.

I stood in a study very much like Michael's. I knew beyond a doubt, however, that this was not my father's. The wood paneling was lighter, the furniture different, more modern. A purple and red Lucite column towered over the desk. Bookshelves of fuchsia and yellow lined one wall. Silver-plated side tables and a faux-fur ottoman occupied a corner. Bloodred carpet covered the oak floors, and a large portrait of a nude redhead—obviously a natural redhead and Jonathan's third wife—hung over the unlit fireplace.

My attention slid to the center of the room.

Lucius lounged atop a lime green couch, a brandy in one hand and a cigar in the other. He'd colored his hair again, this time a rich walnut brown. A scar slashed down his right temple. He wore contacts, darkening his ice-blue eyes to the same shade as his hair. As I'd predicted, the piercings and tattoos were gone. He'd fit his muscled body into an expensive silk suit.

I almost didn't recognize him. His lips gave him away, though. He couldn't change the lush, rosy softness of them. I licked my own as a picture flashed through my mind, a picture of him kissing me, devouring me. Setting my body aflame.

Was I destined to always respond to this man?

Another man sat across from him. Jonathan Parker. The self-indulgent, wife-killing playboy. His picture failed to reveal the aura of depravity that encompassed him, a depravity he couldn't mask in person. Cigar smoke drifted around him as he chuckled devilishly over something Lucius had said.

"So you met an otherworlder who fires your blood, did you?" Jonathan said. He sipped amber liquid from a glass, his feet propped on top of an expensive coffee table. His grin widened, revealing too-white, too-perfect teeth. "And she's a Rakan, at that." He sighed wistfully. "I'll be honest. I've always wanted to fuck a Rakan. All that gold . . ."

"This one's mine," Lucius cut in sharply. His gaze narrowed, leaving no hint of humor. Only deadly menace. "She's the only reason I came back here. I want her. She's mine," he repeated.

Leaning back, Parker tugged at his earlobe with his free hand. "That hot, is she?"

"She's fire and ice. Lava one minute, glacial the next. And she won't have anything to do with me," he admitted, losing his darkness and assuming a sheepish quality.

"Ah, Hunter. I wouldn't let it worry you. Women like to play hard-to-get. They want us to romance them. They're desperate for it. How else do you think I won each of my wives?"

"I thought that was what women wanted, too. I sent her three hundred orchids, and she used them as fertilizer. I bought her a 'Vette, and she used it for a crash-test demonstration. I sent her a diamond necklace, and she sent me a restraining order."

Jonathan chuckled. "If she's that difficult, why don't you find someone else?"

"I want *her*."

I stepped toward Lucius, coasting my fingertips over the buttery soft leather couch. With each step, I imagined his scent, that soapy pine scent I so admired. I even imagined the heat of him. *What are you doing? Stop!*

Lucius's shoulders tensed slightly. Had I not been so focused on him, I would have missed the action. My head tilted as I watched his gaze flicker left and right, as if searching for something—or someone? A cold shiver racked me, and I paused. There was no way he could see me. Right? Was something wrong? I scanned the room, looking for anything that might have raised his guard. I found nothing out of the ordinary.

"I'll win her one way or another," Lucius said, but there was now an edge to his voice that hadn't been there before.

"I hope you're right." Jonathan didn't act any different. He dropped his head back to stare up at the vaulted ceiling, the action causing the liquid in his glass to slosh. He puffed at his cigar. "If the woman's as reluctant as you say, she might not like it that you followed her here. Well, beat her here, I should say."

"I can guarantee she won't like it." Determination gleamed in his eyes. "But I'll persuade her to see things my way, I have no doubt."

"You're confident." Parker straightened and gazed pointedly over at Lucius. "That's what I've always liked about you. Nothing dampers your determination."

Lucius nodded in acknowledgment of the compliment. I resumed my journey toward him. I hadn't seen him or touched him in a week. It felt like years. The urge had never left me, of course, but now that I was here—well, kind of here—the craving intensified.

When I reached him, I allowed my fingers to drift through his hair. I couldn't feel the strands, but I imagined their silkiness and wished I could somehow solidify my fingers. The best I could do was gather energy and push *that* through his hair. But such an action required more concentration than I was willing to devote at the moment. Besides, Parker and Lucius might wonder at a sudden breeze.

Sighing, I moved to caress his jaw. He stiffened, even sucked in a slight hiss of breath. My hand froze in place. What the hell was going on? He should not feel me. Not even a little. No one, not even Michael, had ever guessed my secret. I hurriedly drew back my hand.

"Do you smell cinnamon?" Lucius asked.

My knees nearly buckled in shock.

"No." Parker's brow furrowed. He regarded Lucius silently for a moment, then tilted his chin and said, "Are you all right?"

"Fine, just fine," Lucius said. "Just thinking of Eden. She's likely to spit on me when she realizes I'm here."

"Even if she despises you, you're a lucky man. No woman has ever consumed me like this one does you."

"Not even your wife?"

"Which one?" Parker snorted. "Never mind. Which one doesn't matter. They were all bitches."

Lucius's eyebrows descended low over his eyes. "Were? Isn't Cybil still alive?"

"Barely. If I'm lucky, she'll soon drug herself to death."

My focus whipped to Parker, darkening. If I'd had a weapon, I might have used it. Such casual disregard for his wife deserved a bit of punishment.

"Being consumed by a woman isn't a pleasant experience," Lucius grumbled. "I almost wish I'd never met her."

There was a ring of truth to his voice that insulted me. Turning to face him, my eyes slitted; I reached out and jerked his hair. Childish of me, I know, the actions of a spoiled princess. Just like before, he stiffened. I frowned. How was he doing that? Did the connection between us allow him to sense me?

My blood chilled with the thought. I didn't want to be connected to him like that. I gulped and backed away until I stood in the corner, out of reach. Out of temptation's way.

"Speaking of Eden," Lucius said, resuming the conversation as if it had never stopped, "I need you to host a party for me."

Parker grinned slyly. "One to welcome her to town, perhaps?"

"No." Lucius shook his head. "I don't want her to know she's the guest of honor. A political gala will do. A gala that I, of course, will attend."

"What about the restraining order?"

"The law can kiss my ass. She's an alien, so she doesn't really have rights, does she?"

Parker's grin widened, and he sipped his brandy. "Who's your Eden working for?"

"Ambassador Claudia Chow."

A heavy pause slithered around the room while Parker mulled over his next words. "I don't like Claudia Chow," he said. "And I'll be honest. I don't really have the time to host a party."

It was a lie. I knew it, and Lucius knew it. Parker was simply hedging for some type of favor.

"I'll owe you," Lucius said.

Head tilting to the side, Parker studied him. "The woman really means that much to you?"

"I told you. I'm obsessed with her." He sighed.

"I know she's a Rakan, but damn. She's still pussy, and you can get that anywhere. Tell me again what's so special about this one."

A wicked gleam lit Lucius's eyes. "She's got a mouth that could suck a man dry."

Yes, a weapon would have been nice. I'd carve my name in his balls, then drain every drop of his blood so there would be nothing left to suck.

"Then, of course," Jonathan said, "I'll take you up on that favor and happily arrange a party where the two of you can renew your acquaintance."

The two men continued to chat for a while, before finally saying their good-byes. Parker walked Lucius to the door and with a slap on the shoulder, sent him on his way. Lucius was doing his job—quite nicely, too, I grudgingly admitted—so it was best I get some rest so I'd be in top shape when I joined him.

Though I wanted to follow him, I closed my eyes

and pictured my bedroom. That ghostly wind soon returned, and I felt a strong tug. Felt the foundation shift, saw twinkling white lights. Within minutes, my spirit glided back into my body, and I opened my eyes.

Moonlight pushed through the familiar velvet curtains of my bedroom. The feather-soft mattress I'd grown accustomed to cushioned my back. Unlit, vanilla-scented candles fragranced the air, blending with a hint of Michael's cigar.

I rolled to my side, forcing Lucius from my mind. I'd never sleep otherwise. Odd, though, that I felt more bereft and alone than I had in a long time.

Damn that man.

CHAPTER
9

The next day, I lugged my newly waxed body through a grueling three-hour workout, followed by two additional hours of assault and defense training using a diverse range of weapons. A girl never knew when a specific skill would come in handy. Knives, pyre-gun, hand-to-hand combat in the virtual reality chamber, they all took their toll.

I opted out of the final wardrobe fitting. The seamstress had my measurements. What more did she need from me?

My failure with EenLi was becoming a heavy mantle of guilt on my shoulders. More so than before. Perhaps that was why I had pushed myself so hard today. Or perhaps watching Lucius so easily insert himself into Jonathan Parker's life had made me jealous. He was a much better agent than I'd given him credit for at our first meeting. Now *I* had to prove my worth to *him*.

Only when completely exhausted did I retire to my room. I didn't nap, however. There was much yet to be done. I showered, changed clothes, then jogged downstairs for a quick meal to boost my energy. Chocolate truffles, strawberries dipped in cream, peaches, all sprinkled with sugar. My favorites. I ate them quickly. As I downed two glasses of sugar water, I heard Michael's voice over the speaker system.

"Eden, sweetie. I need to see you in my office."

Curious, I abandoned the kitchen and my delicious treats and strode into his office. He looked exactly as I'd left him yesterday—dressed in a suit, hair slightly rumpled, cigar at his side. He sat at his desk and glanced up from a thick stack of papers. He grinned at me welcomingly.

"That was fast. Finish your fitting already?"

"No, I decided not to go." Before he could respond, I sank into the chair in front of him and said, "What did you need to see me about?"

He leaned back in his seat and watched me silently for a long while. "I know you've been anxious. I also know there's nothing to be done on EenLi's case right now."

"Yes," I said, confused. What was he getting at?

He folded his hands over his stomach. "I have another case for you."

Excitement bubbled inside me. How much did I love this man? "Go on."

"There's a Morevv in New Florida raping human

women. Local AIR have been unable to act because of political bullshit. The Morevv is the mayor's lover. Mayor Jeffries, to be exact, a woman known for her political iron fist. The man's death needs to look like an accident."

"Does he have guards?"

Michael shrugged. "Two burly humans, but they always make a hasty exit when the mayor visits him."

Which meant I needed to catch him with his pants down. Literally. "Does AIR want to interrogate him first?"

"No. They just want him dead. He's due to meet the mayor tomorrow."

I could get in and out in no time. It was exactly the challenge I needed to combat my restlessness. Michael knew me so well. "I'll do it," I said. "Thank you." Perhaps, with this success, I could begin to wipe away my last failure.

He uttered a sigh. "Please, please, *please* be careful. After all the resources you've put into EenLi, I don't want you knocked out of commission on a routine takeout."

"I'm always careful." I blew him a kiss. "I'll leave within the hour and hopefully return by tomorrow night. If you'll reschedule my fitting, I'd be grateful." I winked and shoved to my feet, then sprinted from the office.

*   *   *

My target's name was Romeo Montaga.

Yes, that's what the Morevv called himself. Romeo.

Morevvs were known for their beauty, so I suppose the name fit. Especially since this alien's beauty surpassed any I'd ever seen. He possessed sun-kissed hair that flowed past his shoulders and an innocently divine face only an angel should have. Only his forked tongue gave away his alien status. He dressed his tall, lean frame in black leather pants and an open white shirt. I think he fancied himself a Casanova pirate.

He owned a wolfhound instead of a parrot, but the dog was about as menacing as a bird. She sprawled on her velvet pillow beside the bed and hadn't blinked twice when I entered. With her head resting on her paws, she watched Romeo with complete disinterest, even a little fear.

I'd spent the day following him, learning his patterns. He liked young girls, liked watching them and rubbing unceremoniously against them as he sauntered past them.

He disgusted me.

And right now the disgusting bastard had New Florida's fifty-four-year-old mayor naked and tied to his bed. I'd known I needed to catch him with his pants down, but I'd hoped to arrive after the act was completed. Not before.

Amid the woman's cries of encouragement, he quickly undressed, ripping off his clothes in a single, dramatic sweep. Seeing his naked body, I blinked.

Shook my head. Nope, still there. I guess Morevvs had more than one alien quality. A forked tongue *and* a doubled-pronged penis. Two penises, of all things.

As Romeo stood naked at the edge of the bed, the mayor moaned and thrashed like she'd just entered the corridors of paradise. I noticed the Morevv remained unaroused. He had to close his eyes and stroke himself to achieve a (double) erection.

Being inside the closet as I was, I yearned to jab out my eyes and cut off my ears. These memories were going to haunt me. If only the closet door wasn't slatted.

"Ride me, my stallion," Mayor Jeffries cried. "Ride me hard. Just like you know I like it."

"No talking, woman," he growled. He slapped her ass, only a mild tap, really. "I'm in charge here."

She moaned with rapture.

He slapped her again, harder this time.

Though he would never have admitted it aloud, I think he was turned off by her enjoyment. I wouldn't have doubted if this was how Romeo raped the others. Chained them to a bed, and let them see his goods.

"Now you're mine." The words held no hint of possessiveness. No, they sounded rehearsed. He climbed up the bed and slammed into the mayor. That brought forth another round of moans from her. Thankfully, only five minutes passed before the Morevv stallion finished his ride. Well, before his bedmate finished, that is. Her entire body convulsed in orgasm. With his features drawn tight, the alien hefted himself off her, even though it was obvious he hadn't come.

He untied the sated woman and said, "Did you like that, sweet?"

"You know I did. Maybe . . . maybe do it even harder next time," she whispered, almost as if she were ashamed by her desire.

"Harder?"

"Yes." Mayor Jeffries lumbered off the bed. She retrieved a mint green suit from the floor. Once the wrinkled material was secured over her equally wrinkled body, she withdrew a stack of bills and placed them on the table. She stared over at Romeo.

"You will be free tomorrow," she said, her voice going crisp. When she donned her clothes, I guess she also donned her sense of power.

Romeo glanced at her. He grinned slowly. "Of course. I'll ride you so hard your screams will be heard all over the world."

"Tomorrow, then." She shivered before striding from the room. The door closed behind her automatically, locking her out.

Romeo quickly lost his smile. "Bitch," he muttered.

If I hadn't realized before, I did now. He didn't like her. Not a bit. He was a paid lover, and gave her what she wanted. Domination. It was ironic that a public figure known for her iron fist in the political arena allowed a man, and an alien at that, to so control her privately.

Alone now, Romeo scowled down at the dog. "You should have bitten a chunk out of her ass, you worthless piece of shit."

The dog whimpered at his tone.

I frowned.

Romeo closed his eyes and began stroking his erections—he needed two hands for the job. Added new meaning to the term "double your pleasure." I rolled my eyes. I could stun him now, then poison him while he couldn't fight me. He'd be dead by morning, and no one would know why or that I'd even been here.

But . . .

I'd broken in several hours ago, bypassing two guards and a cutting-edge robotic security system. A robotic system that used artificial intelligence to systematically learn the homeowner's behavior patterns and adjust itself accordingly without the need for programming. Security components integrated into such a system armed and disarmed automatically, while making accommodations for those still on the premises. To even enter the home, I'd had to program myself into the system. Very time-consuming, but worth it.

There should have been more guards, but I guessed the mayor preferred to keep their liaison as private as possible. Probably because she was nothing more than the Morevv's bitch. I wouldn't want people to know that, either, if I were her.

Upon first entering this room, I'd taken the time to glance around. I'd found Romeo's holograph appointment book. Why did people use those? They left a clear trail to follow. Anyway, there'd been an interesting tidbit there.

Visit home, 9 p.m. Return 11:30.

What did he mean by *home*? Did he have family here? Or did he mean something else entirely? Did he mean to travel through a portal and return for a while to his home planet? I suspected the latter, and that piqued my interest. Actually, I hoped the latter. EenLi was using those damn portals. Michael wanted to know where they were. Lucius wanted to know where they were. If *I* could supply that information . . . The intoxicating thought seduced me as surely as a passionate lover.

When Romeo (thankfully) finished his business, he rolled to his feet. "Like what you saw, Killer?" he asked the dog, his tone snide. "Bitch," he said. "You're all bitches."

He kicked Killer in the stomach, and she yelped. She tried to bite him, but he kicked her again. Head ducked between her paws now, she crawled backward, away from him. I bit the inside of my cheek. Kick her one more time, I thought darkly, and I'll forget the portal and kill you now.

Naked, he padded to the closet to find something

to wear. As huge and filled to bursting with clothing as this space was, I didn't worry that he'd see me lying on the top shelf. Hell, I wouldn't have been surprised if a dozen other assassins were hiding in here, and I simply hadn't seen them. The only thing that bothered me about the situation was how clichéd it was. I mean, a sophisticated killer forced to hide in the closet? Please. But I'd been stuck like this before, and I'd most likely be stuck like this again.

Romeo quickly chose another pair of black leather pants. He opted not to wear a pirate shirt, instead choosing a tight V-neck. I supposed I could see why some women fell for him—besides the double penis. His outward beauty bordered on illegal. He left me cold, however. Partly because I knew he possessed the heart of a monster underneath all that masculine beauty, but also because he lacked the rich vitality Lucius possessed. Comparing the two men was like comparing a still-life portrait with a carved sculpture. The sculpture, at least, boasted three dimensions.

Finished dressing, Romeo closed the closet. I quietly climbed down and moved to the slatted door. He was admiring himself in a full-length mirror. I glanced at his digital clock. He was scheduled for "home" in thirty minutes. The ticking of time didn't rush him. Humming under his breath, he ambled to his dresser and slipped a necklace around his neck. I remembered seeing the necklace earlier when I'd searched his room. It was small and triangular, with a platinum chain and an odd stone in the center—a stone unlike any I'd ever seen. Crystal-like, yet shiny and smooth as brass.

After spritzing himself with cologne, Romeo finally left the bedroom. The dog growled at the door. I desperately wanted to spirit-walk and follow his exact steps, but I didn't dare leave my body unprotected in this home. Instead, I pulled my duffel bag from the shelf. I strapped it to my back before stealthily slipping from the closet.

Killer stopped growling and glanced up at me through soulful eyes. *Save me,* she seemed to say. She didn't attack me, didn't act as if she wanted to hurt me in any way. Something inside me lurched. I didn't have time for this, but I found myself bending down, cupping her face in my hands and meeting that big, brown gaze.

"Don't worry," I whispered to her. "That's the last time you'll ever have to see him." Then I left the same way I'd entered—through the bay window. I didn't think the portal would be located inside the house. That meant he had to exit sooner or later.

I pulled my face mask down. As I hooked my belt to the clear wire I'd left dangling, cool, moist air penetrated the knitted fibers of my black body stocking. I already wore gloves, so I pushed myself over the window's ledge. Amid the sound of nearby swishing waves, I propelled down the five stories. The evening darkness offered some protection. Unfortunately, the home's security lighting cast away most of the shadows.

I'd scaled walls brighter and more visible than this with no problem, and this proved no exception. I floated to the ground undetected. The key was to stay close to the corner, move quickly and silently, without pause.

I unlatched the clear metal tether and crouched low to the ground as I maneuvered to the front of the house. Romeo's car still sat in the driveway. I pushed out a relieved breath as the Morevv exited the house's front door. I'd guessed correctly.

He didn't go to the parked, empty Porsche, however. No, he strode purposefully to the wooded area behind the house. Confused, I silently followed, wondering all the while if I'd made a mistake after all.

CHAPTER
10

Romeo stopped in a small circular clearing at the edge of the property, away from the ocean and allowing me an unobstructed view of him. Over the years, other targets of mine had come to clear areas like this. I'd never known why; I hadn't cared why. I'd always used the isolated surroundings to my advantage and struck. Perhaps I should have had more patience.

For a long while Romeo stood motionless, silently watching the darkening sky. Was he meeting someone? Did he suspect I followed? Or . . . was he expecting a spaceship? Perhaps the word *portal* actually meant "ship."

Minutes passed. I unsheathed my gun.

Brittle grass bit into me. Salt stung the air. Concealed by shadows and bushes, I crouched motionlessly, waiting as time continued to pass and nothing happened. Nothing at all. No one arrived. At least his movements didn't indicate suspicion. I uncovered my wristwatch by pushing back my shirtsleeve. Three minutes after nine. I frowned. What or who was he waiting on? Did he expect to world-travel simply by standing there?

If Lucius were here, he'd grab Romeo and beat the answers out of him. I could do the same, I suppose, but that wasn't always effective. I preferred to observe the otherworlder's natural tendencies.

I only prayed my patience would be rewarded.

A quiet whistling sounded several feet behind me. A person? Merely the wind? Heart drumming with adrenaline, I shifted my focus, switching my aim as I searched the trees. No one was there that I could see. Leaves rustled, then stopped . . . rustled, then stopped . . . like the beat of a drum, ever increasing in intensity. Not wind, for I felt nothing on the ground. An animal?

Romeo didn't seem to notice or care.

The sound steadily crescendoed to a thousand disharmonized screams, like blades screeching through metal. The noise ripped through me, tearing me apart inside. Pressing my lips together to cut off my own scream, I squeezed my eyes shut and dropped my pyre-gun, covering my ears with my hands. That didn't help.

When I realized what was happening, I cringed. Solar flare. They always affected me this way. Humans never seemed to hear them, or feel the searing, violent bombardment of charged particles. Other-worlders always seemed to be affected. For most, the experience was a pleasure. For me, it was a nightmare. Flares were stronger out in the open, with nothing to obstruct their destructive waves.

I forced my eyes open, forced myself to watch Romeo. He basked in the sound, spreading his arms wide, welcoming the disharmony. Had he caused this? How? Why? I didn't understand.

The wind kicked up, lifting and scratching like a desperate lover. Trees shook and rumbled ominously. A bright light pulsed in the purple sky. Too bright. Getting brighter. Getting closer. What was happening? What—

Romeo vanished.

One second he stood there, in the center of the circle, the next he didn't. The screaming ceased. The light dimmed. The trees settled.

Gaining my balance, I shoved to my feet. My head whipped to the side as I searched for my target. I searched the entire clearing for tracks. None led away from the circle.

My confusion doubled.

I replayed the scene through my mind. The screaming, the wind, the lights, and the way Romeo embraced them. My eyes widened as realization struck me. He'd somehow traveled from one world to another through the solar flare. What. The. Hell?

Knowing what he'd done, however, merely increased the number of questions I had. Why hadn't I traveled with him? I'd been no more than ten feet away. I should have disappeared, too.

He was scheduled to return in two hours. I'd question him then. Brimming with anticipation, I settled into my hiding place. And waited for his return.

Eleven thirty came and went.

I should have returned to Michael by now, or at least called, but I didn't dare move from this spot. I kept myself awake all night, well past the time allotted for the trip on Romeo's daily planner. Another solar flare did not erupt, so Romeo didn't return.

Morning brought the harsh rays of the sun, causing heat to envelop me. Causing the grass to stiffen. Maybe I'd miscalculated. Maybe he'd meant eleven thirty this morning.

I'd wait.

Sweat dripped down my face and chest. I wished to God I'd brought a canteen of sugar water. But this was supposed to be a quick job. In and out. So I'd brought no provisions for anything other than killing. One hour after another dragged by, the sound of the insects my only companion. I wouldn't doubt if Michael had sent out a search party for me by now. The man did like to worry.

Eleven thirty arrived without any signs of a solar flare. Romeo, however, arrived right on schedule. I kept my gaze on the circle, and before my eyes, he simply appeared. No warning. Just blink, there he was.

Excitement and anticipation renewed, flooding me. He shook his head to orient himself, and I made my move. I jumped up from my crouch and bolted toward him, taking a controlled, don't-fuck-with-me stance right in front of him. My pyre-gun locked on his heart. His eyes widened when he saw me. Covered from head to toe in black as I was, I looked every bit as menacing and deadly as I actually was.

Without a word of warning, I punched him in the nose to get his attention. His head whipped to the side, and blood poured down his lips and chin. "Where did you go?" I demanded.

His mouth gaped open, and he stumbled backward, away from me.

Instead of trying to overpower me, he wanted to run. I expected no different. Most people, even those who used physical force when angry, backed down when faced with physical force against themselves. "You have three seconds to answer my question, or I'll melt the flesh from your bones. One."

I saw the wheels turn in his head before he morphed into seductive mode and offered me a let's-go-to-bed smile. "There's no need for this. We can—"

Disgust welled inside me. "Two."

"I know how to pleasure women," he whispered suggestively.

"Thr—"

"Home," he gasped out, his body beginning to tremble like a little girl's. "I went home to Morevv."

"Through the solar flare?"

"Yes, yes." He licked his lips, and his gaze darted from side to side. "Please don't hurt me."

"How does the solar flare work?"

"I—I don't know."

"You're lying." I stepped toward him and punched him again.

Tears filled his eyes and spilled onto his cheeks. He dropped to his knees. "I swear I don't know how it works. I only know it's the transit portal. Please don't hurt me. Please."

I wished he could see my expression when I said, "Is that how women have begged for your mercy? On their knees, pleading? Did you show them even an ounce?"

His sun-kissed skin paled, giving him a ghostly pallor. "I've never raped a woman."

Busted. "I didn't mention rape. Did I?"

"So what?" he said with sudden bravado. "They liked what I gave them in the end. Every woman does."

"Now I know you're lying, angel cakes, and I don't like liars." I pulled the trigger. A blue light flashed, hitting him directly in the chest.

He froze, locked in stun. His features projected shock and fear. I withdrew a small vial from my pocket, closed the distance between us, and poured the liquid down his throat.

"Onadyn," I said, knowing he heard every word. "Completely undetectable. A deoxygenating drug that some otherworlders use so they can breathe Earth's air. You—someone who needs oxygen to live—will suffocate in minutes, your every breath ineffective, making it look like you came out for a walk but suffocated."

I saw a muscle twitch in his jaw, and abject terror filled his eyes. I patted his cheek and gave him my sweetest smile. "Don't worry. I'll take care of your dog."

Romeo had named the dog Killer. Since that wouldn't do, her new name became Agent Luc. A play on the name Lucius. Hopefully he would be properly irritated, especially when he learned this shaggy brown dog with the big, watery brown eyes was female. I smiled. Ah, life was suddenly good.

Agent Luc and I negotiated an understanding on the flight home. She craved affection, and I gave it to her. She'd been nothing more than Romeo's punching bag. She deserved a little pampering.

When we exited the ITS, she saw Michael waiting at the bottom of the exit steps. His expression was concerned until he saw me. Then a big, relieved grin lit his face. Immediately, Agent Luc began whimpering. I guess she didn't like males—even those who smiled.

Wise woman, I thought. I gently patted her neck,

cooing, "He won't hurt you. He just looks mean." I squinted in the harsh daylight, heard another ITS pass overhead, a gentle hum.

Michael's confused gaze flicked from the dog to me. "You're late, and you didn't call" were the first words out of his mouth.

"I was delayed. I'm sorry." I hoisted my bag over one shoulder. Gripping Agent Luc's leash in the other hand, I strode from the private airstrip toward Michael's waiting sedan.

Agent Luc resisted at first, watching me with those sad brown eyes. "Come on, big girl," I said. "Think of this as an adventure." She reluctantly fell into step beside me, hopped into the back seat, and curled into a protective ball. She looked out of place against the fine black leather.

"Who's your friend?" Michael asked, motioning to the dog.

"She used to belong to the Morevv, but now she's your newest agent."

He rolled his eyes. "Do I have to pay her?"

"Of course." I slid into place beside Luc, and Michael settled behind the wheel. "Mission complete," I told him.

His motions clipped, he spun to face me. "That's it? That's all you have to say? I was beyond worried about you. After your last injuries . . ."

"I'm sorry I didn't call." I reached over and squeezed his hand. "I got caught up. I should have made the time, anyway, and I was wrong not to. I admit it." I knew he was a worrier, and I needed to take better care of him. "Forgive me?"

"As if I could stay mad at you," he said with no heat. Only affection.

I grinned. "What do you know about solar flares?"

"Only a little, and only because they bothered you so much as a child. Why?"

I sidestepped his question. "Tell me what you know first."

He programmed the self-navigating vehicle to take us home, then shrugged. "They're sudden eruptions of energy, heat, and light."

The car jolted into motion, but Michael didn't have to turn his attention away from me. The car drove smoothly along the road, expertly weaving in and out of traffic. A typical male, Michael had always liked his toys to be expensive, fast, and state of the art.

"What else?" I asked.

"Humans can't see them, but we think a lot of otherworlders can. They happen more frequently when the sun approaches the maximum apex of its cycle. Now, you tell me something. What's this have to do with anything?"

"I experienced one."

"And?" he prompted.

Leaning back in my seat, I propped my feet on the dash. "And I watched an alien disappear in the midst of it."

"Disappear?" Michael frowned. "Until a few weeks ago, I'd never heard of anyone mastering molecular transfer."

"I don't think that's what happened."

"Because—" he prompted.

"Because of what was happening around him. Violent winds. High-pitched screams. It wasn't just molecular transfer. What if solar flares aren't what we think they are? What if they happen when aliens open portals?"

"Then why can't *we* open one? Why can't you?" Michael's frown deepened. "Maybe you missed the guy. Maybe—"

"No," I interjected. "I looked for him, for his tracks. He didn't simply run or hide, Michael. He vanished."

"So you think . . . what?"

"Remember what EenLi said about the portals not always being open?"

"Yes, I remember."

"That means they are opened and closed. They could be opened and closed through solar flares. Because of solar flares. Cause the solar flares. *Something*."

"Possibilities, yes, but they raise the question of why *you* have never vanished during one. Over the years, you've been in the middle of several."

True. My hands curled into fists. I was so close to the truth. I knew it. But so close wasn't what I needed. "There has to be a reason, a catalyst that sucks someone through. When is the next flare due, do you know?"

"I'll check on it."

I rubbed my forehead. "I wish my parents were alive. I could ask them how we came to this world."

Michael stiffened, just as he always did when I mentioned my biological parents. I immediately regretted my wistfulness. I suspected when I spoke of them, Michael felt I was somehow dissatisfied with him. I wasn't. Michael had worked hard to raise me. Very hard. He hadn't hired nannies or shuffled me off on other people. No, he'd kept me near him, seen to my every need and want. I loved him all the more for it.

I hurried to change the subject. "Could the other-worlders be using some sort of homing device?"

"Again, it's a possibility," he said. "I'll do a little research on solar flares and keep you posted on what I find."

"Thank you."

He patted my hand. "I hope you'll go to your fitting when we get home," he said. "That seamstress, what's her name, Celeste?"

I shrugged. I didn't know, either.

"She nearly cut out my heart with her needle and thread when I told her you would be gone for an entire day."

I laughed. "Give her a raise. I like her style."

We reached the house a few minutes later. I shifted to command the door to open, but Michael caught my wrist in his hand. His features tightened. "Eden," he began. "You know I love you, right?"

My stomach instantly clenched. "What's wrong?" I asked, my concern making the words sharper than I'd intended. He told me he loved me all the time, but there was something in his voice this time—something deep and filled with pain.

"Nothing," he said, turning away. "Nothing's wrong. I just wanted to remind you how I feel about you, that's all."

"Michael—"

He emerged from the car without another word to me, leaving me mystified.

CHAPTER
11

Still reeling from Michael's words, I grabbed my bag and tugged Agent Luc from the car. We quickly stormed the house, leaving the heat of the afternoon behind us, along with the trees and birds and colorful flowers that encompassed the home. I had every intention of hunting my father down and demanding an explanation. I didn't buy his "I just like to remind you" line. He liked to remind me, sure, but never with such stark pain in his eyes.

Before I found him, however, the seamstress—Celeste—found me.

Agent Luc plopped protectively at my feet as Celeste bounded down the stairs, needle and thread in hand. "Where have you been?" she scolded. "I have eleven dresses and six pantsuits to finish, and yet you abandon me at the most pivotal part of my work."

"You don't need me here to finish." Frowning, I

hoisted the weight of my bag over my shoulder. "You have my measurements."

Exasperation flittered over her pretty features, and she tossed her hands in the air. "Fine. You want the clothes to slip from your shoulders, tear when you run, and reveal your precious weapons, that's fine with me. I will sew another's name in the garments so no one knows they are my creation."

"Great idea," I said and turned toward the study where I knew Michael had gone. The doors were closed, most likely locked.

Celeste screeched, the high-pitched sound echoing off the walls. "Go to your room and try on those clothes, Eden Black. Now!"

I spun and faced her. I opened my mouth to offer her a stinging retort, but noticed how her chest heaved, how her eyes gleamed. She was as passionate about her work as I was about mine. I respected that.

"What are you waiting for?" she prompted. "An engraved invitation from the Rakan king? Go."

"This isn't a good time."

She pushed a breath from her pursed lips, and her shoulders drooped slightly. "There is never a good time with you."

I cast one last glance toward the study door, then reluctantly leapt up the stairs with Agent Luc close to my heels. "Next time someone talks to me like that, you attack. Understand?"

She whimpered.

I rolled my eyes. Useless canine. Thankfully, the pinching and poking of my fitting only lasted an hour, and Celeste quite happily went on her way.

While Agent Luc slept on the bed, I allowed myself a long, lingering shower, letting the steamy water wash away the trials of the last few days. Afterward, I brushed my hair and changed into comfortable lounge pants and a shirt, then strode into Michael's office. He was absent, but two women were cleaning and dusting. I fought a wave of disappointment.

"Come back later," I told the women.

They nodded and hurried out. I really *did* need my own place, I realized. Somewhere private and all my own. Unlike Michael, I'd do my own damn laundry and cleaning. I didn't like how freely he admitted his staff. Yes, he took precautions against theft and spying, but was that ever enough?

Alone, I logged onto the computer with a spoken "Eden F. Black." I e-mailed Colin Foley, a quantum physics instructor I'd once dated, asking for information on solar flares and potential transportational properties. He might know nothing; he might know something. We'd ended our two-year relationship amicably, so I didn't doubt he'd return my message. I stressed the importance of a speedy reply—which I hoped to receive before I left for New Dallas.

As I stared at the screen, willing him to reply *now*, my eyes began to burn and water. I yawned. I'd been up the last two days and needed sleep. Pushing out a breath, I shut down the computer and left the comforting familiarity of the office.

I trudged up the stairs into my room and flopped onto the bed beside Agent Luc. Hopefully taking an hour or so to rest and center my energy would grant me a measure of peace and sanity.

I closed my eyes and commanded every limb, cell, and organ to relax. Slowly my mind smoothed, beginning its gradual slide into calmness and tranquillity. In gentle increments, my chaotic thought patterns coalesced into a focused whole. The pulse of my heartbeat harmonized with the steady stream of my mind.

Just when I was congratulating myself on a job well done, an image of Lucius appeared, upsetting my equanimity. My heartbeat sped up and thumped eagerly; my blood heated. I bit my bottom lip and mentally shoved his picture out of my mind.

It slid right back to center, taunting me.

My eyelids fluttered open, and I shifted to my side. The dog opened her eyes, checking her surroundings. When she realized all was well, she closed her eyes again and continued slumbering peacefully—taking up half the bed. If only I could find such peace. Lucius, I decided in the next instant, was a disease. A stinking, festering disease that rotted my common sense and might very well be the death of me. I needed some sort of antidote.

The battle to cast out the haunting presence of his

image was in full force when my phone erupted in a series of beeps.

I uttered a low growl and picked up the cell unit from the side table, anchoring the main piece to my ear. "Yes."

"Miss me?" A rough voice crackled over the other end.

"I miss you about as much as I miss the copper bullet I had to dig out of my stomach."

Lucius laughed, the sound husky and rich as it washed over me. Neither of us commented on the fact that we didn't have to state our names, that we'd only known each other a short time but already recognized each other's voices.

"I love it when you play hard-to-get. Tell me how things are going," he said with barely a breath.

"On schedule."

"What's this I hear about solar flares?"

My eyes narrowed, and I glared at the far wall. "When did you talk to Michael?"

"Answer me first."

I did, and my speech was followed by a long silence.

"We need to investigate this," he finally said. "Michael's doing some research, but I think we need to do some on our own. The more the merrier, right?" He paused. "There's got to be something to this flare shit. You did good."

To be validated by someone as stern and unbending as Lucius was intoxicating. "Thank you," I said. I tried to keep the elation out of my voice.

I must have failed because he said, "You cryin' tears of joy over there?"

My cheeks heated. "Shut the hell up."

"Don't bite my head off." He laughed.

"Which one?" I muttered.

"Either." Another pause reigned before he blew out a breath. "I like you more every time I talk to you, you know that, cookie?"

I faked a southern drawl (quite well, I might add). "Is that why you're calling me, Agent Luscious? So you can like me more?"

"Don't call me that," he snapped. "I had a spare minute and thought I'd check on you."

"Didn't Michael tell you how I was doing?"

"I wanted to hear it from you, all right?"

"All right," I said, and let the subject drop. I didn't admit that I was glad he'd called, that I'd wanted to hear from him. "Let's finish our conversation about the solar flares, and you telling me what a good job I did."

He snorted. "Just look into them. We can compare notes when you get here."

My eyebrows winged up as a tide of anticipation hit me. "I bet I'll have more information than you."

He chuckled huskily. "Are you for real?" he said.

"What?"

"Did you hear yourself? I'll have more information

than you," he mimicked. "I doubt I've ever heard a more obvious challenge. You have got to be the most competitive woman in the entire world."

"Now that's hardly a fair statement. You haven't met every woman in the world."

"Doesn't matter. I accept the challenge. We'll just see who has more information."

I grinned, invigorated. "So, how are things with you?"

"Parker sympathizes with my obsession for you and plans to help me win you. He's throwing a party and made sure your new boss received an invitation."

I knew that, I almost said, but thankfully stopped myself. He had no idea I'd listened and watched his interaction with Jonathan Parker, and I needed to keep it that way. "What exactly do you plan to do to win me?"

"Let's keep that a surprise so your reaction is real. I wouldn't worry except that your acting sucks."

My grip on the unit box tightened, and I lost my grin. "I can act."

He didn't comment.

I heaved a sigh. Fine. "What's my apartment like?" I gritted out.

He offered no denial about the fact that he'd sneaked inside. "Looks good. Spacious. Well guarded. Expensive. You'll have no trouble fitting in. And in case you were wondering, your bed is big enough for two people."

"That's good to know. I'm sure Agent Luc will be glad we can both fit."

Silence. Dark, heavy silence that crackled with tension.

"Who the hell," he said haltingly, "is Agent Luc?"

"A friend of mine." I stroked a hand down the dog's soft fur, and she snorted blissfully in her sleep. "Luc is helping me with the case."

"You did not have my permission to include this man in our mission."

I didn't correct his assumption that Luc was a male. *How's my acting now?* "I don't need your permission for anything."

"Damn it, Edèn. Does Michael know?"

"What? Are you going to run and complain to the boss?" I taunted.

I heard a sharp grinding noise and pictured Lucius working his jaw. I smiled because I'd just ensured he wouldn't ask Michael about Luc for any reason. Ah, male pride. So predictable.

"If this man steps one foot—one damn foot— inside your apartment, I'll shove those feet so far up his ass he'll vomit them out. Understand?"

My smile grew wider. I couldn't help myself. "Oh, I understand all right."

He paused. "What's that supposed to mean?" He no longer sounded angry. He sounded hesitant.

"Your jealousy is cute, that's all."

Click.

The abrupt disconnection and sudden silence caused my ears to ring. My smile became a chuckle. I rolled to my back, letting the cell unit drop beside me. I even kissed Luc on her wet nose.

A few minutes later, the phone rang again. Still grinning, I picked up on the fourth ring. "Yes," I said.

"I never make threats, Eden. Only promises. I didn't want a partner, but I've resigned myself to you. I will not tolerate anyone else on this case."

I wouldn't either, but I was not about to let this man think his threats—oopsie, *promises*—cowed me. I would not let him think he called the shots.

"Agent Luc and I will be there on schedule," I said. With that, *I* severed the connection.

Feeling more at peace than I would have after a ten-hour slumber, I affectionately scruffed Luc atop her shaggy brown head. She opened her eyes and stared up at me adoringly. "Better watch your paws, girl. Agent Luscious is a jealous man."

I laughed happily.

CHAPTER
12

Finally, the day arrived.

Pretending to be an employee of Michael's sent to check on his daughter's accommodations, I flew into New Dallas. After a quick stop at Michael's farmhouse, I visited my apartment. For the event, I dressed in a short, spiky black wig and wore a fake pregnancy belly under a synthetic cotton dress. My skin was heavily caked in makeup. I looked a sight, I'm sure, but I needed to map an escape route. Or two. I needed to know what to expect when I, as pampered Eden Black, arrived.

Honestly? This sucked. It was hot. Sweat dripped from me as I walked down the sidewalk.

I blamed EenLi for the extreme heat and wouldn't have doubted if he was one of the Mecs who could control the weather. They did like it hot and dry, but the boiling temperature nearly felled me.

Situated in the bustling heart of New Dallas, the apartment building was enhanced chrome and bullet-resistant glass. Eighty-seven stories high. I stepped inside. Fingerprint scanners were at every door. Holographic guides. High-tech, just like Lucius had said.

Grateful for air-conditioning, I maneuvered my way through the throng of people in the well-lit, computerized lobby and entered the farthest elevator, exclusively used for the penthouse. My data—both real and fake—had been programmed in, and the scanners readily accepted me as who I claimed to be. The ride inside the decadent box was long but smooth. A satin-covered bench occupied the far wall, and a cooler with single-serving wine sat next to it.

When I reached the top, the doors slid open and I stepped into a world of utter self-indulgence. Gazing around, I inhaled the aromas of leather and cotton, expensive commodities in this synthetic world, where alien and human wars had destroyed so many precious things. Plush recliners, overstuffed couches. Glass tables. Double holoscreen TVs. Two wet bars, fully stocked.

Everything was voice and fingerprint protected.

I did a quick walk-through, making sure that I was alone. I was. Good. I found the two hidden doorways that Michael had installed, making sure they opened properly. The one located on the kitchen floor squeaked, so I oiled it down. Wouldn't do to let the bad guys know my location. It led to a safe room. The other door, which opened smoothly, led to a slide that would take me straight to the bottom of the building.

My bed, I noticed, was covered in blue silk and lined with what looked to be sheer lace. I knew the material was a protectant and would seal out poisons and gases. And yes, two people could easily fit inside it.

Everything was in order. That was all I'd needed to know.

I took a cab for several miles, then walked the rest of the way to the farmhouse, all the while making sure I wasn't followed. A girl could never be too careful.

Agent Luc was waiting for me. The moment I stepped through the door, she bounded from her floor pillow. Ren, the agent I'd left in charge of her care, growled a clipped, "Be still, dog."

"Watch your tone," I snapped. I crouched down and petted Luc's soft, clean fur. She sighed happily. "Missed me, huh?"

I quickly showered and changed into a fancy dress suit, then Marko drove Luc and me back to the airport to await pickup. What a busy day so far, and I knew it was only going to become more hectic from this point on.

Thankfully my civilian driver, or rather Claudia Chow's, arrived not long after, and I soon found myself gazing out of a limousine window. I shifted impatiently in the soft leather seat.

The mission, for me, had officially begun.

Agent Luc lounged next to me and rested her chin on my leg. Absently I stroked her fur and tapped my high-heeled foot against the floorboard. This part of New Dallas offered a plethora of scenery, most of it bleak. One moment a series of towering buildings and speeding cars could be seen; the next I saw wide-open spaces, tumbleweeds, scrubby trees.

I'd always thought of myself as a patient woman. But right now, everything inside me screamed to *hurry.* Not because I yearned to see Lucius, I assured myself, but because I wanted, at last, to begin helping with this case.

An hour passed. My lips dipped in a frown, and I shifted in my seat again. Why couldn't the ambassador of alien goodwill live closer to the airport?

I'd read the file on Claudia Chow. She'd been born to privilege. She'd married young—a man also born to privilege. She'd never known a moment's hardship in her life. When her husband had been alive, the two of them had enjoyed hunting cloned animals and traveling the world.

Now she spent her time fighting for alien rights. That didn't make sense to me, didn't seem to fit her background. I was to translate for her at parties, meetings, and any other events she chose to attend. I sighed.

She owned a ranch on the outskirts of the city . . . a sprawling ranch now visible on the horizon. Thank

God. My back straightened, and I grinned suddenly. Happily.

"We're almost there," I told Luc, excitement dripping from my tone.

She blinked up at me and licked my hand.

I patted her between the ears. "Be careful around the ambassador. She used to hunt animals. She might still."

Luc licked me again. She trusted me to keep her safe, and I liked that.

I returned my attention to the ranch. It was red and white, wide and sprawling, with notched wooden posts anchoring the first floor to the second. Armed guards roamed the edges of the property as well as around the home itself. They weren't human. They were purebred Ell-Rollises, creatures so thought-dependent they could only follow the dictates of their master.

"You've got to show total courage while you're here, girl," I said to Luc. "If anyone suggests one of those guards hurt you, they'll do it without a moment's thought. So don't go outside without me." I traced a hand down my braided ponytail and muttered, "Maybe I should have left you with Michael." I didn't want her hurt.

I'd intended to leave her behind. As I'd strode out the front door, however, Luc had bounded behind me, whimpering with every step. I'd been reminded of every time Michael left me behind for a mission—every time I'd cried for him, wanted him to sing me to sleep. I hadn't been able to do the same to Luc.

Who could have known I'd turn to mush over a dog?

She licked my leg.

With such a fierce companion, I thought dryly, I might not need the modified rifle, silencer, and hollow-point bullets in my bag. Of the two of us, though, I was in more danger than Luc. Michael had told me Ambassador Claudia Chow liked to collect otherworlders. All races. "I bet she'd stuff and mount me if it were legal."

Agent Luc gave me yet another lick.

Honestly, I despised humans who used otherworlders as trophies. "Ah, look at my alien," I mimicked with sugary sweetness. And I didn't care if the driver heard me. I was a pampered princess. A diva. "Isn't it pretty?" My lips pursed. If Claudia treated me that way . . .

One of the guards must have notified Claudia of my arrival, because the moment the limousine eased into the long, winding gravel drive, she stepped onto the slatted porch. I studied her. She wore her black hair in a severe twist, had perfectly applied makeup, and her long, elegant body was molded into a conservative black silk suit. I would have put her age at thirty, but I knew she'd just turned forty-six. She was an attractive woman who obviously knew her power and reveled in it.

The car stopped, and my door instantly opened. An Ell-Rollis stepped toward me and extended his hand. "Thank you," I told him coolly. Game face on. Sweet, air-conditioned air became hot and fragrant with the smells of summer and horses. My nose twitched as I stepped outside.

The Ell-Rollis didn't speak. He did smile at me, revealing razor-sharp yellow teeth. The smile seemed out of place on his lizardlike features. He must have been ordered to greet me with a welcoming grin.

Agent Luc jumped beside me and sat, my ever-watchful guard. At least she didn't fall asleep. As if she had heeded my warning, she eyed the Ell-Rollis warily.

With absolutely no expression on her face, Claudia closed the distance between us and folded me in her arms. For show? Most likely. I didn't welcome the embrace, but I did tolerate it. She stood a few inches shorter than me, forcing her to stretch on her tiptoes when she kissed both of my cheeks.

"Welcome," she said, her voice cultured, refined. Her eyes were brown, and up close I could see the freckles scattered over her nose.

"Thank you." I smiled sweetly, not a single hint of falsity. I hoped. "I'm very happy to be here."

"Let me look at you," she said, releasing me and stepping away. Her dark gaze drifted over me, slowly taking my measure in a full body once-over. "So much gold. It's stunning, really."

Want to check my teeth? Perhaps tag my toe? I gave her a wider grin. "Thank you. That's nice of you to say."

"Did someone tinker with your DNA," she asked innocently, "or are all Rakans as glittery and golden as you?"

"We're all like this, I'm told."

"I'm simply eaten up with jealousy. You must look at yourself in the mirror a thousand times a day."

"Yes." The answer of a princess.

"We'll make sure no one tries to de-skin you. I'll take measures to protect you." She patted my cheek, just as I sometimes did to my dog. "You and I are going to get along famously, I'm sure. Giles," she called over her shoulder. She even clapped her hands together. "Take Miss Black's bags to the Yellow Room." To me, she added, "Yellow will blend so nicely with your golden skin."

"I won't need my bags taken to the Yellow Room. I have an apartment in the city."

"Nonsense. I want you to stay here. No reason for you to travel back and forth."

Oh, no, no. "I prefer to stay at my own place. That's one of the reasons I moved away from my father."

Claudia's brown gaze sharpened, and she inched toward me in a subtle I-am-in-command-here pose. "I prefer to have you here. With your dog, of course. It's welcome to stay as well, and will have more room to run and play here."

"I'm sorry, but I must insist—"

"And I must insist that you stay." Her eyes gleamed with determination.

"That was not part of our arrangement," I said, striving to maintain my calm. Should I throw a fit?

"I've now made it a part of our arrangement. If that's a problem . . ."

Then she would find another interpreter. I'd lose my cover. Why such insistence that I stay? I wondered, fists tightening. Still, I gnashed my jaw and didn't offer another argument. Studying the apartment, oiling the secret door, had been for nothing. Great. "The Yellow Room sounds lovely."

The moment I spoke, her expression softened, and she grinned happily. Her teeth were white, perfectly straight. "Wonderful. I knew we'd get along. Giles," she called again.

A tuxedo-clad Genesi appeared behind her. His race possessed wrinkled gray skin that folded over in layers. I'd killed a Genesi once. A female. She'd emitted some sort of humming energy that tinkled like bells as she fought me. Those bells had grown in volume and had nearly burst my eardrums by the time I finished her off.

Without looking me in the eyes, the Genesi walked stiffly past me and to the car, hefted my bags in his arms, then pivoted on his heel. I allowed this without protest. Most of my weapons were hidden securely in everyday toiletry items. Even if he searched my things for hours, he'd never find anything out of the ordinary.

"Now, tell me about your friend," the ambassador said, motioning to the dog. "What's its name?"

"*Her* name is Luc. She's leery of men," I added, patting her head, "so it will be best if your male servants leave her alone."

"I think it's marvelous that you have an Earth-born companion." Ambassador Chow's face blanketed with a hint of sadness. "My companion is gone. A virus took him."

I didn't mention that I myself was Earth-born. "I'm sorry for your loss."

She waved her hand through the air and forced a smile. "It was so long ago. Are you thirsty, my dear? I'm sure you are," she answered for me. "Let's adjourn to the drawing room. We'll have lemonade and get to know one another better."

With Luc clopping at my side, I followed the ambassador and strolled eagerly inside, my form-fitting calf-length skirt crinkling with my every movement. Cool air blasted me, shivering through my clothing and onto my too-warm skin. That brief stay in the sun had overheated me, I realized.

I blinked away the red-gold sunspots and studied my new, temporary home. Comfortable looking, yes. But . . . My hands curled into fists again. I wanted my apartment. As we sauntered down a long hallway, one of the first things I noticed were the animal heads that decorated some of the walls. Deer, coyote, and wild hog, all of which were endangered and illegal to possess or kill, even the clones.

I'd expected something different for the elegant Claudia Chow. Yes, I'd known she hunted animals, which was now something that required a government license, but I'd thought . . . I don't know what I'd thought.

She glanced at me over her shoulder. "What do you think of my home?"

I decided to be truthful. Less complicated that way. "The animal heads give me the creeps."

"Really?" She frowned, genuine surprise flicking through her eyes. "Almost all of your people seem to enjoy them."

My people? Did she mean Rakans or all otherworlders? Either way, it didn't seem like something an Ambassador of Alien Goodwill should say.

We finally stepped inside the drawing room, a room boasting animal skulls and bird feathers. Interspersed throughout the carcasses were lace doilies and flower-filled vases. Are you kidding me? This had to be hell.

Hiding a grimace, I waited until Claudia seated herself in a floral chair before I claimed the rosy pink settee across from her. Luc sat at my feet, still looking wary. Between Claudia and me was a small, rolling table piled high with cookies and lemonade.

Except for the dead animals, the scene reminded me of a period piece. An old movie, perhaps, with ladies and gentlemen and proper manners. I suspected Claudia cultivated the image purposefully. To relax her guests? To disarm them?

Ever the gracious hostess, she poured me a glass of tangy lemonade, and I tentatively sipped. I hated anything sour, and this proved to be completely devoid of the sweetness I preferred.

"Martha," she said, "please bring Luc a bowl of water." Orders given, Claudia offered me a cookie.

I readily accepted. It, at least, possessed *some* sugar. If I could have only one food in the entire world, that would be it. Pure, granulated sugar. I nibbled on the edges of the cookie and sighed with satisfaction.

"I'm not sure what you've been told of your duties," she said, "but all I'll require of you is your presence at every political and social function I attend, to accompany me when otherworlders visit to tell me of their problems and concerns, and to interpret any calls I receive."

That's all, huh?

"My last interpreter spoke only six languages, so aliens often left my presence frustrated with their inability to communicate with me. Your father mentioned you speak twenty-seven languages." There was a ring of disbelief in her tone.

"He didn't exaggerate, I assure you."

Surprise flittered over her refined features, as if she'd expected me to deny it. "How did you manage to learn so many?"

A female servant arrived with Luc's water bowl. The girl was alien, a Brin Tio Chi, a race that was dark as mocha and moved with fluid grace, practically floating, with a shadow-mist enveloping their bodies. She placed the bowl in front of Luc and drifted away like a dream, her white robe wisping at her ankles. The dog drank greedily.

"A tutor of mine once told me Rakans have an affinity for languages. That all of our kind seem to learn them as easily as human children learn the alphabet."

"That's wonderful." Grinning, Claudia clasped her hands. "There's a party we'll be attending tonight, and I expect many different alien races to be there. Some of them haven't yet mastered English, so you'll have to translate for me."

The party. Lucius. I could hardly wait. "That will be my pleasure."

She sighed. "Something you need to know about me is that I always mix business with pleasure. I expect many otherworlders to approach me tonight with problems they've been having. They know they can come to me anywhere, anytime."

My head tilted to the side. "What kind of problems?"

"Discrimination, mostly. Humans often act superior to their alien counterparts—and jealous when someone they feel is undeserving has money and power. That's when I step in. I make sure alien needs are represented in the Senate."

A pretty speech. Rehearsed? Or truthful?

"When Yson—he was my husband—was alive, we traveled the world and witnessed so many atrocities against aliens. We vowed to do what we could to help." Her face gleamed with sadness. "Then the Zi Karas came over and brought that horrible plague that killed so many humans and animals. Yson was one of the first to die, leaving me to help on my own."

"I'd think that would have made you hate all aliens." I stated the words as an observation, an afterthought. Casual. But I watched her expression intently.

The fine lines around her eyes seemed to deepen. "For a while, yes, I did hate them. But Yson would not have wanted me to harbor such hatred. He would have wanted me to keep my vow. And so I have." She waved a hand through the air. "Now enough sadness. Let's talk about happy things."

What a puzzle she was—a puzzle I planned to solve. Whether the pieces would fit together in an innocent or betraying manner, I didn't know. I only knew I'd have to stay on my guard with her. Michael seemed to trust her (somewhat), but I couldn't. Not yet.

We chatted for a few more minutes about the weather, about my food preferences and sleeping habits.

"Why don't you go upstairs," she said. "You can unpack or rest or whatever you need to do before the party."

"Where's the party located?" I asked, unable to keep anticipation from my tone. I already knew the answer.

"At Jonathan Parker's estate. He's wealthy and powerful and a good man to have on your side." She paused, grinned. "He insisted, absolutely insisted, we attend."

I returned her grin with one of my own. "I look forward to meeting him."

CHAPTER
13

I spent the next hour searching my new bedroom for bugs and cameras.

A single dead animal head hung from my "yellow that blends well with my skin" walls. A deer. The rest of the decor was tasteful, if purely Texan. Cowbell chandelier, horseshoes on the walls, wooden bedposts that supported a wheelbarrow-shaped bed. Snakeskin baskets rested on the side tables.

I found two cameras, but no bugs. The ambassador of alien goodwill had replaced the deer's eyes with round, black lenses pointed toward the bed. Whether Claudia Chow was simply a pervert who liked to watch, had nefarious reasons for wanting me under surveillance, or wanted the camera here to help "protect" me from gold lovers, I didn't care. I renewed my determination to be cautious around her. She didn't know my true purpose for being here, but she was going to get me inside Jonathan's party. For that I'd endure her creepiness.

I didn't care if she knew I'd found the cameras. I openly removed and disabled them. Picture splicing had become common years ago, so the government had made cameras like these illegal without a permit. I doubted she had a permit.

"Lord save me," I muttered. I could handle the camera problem one of two ways. Hand the cameras to the ambassador personally with a warning not to place them in my room again, or not mention them at all.

After a moment's debate, I decided not to mention them. I'm willing to bet she knew the exact moment I found them. If I kept quiet, she'd wonder about my thoughts, my reaction, and perhaps tread more carefully around me.

Assured now of my privacy, I began memorizing the layout of the room by sight, then with my eyes closed, learning the spacing between furniture and the length of the floor. Luc watched me curiously the entire time. She even paced beside me for a while before becoming bored and flouncing to the bed.

A time might come when I needed to navigate this room in the dark, simply to survive. I charted the best escape route, as well as a second in case the first was blocked.

Afterward, I allowed myself a lingering shower.

The dry enzyme spray did not offer the same relaxing sensation as the warm, steamy water at Michael's, but I enjoyed the feel of clean skin.

Especially now, knowing I would soon see Lucius. Knowing I would soon meet Jonathan Parker face to face. Knowing a "slave" order would soon be placed for me, and I would be stolen away, perhaps locked underground. Dirty and cold.

Soon . . . yes, soon.

Lucius would be attending Jonathan Parker's party tonight. I'd see him in person. Talk to him. And I would think only of our case, I vowed. Had he learned anything new about the solar flares? About EenLi? According to Michael, the bastard still had not been spotted. It was like he'd disappeared.

Maybe he had.

Maybe, like Romeo, he'd used a solar flare to return home.

If that proved true, I'd find a way to chase him all the way to Mecca.

The spray began to sputter, so I shut the unit off and stepped from the white tiled enclosure. Heated air billowed from vents above, beside, and below me to keep me warm until I dressed. I restrapped my weapons onto my body: a small pyre-gun on the inside of my thigh, one knife, and a tiny vial of Onadyn. I never knew which I'd need, so I liked access to all three.

I decided, though, that I needed something else

this time. Something more than my usual arsenal. Just in case. These were new surroundings with people I didn't know and hadn't followed. I locked an anklet around my ankle—an anklet that possessed hallucinogens in the shapes of diamonds.

That done, I slipped the ice-blue sheath dress over my head. The sheer material kissed my breasts and hips, but flared freely around my calves with different lengths of scarves. I left most of my golden hair down, clipping only the sides back and out of the way with sapphire-studded combs—which also doubled as retractable blades.

"Not bad," I muttered, studying my reflection in the mirror. Iced gold.

I'd come to loathe high heels, but I supposed I could tolerate them for tonight. Who knows? If needed, I could use the heels as a weapon. I anchored a strappy pair the exact shade of my dress onto my feet. A little mascara, a swipe of gloss. There. Done.

Luc barked her approval.

I checked my computer for a message from Colin. Nothing. I sighed. The wall clock ticked the hour. Five o'clock, two hours before the ambassador and I needed to leave. That gave me plenty of time to question her about Jonathan Parker.

Claudia, as it turned out, was a certified gossip and more than happy to tell me everything she knew about everyone she'd ever met. Our conversation lasted the entire two hours before she rushed upstairs to change for the party.

During our chat, I'd learned the following tidbits of information:

1. River Garwood preferred homemade beer to expensive champagne, although he did have an excellent wine cellar.

2. Norine Smith's breast augmentation had left her with one breast larger than the other. The woman now wore a one-sided padded bra.

3. Jonathan Parker hated peas with a passion that could not be surpassed (perhaps this knowledge could be used if we ever decided to torture him?).

4. Gladys MacGregor, who lost all her money to bad investments and everyone knew it, had paid her dentist for her porcelain veneers with a little oral surgery of her own—performed on her knees.

I brooded over the fact that those were two hours I'd never get back. Not one of my better plans.

When Claudia rejoined me ten minutes later, she wore a shiny violet sequined dress that hugged her body. It glinted like rich oil in the light. Her hair was wrapped in a matching turban. She looked elegant. Refined.

"Claudia," I said as she descended the stairs, "do you mind asking one of your female employees to walk Luc sometime this evening?"

"Of course." She eyed her servant, the floating, velvety dark Martha, who nodded. "Martha will see to it. Are you ready?"

"More than I can say."

We climbed inside the limo and made our way to Parker's. Claudia picked up our conversation as if we'd never left off. Who knew a cozy limo with its black leather and mini-bar could be used as a torture device? I half listened, hoping there'd be information I could use.

At long last, she mentioned the name Hunter Leonn. *Lucius.* I perked up and adopted an expression of feigned distress and dismay. *Remember, he stalked me. Abused me.* An intense rush of impatience and excitement gripped me.

"Hunter Leonn, did you say?" I asked sharply, jolting forward in my seat.

"Yes," she said, blinking over at me. Her features lit with eagerness, and she leaned toward me. "Why? Do you know him?"

I gave her the same story Lucius had given Jonathan. "He chased me relentlessly. Ruthlessly! Every time I turned, he hovered beside me. I tried to tell him I didn't like him, that I didn't want him in my life, but he wouldn't listen. He refused to leave me alone."

"Oh, how awful."

"Yes, it was. Hunter is the real reason I moved away from Michael. I wanted so badly to escape him." I gripped my knees in a show of agitation. "And now you tell me he's here?"

"Are you worried he'll bother you again? Well, don't be. My home is well guarded, Eden. He won't be able to reach you."

"I thought that before. With Michael. But because I continually told Hunter no, he jerked me off the street one day and into his car. He took me to his house and locked me inside. He said he only needed time with me, but I was so scared. Finally he let me go. What am I going to do?"

"Oh, darling. I'm so sorry. I didn't realize the seriousness of the situation." Features tight with concern, she grabbed my hands. "You must have been so scared, and now you're finding yourself in the same predicament. I wish we could have him arrested, but—" She sighed with dejection. "Humans simply aren't punished for hurting aliens. Not yet, anyway."

"What if he tries to steal me again?" I asked. I bit my lower lip. Was I laying it on too thick? "I bet he learned I would be living here and decided to move here, too. He's probably there right now, waiting for me."

"I'm sorry to say he will indeed be there, but I don't think he'll make a scene. Too many people will be there to act as witnesses." She squeezed my hand. "Please don't worry. I won't let Hunter harm you in any way. That I promise. I'll talk to Jonathan, and make sure Hunter is kept at a distance from you. All right?"

Such adamancy from her surprised me. Her perfectly made-up features were bathed in concern and affront, and tension hummed from her body. Authentic distress? For me, an otherworlder? If this was indeed real, such concern for alien safety was probably why this vain, pampered, gossiping woman had been chosen as ambassador of alien goodwill.

I hadn't expected this from her. Rarely did someone prove to be more than I'd anticipated. First Lucius, now Claudia. Had I lost my edge?

"Thank you for your concern," I told her, letting myself visually calm.

"I just wish I could do more. Aliens have feelings, just like humans. Why can't more people see that?"

"Have you met him? Hunter, I mean?"

"Once." She released my hand. Her gaze flicked to the window, and she stared out at the moonlit landscape. We passed Michael's lush little glen, a dewy and sparkling emerald haven. A total contrast to the dry land everywhere else. "He's an intimidating fellow, I must say. His eyes are . . . there's something about them. They're dark and cold and so unfeeling."

"Yes," I agreed, shivering. "I remember that about him." This had worked out so much better than I could have ever planned. "You speak so highly of Jonathan Parker. How can he be friends with such a man?"

"I'm sure Hunter pretends to be civilized when he's with other men. Men like him always do. But I can assure you I will tell Jonathan everything, and something will be done."

By telling him, she would completely validate the story Lucius had given him. Why, thank you, Ambassador Chow. "That would set my mind at ease." I placed my fingers over my heart in a show of relief. "You are wonderful, Ambassador Chow. Truly."

"Please. Call me Claudia. And I would do the same for any other alien. I believe otherworlders should have the same rights as humans."

"Claudia," I said. "If only everyone believed as you do."

The limo slowed, then stopped altogether in front of a towering white stone mansion, surrounded by a narrow cerulean river and an electric fence. My heart began a fast, erratic dance. We were here. Multicolored and multisized cars littered the grounds, and throngs of formally clad people meandered toward the arched bridge that led to the house. Moonlight stretched and yawned over the entire enclosure, as golden as I was.

I tried not to smile, but I felt, actually felt, the hum of Lucius's energy. He was inside. And he was waiting for me.

Our mission was about to reach the next level.

CHAPTER
14

The party overflowed with humans and other-worlders, twinkling jewelry, and rich fabrics. Real cotton, real silk, not the synthetic versions worn by the masses. The room fairly buzzed with activity. Amid a thick haze of illegal cigarette smoke, expensive perfume, loud, laughing voices rolled through the air like a cadence of ocean waves. Candles glowed from wall sconces, giving off a dim, antique light. Alcohol flowed like a giddy river.

Mahogany floors, plush carpets. Every piece of art hanging on the walls depicted a woman in different stages of dishabille and seduction. Several alabaster columns with ivy twined around their entire lengths stretched to the vaulted ceiling. The elegance surprised me. This foyer and living area did not resemble the modern, vibrant office I'd seen when ghost-walking.

I remained at Ambassador Chow's side as we worked our way through the throng of guests. Both men and women, humans and otherworlders, constantly slid their gazes over me in speculation. The humans speculation soon turned to appreciation for my golden color. I could almost see the direction of their thoughts—my skin and hair decorating their walls.

I scanned the crowd for Lucius, for EenLi, for Jonathan, but I saw only strangers. Every few minutes, Claudia paused to speak with someone. I forced a casual, this-is-exactly-what-I-want-to-be-doing tone each time I translated her conversations with the otherworlders.

Most of the complaints, as Claudia had predicted, were about discrimination. A Mec's office was wrecked by humans. An Arcadian—a race known for their white hair, psychic abilities, and dabbling in mind control—wanted the laws changed so he could marry his human lover. A catlike Taren had been locked in an AIR jail for two weeks because he'd been accused of stealing a dress from a human. When the dress had been discovered in the back of the human's closet, the alien was released but without an apology.

Claudia offered each of them a fervent assurance that she would speak to the Senate and do everything she could to get their problem resolved. I hoped she followed through. I was an otherworlder, but I'd never known these prejudices, and it struck deep that others had. Michael had always protected me. If someone had looked at me oddly, they were never again allowed inside Michael's house. If someone said a derogatory word to me, they were never heard from again.

"You're not too bored, are you?" Claudia whispered when we had a rare moment alone.

"Of course not."

"I haven't seen Hunter." Her gaze darted left and right as she made sure we weren't overheard. "Hopefully I was wrong, and he won't dare show his face here."

Just then a tall, handsome man stepped from the crowd and approached us. Jonathan Parker. I recognized him instantly. Blond. Strong. He wore a black silk suit that fit him perfectly. Our gazes met, and his thin lips played in a welcoming smile. Up close, he reeked of money, self-indulgence, and confidence.

"Hello," he said to me, barely sparing Claudia a glance. His low, seductive timbre scratched across my nerve endings.

"Hello," I returned, using my huskiest voice. I even managed a soft, welcoming smile without gagging as I held out my hand.

"I'm Jonathan Parker." He clasped my fingers and lifted them to his mouth, then placed a line of kisses between each of my knuckles. "You must be Ambassador Chow's new assistant."

"Yes, I am." Did he think I'd be charmed by such a display? Of course he did. He fancied himself a smooth-talking ladies' man. I shook off my revulsion as images of his dead wives flashed inside my mind, and fluttered my lashes. Coyly I withdrew my hand. "I'm Eden Black."

"Such a lovely name." His heated gaze swept over me, lingering on my cleavage. "Eden . . . a man's paradise."

I chuckled seductively, as if I'd never been so flattered. The action stretched my acting talent to its limits. "I certainly hope so." Bastard. The man was married, was supposed to be helping Lucius win me, yet here he was hitting on me as if I'd jump instantly into his bed. Naked and ready.

"Jonathan," Claudia said, a stern edge to her tone. In that moment, she was all business. She pinned him with an equally stern stare. "I'm glad you found us. I need to talk to you about something very important."

Still his gaze remained on me. "You know I'm always willing to listen to your causes, Ambassador Chow." His voice had lost its sensual edge and was now crisp with formality. "First tell me where you came to find this vision of loveliness."

"She found me, and I'm grateful that she did."

"I needed a change of scenery to escape a bit of . . . unpleasantness at home," I said, "and Claudia needed a translator."

"Unpleasantness?" Jonathan replied, his eyes

locked with mine. "Please tell me you were not subjected to the types of discrimination Ambassador Chow is always complaining about."

I glanced (shyly) away. "I wish it was that simple."

Maybe I'd take Parker out after EenLi. An employee perk, if you will. Everything about him irritated me. Changing the subject, I said, "Claudia has spoken so highly of you, Mr. Parker."

"Please, call me Jonathan."

"Jonathan," I said, pretending to savor the name. I definitely deserved an award for my performance. How could Lucius say I wasn't a good actress?

"Jonathan, I *must* speak with you." Claudia stepped in front of me, a silent demand to be heard. "I'm afraid Eden is in danger. The unpleasantness she mentioned has followed her here."

I moved beside her and watched Jonathan arch a perfectly sculpted brow. "Danger?" He grinned slowly. "How ominous that sounds. Whoever would harm such a delicious creature?"

"You," she said.

"Me?" His face darkened and twitched with affront and I caught a glimpse of the killer he tried to hide. "I can assure you I would never harm a woman, and certainly not this one."

"Not you personally, but through your association with a certain individual." Claudia's voice rose, projecting to those hovering around us.

He frowned, and his gaze moved over those people

in a silent command to go about their business. "Perhaps we should move this conversation elsewhere," he suggested.

Claudia shot me a triumphant grin. "I knew he would help us. I'll only be a minute, Eden. Jonathan, can you guarantee she'll be safe while we're gone?"

I think he wanted to ask who she thought would hurt me, but thought better of it out here. He already knew the answer, anyway. "Of course," he said. He turned to me. "If anyone accosts you, there are Ell-Rollises posted along the edges of the room. They each have pyre-guns under their jackets and have been ordered to subdue unruly guests."

Claudia employed Ell-Rollis guards as well. Had Jonathan given them to her? They could be in league together. After all, I had to wonder why she wanted to talk to him without me. "You two go on," I said. "I'll be fine. I'm going to make a quick trip to the ladies' room."

Jonathan's gaze lingered on me for a long while, classical music floating around us like a gentle breeze, before he led Claudia away. When they disappeared in the crowd, I followed the path they had taken. They passed two half-man, half-lizard Ell-Rollises, then Jonathan scanned his fingers into an ID box. A bright blue light enveloped his hand. A door slid open, and I caught a glimpse of light wood, those red and purple columns, and those fuchsia and yellow bookshelves before the door shut, cutting off my view.

I had to get into that room. But how? Secret door? I blinked. Yes! Of course.

In all of Michael's homes, he had installed a secret door to every room. He wanted to be able to get inside anyplace at any time, as needed. I bet Jonathan was the same. Men with something to hide, as well as men with something to find, liked unlimited access. Liked watching and listening when others didn't know they were watching and listening.

Michael could get to any room in his house through a hidden corridor that began in his bedroom. Jonathan would have that, too. I knew it. *Felt* it. In his bedroom, he would be able to lock himself away for hours, do anything he wanted, no one the wiser.

I didn't have long before Jonathan and Claudia finished their chat, so I had to act quickly. During one of our phone conversations, Lucius had given me the layout of this house—just in case. Well, just in case had arrived. I knew Jonathan's bedroom was upstairs, third door on the left. There were probably guards upstairs, so I'd have to be careful.

I'd need a distraction. Nothing overt, just something to draw attention away from the stairs. I spun around slowly, thinking, gazing, studying. An idea hit me and I grinned. When a waiter passed me with a tray of red wine, I claimed two glasses. There, below the steps, was a woman in a sleek white dress, speaking with several men. Her hair was salon red, her skin sun-kissed, her makeup perfectly applied. She'd obviously spent hours preparing for this event.

Determined, I strode toward her. The different layers of scarves I wore danced at my ankles. Another female passed the group just in front of me, and she was holding her own glass of wine. When I reached her, I tripped her and "accidentally" tripped myself, spilling both of my wineglasses. Both women screamed as red liquid cascaded over their hair, their clothes.

The entire room seemed to turn toward them, intent on finding out what had happened. "Towels," I said. Several others began muttering about towels. "I'll get them towels." Without another word, I slunk up the staircase as quickly as possible.

No one tried to stop me. When I reached the top, I smashed myself behind the wall and into a shadowed corner. Just beyond, I could hear footsteps pacing back and forth. One . . . two sets, I realized.

I didn't have time to spirit-walk. Didn't have time to learn their nuances and sneak around them. Determined, I reached up to remove my hairpins—but I paused, dropped my hands to my sides. Killing them wasn't necessary, and I didn't want blood on my dress. I quietly palmed the miniature pyre-gun strapped to my thigh and programmed it to stun. My adrenaline spiked—even as my feet ached. Damn heels.

Say hello, boys, I thought, leaping into action, racing straight for them, not even pretending to be lost.

My hair swished back and forth down my back. Immediately I saw that both Ell-Rollises were holding pyre-guns. They were startled to see me and raised those guns to shoot. But they paused when they realized I was a woman, and their scaled, yellow faces darkened with confusion. That pause cost them.

I fired two shots in quick succession. A stream of blue light erupted, nailing one. The second stream slammed into the other. They froze in place, where they'd be locked in stun for hours, unable to move. But I couldn't allow them to later tell Jonathan what they'd seen, so I fed them the hallucinogens. They wouldn't know what was real, what wasn't. They might even be blamed for stunning themselves. I bypassed them and quickly worked at the ID box that locked the bedroom door. A few seconds and two cut wires later, I was inside the room, the door closed behind me. I sheathed my gun.

Before I could revel in my victory, a hand smashed over my mouth and jerked me into a hard, hot body. I recognized Lucius's decadent scent. Recognized the contours of his chest. I'd felt it that day in the woods, had seen it in my dreams. Still. Grab me, would he? My eyes narrowed. It was time to prove to this man he wouldn't always get the upper hand with me.

I shoved my elbow into his stomach once, twice. He puffed out a breath, and his hold on me loosened. Spinning around, I kneed him. Hard. I didn't curb my strength. He dropped to the fluffy white carpet with a pained moan. While he was down, I slammed my fist into his temple, and his head whipped to the side. I didn't want to break his nose or blacken his eye. Not because I liked him, but because it wouldn't do for people to know he'd been in a fight.

"Don't ever grab me again," I told him quietly.

"Dear God," he said. There was pain in his eyes, but also respect. And admiration. "You're in a slinky dress, and you look like a lady. You shouldn't do that to a man."

"I'll do whatever it takes. Always."

"Good to know." He lumbered to his feet and massaged his balls. "Don't ever hurt the boys again. I get vicious when they're threatened."

I rolled my eyes. "What are you doing here?"

"Same thing you are, I'm sure, and there's no time to waste. This way." He grabbed my hand—I didn't hurt him this time—and led me to a mural of naked, frolicking couples. He reached out, caressing his fingers between a redhead's splayed legs.

"What are you—"

The mural parted, revealing a dark entryway. I almost clapped in excitement. I'd been right about the corridor! Lucius tossed a grin (still a little pained) over his shoulder before tugging me inside. The door closed, and total darkness surrounded us. Total silence.

Lucius never slowed as we descended a staircase.

"I hope you know where you're going." My words echoed through the small, cramped space.

"I've been here a thousand times. I know the way."

An eternity had passed, or perhaps only a few minutes, when he ground to an abrupt stop. He released my hand. I heard a scratch, a *clang*, a muffled curse from Lucius, and then another door was sliding open. Rays of light seeped into my line of vision.

"In here," he said.

"Should we be talking?" I whispered.

"Soundproof walls."

We stepped into a plain gray room that boasted a single wall of windows, nothing more. Those windows gazed into the library, where Jonathan was lounging on the lime green couch, Claudia seated across from him. They each held a glass of dark, rich liquid.

I stopped and stared, but Lucius walked to the window and pushed a panel of buttons. The speakers came on, and we could suddenly hear what was being said.

"—won't hurt her here, I promise you," Jonathan was saying.

"Oh, really? Your friend came to New Dallas because he knew Eden would be here. He's a stalker, Jonathan. A dangerous criminal who once kidnapped her and locked her away. Now, can you offer me a hundred percent assurance that he'll leave her alone?"

Jonathan chuckled. "That certainly sounds like something Hunter would do. The man has balls of steel. But I'm not his father, and I can't control him."

Anger gleamed in Claudia's dark eyes. "You're laughing about this?"

"Claudia—"

"No. Eden is an alien and my employee, and therefore I am her protector. You'll either keep your friend under tight watch, away from her, or I'll bring in the media. You know several of them are sympathizers and will crucify you."

I blinked in surprise. She was defending me, fighting for me. Wasn't backing down. Was determined to help me. In that moment, I realized she wasn't working with or for Jonathan. She really did care about her job, about aliens.

A muscle ticked in Jonathan's jaw. "Very well," he said. "I'll speak with him." Done with the conversation, he unfolded to his feet. "Come. I'll escort you back to the party."

Claudia, too, stood. She didn't wait for Jonathan, but turned on her heels and strode out. Before he left, he tossed his glass against the wall, and gleaming shards rained onto the floor. All that sneaking around for a small glimmer of conversation.

I glanced at Lucius, who was watching me. Our gazes met. Clashed. The intensity in his eyes was disconcerting. Confusing. "We better get back, too," I said.

He latched onto my arm, stopping me from movement. "Can you handle this?" he asked roughly. "Once we leave this room, there'll be no going back."

Was he doubting me again? "I can handle it, *Hunter*. You don't have to worry about me."

"These are dangerous people." He stiffened, but slowly, slowly relaxed and surprised me by saying, "The other day, I told you I had a mother. She raised me the first ten years of my life. She was a drug addict and a whore, but she loved me in her own way. I think she was glad when Social Services took me away."

I couldn't open my mouth to save my life. I was riveted by his words. Why he was telling me this now, I didn't know.

"I was given to a nice, conservative family, but I was already street-hard and used to doing whatever I wanted, so that didn't last long."

When he paused, I gulped and finally found my voice. "What happened to you?"

"I was sent to a sadistic couple who liked to rent out their foster children."

A cold sweat broke over my skin at the implication of his words. I should have let the subject drop. Knowing about him, about his past, wasn't necessary and might actually harm my resolve to resist him. To dislike him. I should have let it drop, yes, but I didn't. I had to know. "Rent out?"

His shoulders lifted in a rigid shrug. "The first time they gave me to a man, I was scared and ashamed. Have you ever been raped, Eden?"

My eyes wide, I shook my head no.

"It's a thousand times worse than anything you've

ever heard about it, and it's what's going to happen to you if something goes wrong."

"I can protect myself," I said shakily.

"I thought so, too. But the second time I was sold, I tried to fight. I was strong for my age, and I'd been in a lot of fights. He had me pinned to the ground in minutes, as if my struggles meant nothing. I'd never felt so helpless in my life."

"I'm sorry." I didn't know what else to say. I'd had a childhood of privilege. Yes, I'd seen my parents murdered, but nothing had been done to me physically. I'd known love and safety. "So very sorry."

"The third time, I went into a rage. Before I could be subdued, I stabbed the fucking pedophile in the stomach. He died, and I spent the next seven years locked away."

"But you were a child."

He shrugged again. "I was due to spend three more years inside, but Michael stumbled upon my case and got me out. I didn't tell you that for sympathy, so wipe that look off your face. I told you because I want you to realize those are the type of people we're dealing with here. They don't care about anything except pleasure and money. They'll rape you, sell you without blinking an eye, and we're about to gift-wrap you and hand you to them."

I straightened my shoulders, fortified my determination. "If I don't do this, no one will. People will continue to be bought and sold, slaves to their masters. I *have* to do this. I, at least, know what to expect. I know how to defend myself. They don't."

He didn't speak for a moment. Just watched me, studied me. I don't know what I expected from him, but what he did wasn't it. Without warning, he jerked me into his chest, and his lips came crashing down on mine.

I didn't think to resist. Couldn't. He'd been hurt so long ago, and there was a deep need inside me to soothe that pain. To make it go away, to wrap him up in total safety. His tongue thrust and battled. Mine thrust and battled as well, each of us craving something from the other. Something we shouldn't.

His strong, strong arms wound around me, slithered up and down my back before cupping my butt and lifting me up until I cradled his erection. "You excite me," he growled. He didn't seem happy with the knowledge.

"Yeah, well, you excite me too." I definitely wasn't happy with the knowledge. "You also infuriate me."

He licked the seam of my lips. "You dropped me to my knees today, and that's something no one else has done."

"You deserved it." I nipped at his jaw.

"Yeah, I deserved it." He paused, pulled away from me. "You're a better agent than I gave you credit for."

The unexpected praise shocked me. Thrilled me. *Rocked* me. My heart actually skipped a beat. "Th-thank you," I stuttered.

He drew in a deep, shuddering breath. The beams

of light that couched his face gave him a menacing yet angelic ambiance. Conflicting, like the man himself. "All right, then. Now that that's settled, let's go buy your ticket into hell."

We traveled through the tunnel again and back into Jonathan's room. I needed that time to get myself under control. To stop thinking about Lucius and his kiss, Lucius and his praise, Lucius and his past, and to concentrate on the mission.

He led me through a back way. We soon reentered the party undetected and became part of the laughing crowd. Like a dream, smoke wafted around us. "This dance is mine," he said.

His strong, callused fingers wrapped around my wrist as his rough, husky voice shivered along my spine. Without waiting for my reply, Lucius dragged me onto the dance floor.

Back in character, I cast a helpless look over my shoulder, searching for Claudia or Jonathan. I didn't see either of them.

Soft, lulling music hummed from strategically placed speakers that were hidden in the walls. Lucius wound his arms tightly around me, and I fought the urge to sink completely into him and continue our kiss, picking up where it left off.

I gave him my complete attention, trying to appear fearful and furious. Meanwhile, my body thrummed with the pleasure of his heat and pine scent. If only he hadn't praised my abilities . . .

In the light, I saw that his dark hair framed around his chiseled face, and his faux-brown eyes glowed with . . . what? I couldn't read the emotion there, only the extreme intensity. My fingers itched to trace the fake scar that slashed down his temple. My mouth watered for another taste of him. The small tastes he'd already given me weren't enough. Not nearly enough.

The music began to fade from my ears, and the people around me vanished from my vision. The gray suit Lucius wore fit him to perfection, molding itself over each and every one of his muscles. Though his eyes were now brown, his lashes were the same: long, black, and spiky.

"Damn it, put up some kind of fight," he growled quietly. "You're supposed to hate and fear me. Not fuck me with your eyes."

Common sense slammed into me. My teeth ground together, and my gaze narrowed. I slapped him with so much force his head whipped to the side. The people around us gasped. Lucius didn't remove his arms from me. No, he tightened his hold. Slowly he turned and faced me again.

"Better," he said, his eyes now glowing with amusement.

Just for fun, I slapped him again.

He lost his amused glow. "I think people get the message."

"You sure?" My tone was dark with suppressed animosity . . . and desire.

A muscle ticked in his jaw. "I'm sure." He jerked me deeper into his arms. "Miss me?" he asked, his voice dropping an octave.

Maybe his kiss had weakened my resolve to dislike him, maybe his praise had, or his confession about his childhood, because I suddenly wanted to give him an honest answer—the one thing I hadn't given him in all our sexual sparrings. But I had to stay in character from this point on, and we both knew it.

"Take your hands off me," I demanded and tried to pull away from him.

His hold tightened even further. "You like to play hard-to-get, Eden, but we both know how easy you'll be," he said, and there was a ring of truth in his tone. He wasn't speaking to my character, but to me. "You like where you are."

"Take your hands off me, damn it!"

"First, admit that you like when I hold you. I want to hear you say it."

I pursed my lips. I'd admit nothing, not for our audience and certainly not for him. "I'll scream."

"Do it. Scream."

"Bastard. You'd like that, wouldn't you?"

"I won't wait forever, you know. I *will* have you." He leaned toward me, placing his lips near my ear, as if he meant to kiss me and whisper sweet words of love. Softly, so softly, he said, "You're the most erotic thing I've ever seen. Your nipples are hard and your sheer dress does nothing to hide them."

I slapped him again, harder than before. It was either that, or sink into him. He stumbled backward.

"Stay away from me." I projected my words loudly, loud enough that the people around us heard. "I don't want you. I've *never* wanted you."

I swirled around and finally found Claudia. Her eyes widened when she spotted me, and her features became pinched with shock and concern. Jonathan's darkened with anger. Claudia said something to him, and he motioned to one of the Ell-Rollises, who immediately raced toward him.

I reached them, and Jonathan's attention veered to me. He forgot the guard as he took my hand, turned it, and kissed my wrist. "I'm sorry if my friend frightened you."

I pointedly withdrew from his hold and glared at him. "He dragged me to the dance floor and wouldn't let me go. He could have hurt me." I stomped my foot, the perfect pampered child.

"I wouldn't have let him, I assure you." His brown eyes were already so dark they appeared black, but they darkened further. "Claudia explained what happened between you and Hunter. Believe me, I won't let anything like this happen again. I'll talk to him."

"Thank you." But I remained stiff.

There, I thought with satisfaction. I'd done my job. I'd effectively established my dislike of "Hunter." I'd proven I wanted him nowhere near me, which would validate his growing desperation for me. I gave my attention to Claudia. "I'm feeling poorly. Are you ready to leave?"

She nodded, her color high with anger. She truly was concerned for me. "Yes, of course," she said. "Let's get you home. You're shaking." Like a mother hen, she wrapped her arm around my waist and led me through the crowd and to the front door.

"See that they make it to their car safely," Jonathan commanded the Ell-Rollis. I felt his gaze boring into my spine—and ass.

I couldn't help myself. I tossed a glance over my shoulder, past the Ell-Rollis now shadowing us, and watched as Lucius approached Jonathan. The two men began arguing. People inched away from them, but not far enough that they couldn't listen. Unfortunately, I was too far away to hear.

Jonathan pushed him.

Lucius balled his hand into a fist, and it appeared like he was going to pound the stupid man into a bloody, lifeless heap. But then Jonathan pointed a finger in his face, said a few words, and Lucius nodded stiffly.

Both men glanced to me.

I didn't pretend to misunderstand what they'd been talking about, and didn't pretend I hadn't watched with interest. Lucius abruptly swung around and stalked toward the back door, widening the distance between us.

Still glowering with anger, Jonathan stared at me, silently commanding me to appreciate his efforts on my behalf. I merely offered him a half smile and turned away. Though I desperately wanted to race after Lucius and find out what had been said, I forced myself to keep pace beside Claudia. What kind of power did Lucius wield over me that he made me forget my job, my surroundings, my . . . everything? If I knew, perhaps I could fight against it. Fight against *him*.

The return drive to the ambassador's residence was filled with chatter—all of it Claudia's. She lamented on the plague that was man, promised to speak with Jonathan again, and asked me over a thousand times if I was all right.

"Not a good first day on the job, was it?" she said.

"I'll be fine," I told her. "I handled Hunter once, and I'll handle him again."

Unfortunately, I was lying on both counts.

CHAPTER
15

"Why the hell aren't you in your apartment?" a rough, infuriated voice growled.

I came awake instantly. I lay in bed—my new, wheelbarrow-shaped bed at Claudia's home. I wore a thin tank and equally thin sleep pants. A soft yellow cover draped my lower half. Agent Luc slept peacefully on the floor at the end of the bed.

And Lucius was crouched at my feet.

When he realized I was awake, he sprang on top of me. I had my knife at his throat before he could take his next breath. He didn't flinch, didn't seem to care that I held his life in my hands. Frankly, I was amazed. Not only had he bypassed the ambassador's security; he'd bypassed mine. I'd rigged the windows and door locks before I allowed myself to fall into sleep.

Lucius's weight pushed me deep into the mattress,

making me all the more aware of the cool material underneath me, and the pure male heat on top of me.

"How did you get in here without waking me?" I demanded quietly, pressing the knife deeper. Not deep enough to draw blood. Not yet.

"Very easily. Now answer the damn question."

"Claudia insisted I stay here."

"Claudia, huh? You two are on a first-name basis?"

"She's not so bad. She wants to protect me from you."

"Baby, nothing can protect you from me." The darkness of his voice cut through the darkness of the room.

I tried to wriggle out from under him, but he had me pinned by his strength. More than that, my halfhearted wriggling wouldn't have dislodged a feather. It did spark my desire for him to new heights, though, causing my breasts to press against his chest. The scent of honey began to encompass us in a fragrant cloud. And perhaps, just perhaps, I intentionally spread my legs so his lower body would sink into mine.

His nostrils flared, and tension radiated off him in decadent waves. "We've got to do something about your perfume."

"Why?"

"It gives a man ideas," he grumbled.

I swallowed. "What kind of ideas?"

"The naked kind." His eyes narrowed. "Did you

bring Luc?" Undiluted and unrestrained menace dripped from his tone.

I almost smiled. Almost. "Agent Luc is here, yes."

Even in the moonlight, Lucius's eyes visibly darkened. His ice-blue eyes. No contacts. He'd come to me as himself. My heart picked up in speed, drumming hotly in my chest.

"I told you what would happen if you brought him. Where. The hell. Is he?"

"On the floor," I said, bending both of my knees. An innocent (I swear) action that cradled him intimately against me. I kept my knife steady.

"The only thing on the floor is a fucking lazy-ass dog."

"Exactly." The word emerged on a smug breath. "And she's not lazy. She's finally getting some rest after a horrible life with a predator."

In that moment, he understood how I'd played him. How I'd purposefully made him jealous. Watching me, he popped the muscles in his jaw. "You're going to pay for that, cookie."

"Yeah, and you're going to pay for sneaking into my room." At last I pressed the knife hard enough to nick him. A tiny drop of blood slithered down his neck. "I named her after you."

"If you couldn't have me, you'd have the next best thing, right?"

"Can't you take an insult as it's intended? Now get the hell off me." If only I sounded convincing . . .

Angry with myself, I pressed the knife a little more deeply into his neck.

He didn't answer or comment; he was too busy staring at my lips. For a moment, however, it *did* look like he wanted to say something, something smart-assed and cutting, but then he changed his mind, pressed against the blade, and swooped down.

He kissed the breath right out of me.

His tongue plunged inside my mouth, and I opened eagerly. Helpless to do otherwise. He tasted like man and heat, firing my blood, igniting my senses. I could become addicted to his flavor, I thought dazedly. His lips were soft, so soft, the perfect contrast to the hard battle of supremacy our tongues waged.

Suddenly he jerked back, his breathing ragged and unsteady. He glared down at me. "Getting involved with an agent is stupid."

I glared up at him as I dragged in my own unsteady breath. The blade winked between us. "Getting involved with your partner is stupider."

"Do you care?" he said, brows arching.

"No." I should have, but I didn't. Not here, and not now.

"Me, either. Drop the knife, Eden. We finish this."

"Do we?" I smiled slowly, seductively, though how I was capable of the action when my mind had long since forgotten everything but Lucius I don't know. I moved the blade over his collar like a caress. "I could kill you, instead."

"Drop it."

"No." I used the blade to cut his shirt. His eyes widened; his nostrils flared. I tossed the tatters of his shirt aside.

He grabbed the knife and cut off my top then flung the blade aside. It landed on the floor with a thump. We were chest against chest. My nipples abraded him, and he sucked in a breath.

"You better be worth the wait," I said.

Neither one of us commented on the fact that we hadn't truly known each other long. It just seemed like we'd waited for this for an eternity.

When he didn't move, I prompted, "Do you need an engraved invitation?"

He groaned a sound more animal than human, and his lips instantly slammed into mine. I moaned when one of his hot, callused hands found my breast and squeezed, then plumped. My nipples beaded. I'd told him once that if he ever kissed me again, I'd kill him. To be honest, I'd kill him without thought or hesitation if he dared stop. We'd been building to this moment since we first clapped eyes on each other. Why not get it out of the way so we could at last focus on our jobs?

"This isn't safe here," he said, tearing his mouth away.

"Then hurry."

"You read my mind." He uttered a ragged chuckle. "Everything about you turns me on." He laved my lips with his tongue. "The way you move. The way you talk."

Weapons were strapped all over him. My hands unsteady, I tugged at the cords holding them to his chest. He let me, too. All the while, his mouth slanted over mine, his tongue plundering deliciously inside. Soon, his knives and guns surrounded us. He jerked off his pants. I jerked off mine. I shoved at the covers that separated our lower bodies until finally, we had total skin-to-skin contact. I sucked in a breath at the sheer heat, the rightness.

Luc whimpered.

Lucius tore away again. "Good girl," he said over his shoulder. His eyes met mine, and his tone changed, deepening with his next words. "Very good girl." Sweat ran down his temples, and he breathed as shallowly as if he'd run a marathon uphill. Lines of tension bracketed his eyes. "You're a screamer. I can tell. Just try and keep it down."

"I am not a screamer," I whispered roughly.

A look of sublime pleasure consumed his features, tempered only by amusement and satisfaction. "Then get ready, baby, because you're about to be."

"Enough talking." I jerked his head to mine, claiming his lips in a kiss that branded my very bones. My hands were everywhere. All over him. His nipples speared my palms; the muscles of his back jumped under my assault, and his ass tightened. I bent my knees . . . and felt the weapons that were strapped to his thighs. Another barrier. I cursed under my breath.

"Take them off," I whispered fiercely. "Hurry."

I'd never seen a man bolt up and discard his weapons so quickly in my life. He watched me while he did it, his gaze so hot it scorched me. My blood flowed through my veins in a rush of need and eagerness as I allowed my own gaze to slide down his body. The long length of his penis strained thick, so thick, and hard. I bit my bottom lip to keep from panting; I clenched the sheets to keep from reaching for him.

I ached. I felt the moisture pooling between my legs. I wanted him all over me, inside me, stretching me, slamming deep.

Finally, he was completely naked. No weapons on him. The next thing I knew, he was on top of me, between my thighs. Guns and knives bounced around us with the swiftness of his movements. Without a word, he pushed his way inside me.

I gasped at the extreme pleasure of it, at the heady sensuality. He was long and thick and stretched me to the point of pain—pain that soon vanished into pleasure. I'd been with other men, of course. Hadn't I? I suddenly couldn't recall the image of any other man. Only Lucius existed. Only the feel of his hands, his mouth, his cock.

"Eden, Eden, Eden." He chanted my name with every inch he sank deeper. Finally, he was in to the hilt. But he didn't move. He remained utterly still.

He stared down at me, his hands by my temples. "I didn't use any fucking birth control."

"Humans and aliens can't conceive." At least, to my knowledge, it had never been done successfully before. Though that did raise the question of why the government had issued a law against it if it wasn't possible. I didn't voice that little gem, however.

Still he didn't move. Didn't answer.

Desperation sparked to life inside me, strengthening all of my desires. My body screamed for completion. I needed it, would disintegrate without it. I twined my legs around his waist; I gripped his ass and tried to force him to move.

"What are you waiting for?" I growled softly. "Finish this."

One of his rough hands coasted over the sheet, then covered my knee and gently caressed upward. That was the only movement he made. "You're impatient, competitive, spoiled, and so damn hot I think about you all the time."

If he wouldn't move, I sure the hell would. I arched my back, rolled my hips. Ah, there. Yes, just like that. I did it again. My eyes closed of their own accord, and I ran my tongue over my lips.

I heard him drag in a tortured breath. He gripped both my hips to still me. "Always determined to go it alone I see."

"Fuck me, Lucius, or I'll fuck you. Either way, we're both going to come."

Fire exploded in his ice-blue eyes. "Some of us are going to come more than others," he muttered darkly, but he slowly withdrew, then surged forward.

I gasped. "I bet I win."

"I bet you do, too. I liked it when you talked dirty. Do it again."

"Again?" The word emerged as a blissful moan.

"Again." Once more, he withdrew.

"Fuck me."

His lips edged in a wicked grin as he slid forward. "My pleasure." He clamped both of my knees and pushed them apart, wider and wider, sending him so deep inside me that I felt him everywhere. Not one inch of me was untouched by him.

That was all I needed to send me over the edge.

I shattered completely, and a scream of fulfillment burst from my throat. Spasms consumed my body, and I clenched him tightly to me. Luc barked.

"Shh, girl," I said, still flying through the stars.

Lucius chuckled, and the sound emerged strained. "Told you," he said. He stilled again with a muttered curse. "Damn it. Do you think we'll have to do damage control?" He pulled out of me and rolled one of my nipples through his fingers. A drop of sweat trickled down his temple and onto my cheek.

I expected the pitter-patter of feet, and waited several moments. When I heard nothing, I said, "I think we're good to go." I bit back a blissful moan as Lucius replaced his fingers with his mouth, sucking hard on my nipple. "I'll be careful next time."

He moved his attention upward and licked my collarbone. I closed my eyes for a moment as I savored the silkiness of his tongue. Reaching up, I traced my hands over the ropes of muscles that comprised his stomach. Heaven help me, but he felt so damn good. Like velvet over iron.

He bit my earlobe, and I gasped. "Want more?" he rumbled menacingly. "'Cause I'm dying here."

"More, more, more."

Once more Lucius pounded into me. Yes. Yes! As I met him stroke for stroke, arching into him, I would have sworn a blood oath at that moment that I'd never felt anything so right. My pleasure was already building steadily again, preparing me for another mind-shattering orgasm.

Surely I had experienced such pleasure with someone else. Surely Lucius did not mean more to me than any other. I tried to close my eyes, to resurrect a face that had given me comparable pleasure.

"Don't you fucking dare look away," he uttered gutturally, having realized my intent. "Watch me. See me. Know *me*."

I almost experienced my second orgasm right then because, as he spoke, he stroked in and out of me with determination, slipping and sliding, our bodies slick with sweat and desire. The scent of cinnamon and honey intensified. My knees squeezed his waist.

"Can you handle a harder ride?" he demanded.

"Harder. Rougher."

That was all the encouragement he needed. He rocked into me deep, deeper still, harder still. Rougher still. As he did, he bit down on the sensitive cord in my neck. I came right then. My body shuddered with the force of it, and I silenced another scream that demanded release.

Lucius meshed our lips in a brutal kiss of warring tongues. He continued to hammer into me, riding the waves of my orgasm. Then his body stiffened, bowed, and spasmed, and I swallowed his roar of satisfaction.

A long while of shallow breathing passed. When both of our heartbeats at last calmed, he collapsed on top of me. I didn't mind his weight; I welcomed it. We stayed like we were, weak in the aftermath, every ounce of our bodies sated, afraid to shatter the lethargic spell.

"I told you," he breathed against my ear.

"What?" I barely had the strength to get that one word out.

"That you'd come more than me."

I smiled into his chest. "That means I won."

"Competitive," he tsked.

We settled into a comfortable silence for several minutes. "Speaking of competitions," I said, "have you learned anything about solar flares?"

"Not much. You?"

"No." Colin hadn't contacted me, and I hadn't had time to do the research I wanted.

"Guess we'll have to wait to crown the winner, hmm. I *will* beat you." He paused and pushed out a breath. "You're not the spoiled princess I thought you were," he said. "Not at all."

Another admission from him. Two in one day. This one weakened me as much as the other. "I was at one time," I admitted. I traced my finger around his nipple. "Michael spoiled me rotten. Whatever I wanted, he bought me. If he didn't buy it fast enough, I threw a tantrum the likes of which you've never seen."

His breath fanned my cheek as he chuckled. "What about your parents? Do you remember them?"

"Not really." Maybe I should keep my past to myself, but he'd shared with me. And for the first time, I had someone I *could* talk to about my parents, people I had loved and still missed. I couldn't with Michael. "I have a vague image of my mother's face, pretty and golden, but that's all. Sometimes, in the quiet of the night, I can still hear her voice singing me to sleep."

"She sounds like a good mom."

"She was. I wish I had a memento of her, something, anything, but the day after she and my dad died, our house was burned to the ground, destroying everything inside. Michael had moved me to a hotel, so I wasn't hurt at least."

"Why did they leave Raka and come here?"

"They wanted something better, I think. To escape the dictator who ruled them. I've always wanted to ask them, but . . ."

Lucius kissed the top of my head. I realized, then, that this kind of bonding was propelling us into another realm of awareness. A dangerous realm. We both knew the drawbacks of becoming sexually involved with an agent. But emotionally . . . did we have any clue about the ramifications?

I forced myself to get back to business. Keep it light; keep it casual. "Tell me what you and Parker argued about at the party, after I left."

He rolled off me, then off the bed entirely. Cool air immediately ghosted over me. A muscle ticked in his jaw as he began strapping his weapons onto his bronze chest and thighs.

"Lucius?" As I watched him, I noticed the bite marks and scratches I'd left all over him. I liked it. I liked seeing my brand on him.

"Jonathan wants me to leave you alone for a while," he said, the words rough and raw, "to give you a chance to settle in before I pursue you."

What was wrong with him? "Why does he even care? I highly doubt he's afraid of Claudia's wrath."

He shrugged, the action stiff. "Why else? I told you it might happen. He got a good look at you, and he wanted to fuck you himself." Lucius ran his tongue over his teeth, his eyes glinting like pressurized steel, but he said nothing more on the subject.

"Will he continue to help you?" Luc appeared at the side of the bed, silently requesting reassurance. I patted the bed and she jumped up beside me, all the while watching Lucius warily. I ruffled her fur, and that seemed to be enough for her because she relaxed.

"I think so," he answered. "Even if it's merely to help *himself* to you." Lucius pushed out a long stream of air. "I know I told you before, but it bears mentioning again. You did good today."

"I know. You roared your satisfaction."

"I don't mean the sex, smart-ass."

I snorted and jerked upright. Stiffly I pulled on my ripped tank and shimmed into my panties. "All I did was turn you down. I didn't do a damn thing to truly help this case." I tried to keep the bitterness from my tone. "I haven't since the day I started."

He whipped around, leveling me with a hard stare. The fierce scowl he wore had enough power to kill anyone in its path. "Who got Sahara Rose to talk? Who got closer to EenLi than any other agent ever has? Who got us the lead about solar flares? Who got inside Jonathan's room undetected and knew to look for a hidden door?" Before I could respond, he added, "You want so badly to prove yourself that you're forgetting to stop and acknowledge what you *have* done."

His intense gaze held me immobile. Only Michael had ever praised me like that. It was astonishing—and wonderful—that Lucius kept doing so.

As if he hadn't just rocked my entire world, he turned away and casually resumed dressing. "I put one of my men in this house," he said. "He'll let me know which parties you're going to attend, so I can make sure I'm there."

I forced my mind on his latest words. "Who is this man?"

"He's now the main driver for Claudia. White hair, violet eyes. Six feet. A human pretending to be an Arcadian. Go to him if you need immediate assistance. Also, I left a cell unit in your bag. It's programmed to dial my number the moment you open it."

Expelling a breath, I shoved my hair out of my face. "You could have given it to me before I flew here. Why did you come here tonight, Lucius?"

He shrugged, didn't turn to me.

"You risked a lot," I persisted.

"I risked nothing."

"You could have been spotted."

"I wasn't."

"How can you be so sure?"

His motions clipped, he shoved a blade into the scabbard on his thigh. "Because I'm damn good at breaking and entering."

"Well, I'm good at getting answers, and you haven't answered me. Why did you come here? Tell me the real reason." I wanted to hear him say it.

"Maybe I wanted to tell you to make sure Claudia Chow brings you to see Jonathan and me tomorrow. I want us all to have a heart-to-heart so you can rebuff me again."

"You didn't have to come here to tell me that."

He bent over and jerked on his boots—I didn't remember him ever removing them—giving me a glimpse of his taut, pants-clad ass. He straightened and paused; his fists clenched. "I wanted to see you. Is that a good enough reason to risk everything?" Without waiting for my answer, he stalked to the bay window and disappeared into the night.

More than enough, my mind foolishly supplied.

The thought made me stiffen. Made me panic. It hinted at deeper feelings, hinted at . . . caring. No. No, no, no. I dropped my head into my hands and forced myself to breathe. He was an agent and my partner. We'd had sex, but it couldn't be more than that. I wouldn't allow it to be more than that. Too much was at stake.

"Nothing matters but the mission," I whispered, then said with more force, "Nothing matters but the mission."

CHAPTER
16

The next morning my body thrummed with sensual remembrance, mocking my resolve. Sunlight poured past the wispy yellow-and-white curtains as I lay in the bed. For a long while, I soaked up Lucius's lingering scent and let the softness of the sheets caress me. My skin felt oversensitized, my thighs bruised, and I still emitted the telltale fragrance of honey.

"You're an agent, Eden Black. Don't forget again. Last night doesn't matter. Remember?" I'd give myself the reminder a thousand times if necessary.

Agents who became emotionally involved were easily distracted (case in point) and constantly put their missions at risk. Michael didn't have a rule against it because he knew the forbidden often became the obsession. Still, we all knew the reality of agent relationships.

I forced myself from the bed. I took Luc for a walk, fed her, then quickly showered in the dry enzyme spray. I strapped on my arsenal and dressed in slim black slacks and a white silk top. Steps clipped, I strode to my laptop, which was perched atop the marble vanity in the sitting area of my bedroom.

As I booted up the blue, jellylike holoscreen, Luc padded to me and I rubbed her head. A message from Colin popped up within seconds, and I nearly jumped up and down in eagerness as the words crystallized. Finally!

"Sorry for the delay. Was out of town. Small solar flares usually have no effect and are basically undetectable," I read. "Large solar flares, however, create auroras. At the right angle, these can reach down and create a geomagnetic storm, which can distort the earth's magnetic field. If that happens, radios, TVs, cell units, airplane communications, basically anything that reacts to magnetism, can be affected. I suppose, in theory, a being or object could be molecularly transported into the belly of another solar flare—*if* they were wearing some sort of magnetic device. To my knowledge, that's never been done. Does this help, or do you need more? Colin. P.S. Let's do dinner soon. I miss you."

A thrill of satisfaction danced through me. I'd been right. My lips curled in a smile. I'd been right! Laughing, I replied, "This helps. Thank you. Can you give me an example of a magnetic device that would work best? Eden. P.S. No dinner. You're a good friend, but an awful boyfriend."

A knock sounded at my door.

I quickly shut down my computer and strolled to the thick cherry wood entrance. Strolled? Yes, I had a spring in my step that couldn't be denied. I couldn't wait to share this information with Lucius—and win the solar flare competition.

After unscrewing the extra cylinders I'd placed in the lock, I pulled open the door. "Yes?" I said to the woman in front of me. Or rather, to the pure white, deliciously fragrant orchids in front of me. No, not pure white, I realized a moment later. Flecks of gold had been sprinkled on the petals.

"These came for you," a soft, lyrical voice spoke in halting English.

As I studied the orchids, a very feminine reaction occurred inside me. I melted. My bones literally liquefied, and my muscles turned to mush. Before I took them from her, I removed and read the card. *Thank you for last night.*

I pressed my lips together to keep from scowling—or smiling, I wasn't sure which. Way to keep it about the mission, Lucius. Anyone who read the card would think "secret admirer," but I knew. "Thank you," I told the woman and claimed the heavy crystal vase. I tried to shut the door with my foot. I'd shut off the automatic sensor.

"Wait," she said. She was an Agamen. Not attractive by human standards because of the small horns protruding from her skull—horns that produced poison when the Agamen was frightened—but her eyes were a pure, liquid silver and very pretty. "There's more."

I placed the flowers on a nearby table and turned back to her. I'd fought only one Agamen over the years. He had rammed me in the stomach, and I spent six weeks recovering from the toxic liquid that invaded my body.

She bent down and hefted another vase, this one stuffed with bloodred roses. "These also came for you."

Again I read the card before taking the flowers. *I'm sorry you were upset last night. I hope you'll give me a chance to make it up to you. Jonathan.*

The only reaction I experienced toward *this* gift was satisfaction for a job well done. "Thanks," I said, taking the roses and setting them behind the orchids.

"The ambassador wishes to speak with you in the formal dining area."

I massaged my neck and stifled a sigh. I'd wanted to call Lucius and tell him what I'd learned. Now there wouldn't be time. "I need a moment." Not bothering to shut the door, I rummaged through my bag for the right pair of shoes. Open-toed black heels. My feet immediately screamed in protest, but I strapped the torture devices on anyway. To the Agamen, I said, "Please, lead the way," speaking in her own language.

She blinked at me in surprise, then smiled slowly, revealing sharp gray teeth. "Come."

Down the elegant hall and winding stairs we went, the fragrance of coffee growing stronger. I tried not to grimace; I truly hated that smell. I didn't know how humans could drink coffee. It was so bitter. If I had my way, only sweet-smelling food and drink would be prepared.

Finally we reached our destination, a dining room with an antique cherry wood table, benches instead of chairs, and pictures of sunflowers on the walls. No animal heads. The ambassador sat at the table, which was piled high with food. Her black hair was pulled back in another severe twist, and she wore a severe black pantsuit.

"Sit, sit," she said when she spotted me, waving to the chair across from her.

I did as she requested. She looked me over and frowned. "Eden, dear, you look tired. Are you still upset about the party?"

"A little," I lied.

"Well, stop that right now. I told you I spoke with Jonathan, and he assures me he will see to your safety, as well as to Hunter."

"Thank you. You've been wonderful about this whole thing."

"Speaking of wonderful," she said. She sniffed the air. "What is that heavenly scent you're wearing?"

Feeling hot pink circles consume my cheeks,

I shifted uncomfortably in my seat. "I'm, uh, not wearing perfume."

Her brow puckered in confusion. "You have to be. You smell. In a good way," she rushed to assure me. "Like honey."

"No. No perfume."

"Oh. Well. Maybe it's the food." She swept her hand over the buffet of choices. "Are you hungry?"

"A little." I filled my plate with toast and eggs. There was a bowl of sugar probably meant for the tea, but I sprinkled several heaping spoonfuls over my food. Everything tasted better with sugar.

Everything except these eggs, I realized after the first bite. They possessed enough salt to fill an ocean, and even the sugar couldn't mask it. I managed to choke down a few bites before pushing my plate away.

Claudia nibbled on a piece of toast. "Did you get the flowers Jonathan sent you? I think he sent you the roses *and* the orchids. He feels terrible about what happened."

Lucius had insisted I find a way to Jonathan's residence today, so I said, "I'd like to thank him in person, if I may."

Claudia brightened and dropped her toast onto her plate. "That's a wonderful idea. I'll call him right now and see if he can fit us in." She clapped her hand and called, "Martha. Please bring me the phone."

A few seconds later, Martha floated into the room holding a silver tray. A black cell unit and receiver rested on top. Claudia anchored the earpiece in place and said, "Jonathan Parker." Pause. She grinned. "Jonathan. This is Claudia Chow. Eden Black and I would like to meet with you—" Her lips pursed, and there was another pause. This one longer. "No. We want to meet with you, not you and Hunter."

"I'll meet with both of them," I rushed out.

She blinked at me in puzzlement. "But . . . but . . ."

"I'm eager to get this settled." I needed to be careful about my eagerness.

"Jonathan," she said into the mouthpiece. "I've changed my mind. We'll meet with both you and Hunter . . . yes . . . thank you. Until then." She tossed the unit back onto the tray, and Martha floated out of the room as gracefully as she'd entered. "We're meeting with them this afternoon, after we make my morning rounds."

"Excellent. Thank you."

Her "rounds," as it turned out, consisted of door-to-door schmoozefests at otherworlders' residences. I spent the next four hours interpreting conversations about health care, dietary needs, and Earth currency as Claudia Chow visited with her constituents. I admit, her concern for the aliens of New Dallas impressed me.

Finally we were inside the limousine and headed for Jonathan's house—the moment I had been waiting for. I enjoyed the lush green landscape, the hills on one side of the window and the flat plains on the other that whizzed past the window.

"I feel like I haven't thanked you enough, Claudia, for championing my cause. You really fight for other-worlders, and I commend you."

Her cheeks flushed with pleasure. "I do what I can."

"I'll be honest," I said, facing her. "You aren't what I expected."

She furrowed her brow. "What did you expect?"

"Someone who saw otherworlders as a prize, but didn't actually care for them."

"Aliens are people, too."

"Yes. We are. But not everyone realizes that."

She leaned forward and whispered, "I'm considering dating a Taren, the one who spent a few weeks in an AIR prison for allegedly stealing a dress. He's asked me out on several occasions, but I've always told him no. Any"—she coughed—"advice for me?"

I couldn't picture Claudia with a feline, for that's what Tarens were. They walked and talked like humans, but their skin was patched with fur and their tongues were abrasive. Some could walk through walls. I'd trailed several over the years, and had seen them do it.

"Advice?" I was not the girl to come to for relationship advice. "Hmm. Well. Treat him like you would a human, I guess. And pet him often. Tarens like that."

She nodded, her expression rapt, as if she were soaking up my every word. "Pet him. Yes. Good idea."

"I don't know what more to tell you," I admitted. "I've never dated a Taren myself." Tips on killing them, I could give her.

Thankfully, our car eased past the tall iron gates of Jonathan's estate, effectively ending our conversation. I saw the towering mansion, white brick and jagged peaks. The lawn was perfectly manicured, but the grass was sparse. My heartbeat picked up speed—not out of fear, but in anticipation. Even now Lucius waited inside, ready to push our prey further.

Several black-clad guards manned the outer walls, I noticed, semiautomatic pyre-rifles strapped to their sides. Interesting. Jonathan had human guards today, rather than aliens.

When the car parked in front of the entrance, we emerged in the afternoon heat, strolled over the bridge, and entered the coolness of the house. The French doors were already open, like arms beckoning us inside. We were expected, after all.

My gaze collided with one of the guards positioned at the side of the door. Another human. His eyes widened with . . . awe? Greed? He took an unbidden step toward me, even reached out to touch me, but an older man dressed in a black suit led Claudia and me past him. His arm dropped to his side.

We were taken straight to Jonathan's office, the very office he and Claudia had occupied last night. Lucius was there and seated on a bloodred chair, his feet resting on the faux-fur ottoman. He watched me through narrowed eyes, his lips firm and unyielding. I pretended to ignore him, though every cell in my body screamed in awareness.

"Thank you for the flowers," I told Jonathan. "And for agreeing to meet with us."

A muscle in Lucius's temple ticked.

"My pleasure." Jonathan, seated behind the desk, beckoned Claudia and me to take the green couch across from Lucius. He had a cut lip, I noticed. "I'm so glad you could come," Jonathan said, his cultured baritone very smooth. He watched me, but I didn't feel *his* gaze boring into me like I did Lucius's, branding me, making me ache.

"This is hard for me." I cast a dark glare at Lucius. That was the only way I could allow myself to study him. The contacts he wore made his eyes as dark as a midnight, starless sky, but there was a spark inside them I had never seen before. There was a bruise on his left cheek. Had the two men fought? "I'm anxious to have this problem fixed."

"As are we." Jonathan nodded to Lucius, a silent you-may-begin.

"I would never hurt you," Lucius said to me, speaking for the first time since I'd entered. His rough voice washed over me in sensuous waves.

"Is that so? You jerked me off the street. Locked me in your home. Yesterday you jerked me onto the dance floor and wouldn't let me go."

"I'm sorry for that." He didn't sound sorry. In fact, he leered at me. "I was . . . overcome, seeing you again. But I didn't hurt you, you have to admit."

I pressed my lips together, admitting nothing.

"We're all civilized adults," Jonathan said. "And I assure you, Hunter has learned his lesson."

"I want to believe you." I forced my eyes to fill with tears. "I really do, but do you see the way he's looking at me? He isn't sorry. Not really." I couldn't accept Hunter's apology or Jonathan's assurances because the stage had to be set for my abduction. It had to appear Hunter couldn't win my affections through conventional means. Later, when I left, he would be able to speak to Jonathan about "buying" me. Jonathan would then speak with EenLi. And EenLi would then come after me. Once I discovered what magnetic device EenLi used to transport his "cattle," I'd have the pleasure of killing him.

Ah, life suddenly seemed so good.

"I think . . . I think I need a moment alone," I said. I placed a shaky hand over my heart. I'm sure Lucius already searched the house, but I wanted to do my own search. He might have missed something. If there was any information about EenLi, the abducted, about the portals or solar flares, I wanted to know it. "Will you excuse me?"

"If you want fresh air, there's a veranda down the hall. Just off to your right," Jonathan said.

"I won't be gone long." I knew Lucius would distract them if I didn't come back in a timely fashion.

This was going to be fun.

CHAPTER
17

Of course, I didn't go to the veranda.

For privacy, the guards had been sent away and were no longer inside. Remaining alert, I strode to the first room I came to. Surprisingly, it wasn't locked. I stepped inside. The scent of bleach and lemon permeated the small, dim space. A cleaning closet, I realized happily. They were often overlooked as inconsequential. I ran my fingertips over several bottles of cleaner as I looked for a trash receptacle.

There, in the back. Grinning, I bent over it and riffled through the contents. Dirty napkins, an old pair of shoes. I sighed. People used computers and digital notepads, so paper—rare as it was—was hardly used anymore. Still . . . a girl could hope.

Next, I found a bathroom. It, too, was open. Blue-and-white marble flooring, an antique porcelain tub. Fake plants in every corner. But nothing of importance.

The only other room in this hallway was a laundry. Large and wide, the area overflowed with clothes and servants, poles for the material, and dry-spray hoses that ejected the cleaning enzymes. I stood in the doorway, watching the women work for a moment, hoping to catch sight of something of Jonathan's. Maybe he'd left something in a pocket.

Suddenly a thick, hairy male arm reached from behind me and clamped over my mouth. I was pulled into a hard body, and it wasn't Lucius's. The scent was different, not as clean. The feel was different, not as muscled and hot.

The man kicked my knees, and I buckled to the floor. I winced, but I didn't fight. Not yet. Not until I knew what was going on. Had Jonathan already contacted EenLi? Was this my abduction?

"I've got her," a deep male voice whispered.

"Hurry," another man said, his voice frantic. "Before someone sees us."

They dragged me outside, and I glanced up, squinting past the intense light. My abductors were human and dressed entirely in black, guns strapped to their sides. Jonathan's guards, I realized. In fact, the one holding me was the man I'd seen positioned at the front door when I first arrived. Excitement at last sparked in my veins. This had to be it! I hadn't expected him to act so quickly.

"Be careful with her. Don't damage her skin. Don't pull her hair too hard."

"Will you shut up? I'm doing the best I can. We've got to hurry, or we'll be seen."

The man who held me by the hair cast me an evil, greedy smile. "We're gonna sell your skin and hair for a fortune, pretty girl." He jolted into motion, hefting me up by the waist and carting me away from the house. The other man followed quickly behind us, tossing nervous glances over his shoulder.

They weren't here to abduct me. They were here to de-skin me!

Cold, haunting fury replaced my excitement. The bastards wanted to flay the gold skin right off my body. Sell it. Hurt me unmercifully. My fury intensified with every step my tormentor made, but I didn't utter a sound of protest. Alien voice was as incriminating as human DNA or fingerprints. That was why AIR had strategically placed high-frequency recorders and satellites all across the globe. If an alien was ever implicated in a crime, his voice was logged into a database, then used to trace his whereabouts.

I doubted my name was located in any of the databases—Michael would have seen to that—but I couldn't risk it.

I didn't want to be linked to the slaughter about to happen. Or did I? As the daughter of Michael Black, arms dealer, I would be expected to know how to defend myself. And if EenLi has told Jonathan about the agency stuff, well, same deal.

My captor squeezed me even tighter, almost cutting off my air. Once we reached a cluster of thick bushes that hid us from view of the house, I tangled my feet in his legs, tripping him. As we fell, I twisted toward him and slammed my palm into his nose. He hit the ground, collapsing on top of me and howling in pain.

Gasping for breath, I rolled out from under him, already jumping into position to attack the second man. I crouched and lashed out with one leg, sweeping both of his feet off the ground. He flailed midair, then landed with such a loud thud, I wouldn't have been surprised if he cracked his skull. As he lay there moaning, I sprang up, whipped the knife from his waistband—the very knife he'd planned to use to peel away my skin—and slit his throat.

He gurgled, became silent.

Everything happened so quickly, the first man only now realized what had transpired. Blood poured from his broken nose as he stared, wide-eyed, at his friend. A roar of rage and horror erupted from him, and he leapt at me, hands raised to choke the life from me.

I held the dripping knife steady, waiting, waiting until he reached striking distance. Only then did I swoop low and gut him, sharp silver sinking into human flesh. His own momentum sent the blade deep.

He gasped as his knees buckled, and in the next instant he was dead, collapsed at my feet. I sucked in a breath of satisfaction. Simple. Easy. They deserved what they'd gotten.

I didn't feel an ounce of remorse.

I couldn't leave them like this. No, I didn't want to be linked to this carnage if I didn't have to be. No need to rock the boat so soon.

Though I didn't possess any fingerprints, I cleaned the knife with the men's clothing to remove any evidence I might leave behind and placed the hilt in one of their hands. The other guy needed a weapon, too, so I performed a thorough search and found one strapped to his ankle. I dipped the tip in the other's blood before wrapping his fingers around it. There. Done. They looked like they'd fought with each other, and both emerged the loser.

Satisfied with my work, I cleaned my hands in the grass as best I could and strolled back to the house. I whistled along the way.

"Where were you?" Claudia asked the moment she spied me. She stood on the porch steps, staring down at me in concern.

"I went for a walk," I said, all innocence.

"But . . ." Her eyes grew wide, concerned. "There's blood on your shirt."

I glanced down and spotted the crimson splotches. Jonathan and Lucius joined her in the doorway, avidly watching and listening to our conversation. I felt Lucius's questioning stare all the way to the marrow of my bones.

"Jonathan," I said, forcing myself to tremble, "two of your men are knife fighting just over the north hill. I was coming to tell you."

Lucius's eye flared.

Jonathan frowned.

Claudia raced to my side. She wrapped her arm around my waist. "Knife fighting? Let's get out of here."

I had to contain my smile as she ushered me to the limo.

That night, I waited for Lucius to come to me.

I stayed crouched under the window, in the shadows, practically glued to the wall. It wasn't a comfortable fit, but I didn't mind the pain. Anything to best Lucius.

I'd reinforced the balcony lock with steel pins, which would force him to crawl into my room through the highest, smallest window above me. I grinned because I knew he'd have to climb down from the roof to fit. Would he make the effort?

Oh, yes. He would.

I heard the gentle slide of glass, which meant he'd already disabled the security box. A moment later, I saw his booted feet peek through. Silently I jolted up, grabbed his ankles, and jerked him inside. Not expecting the action, he propelled to the ground, crashed hard and grunted. The wire he'd used to rappel from the roof snapped his feet back up.

I was on top of him in the next instant, my knife at his throat.

He wore all black, but no face mask shielded his face from view. A bead of sweat trickled down his temple. He remained where he was, silhouetted by shadows and moonlight, staring up at me.

"Think you're funny?" he bit out on a quiet breath.

Like Lucius, I wore black pants and a black shirt. I'd hoped, by wearing these clothes, I'd ensure we wouldn't become sidetracked.

"Well?" he said.

"Yes, I do." I tapped the silver blade against his cheek. "Think I'm funny, that is."

His gaze slitted. "Where's your dog?"

"In the bathroom." I'd locked her in and petted her to sleep on a fluffy pallet. I hadn't wanted her to worry if Lucius and I tussled. "Sneak in on me once, and that's my bad. Sneak in on me twice, and it's yours." I cut the wire to his feet.

His legs dropped to the ground with a thump, and Lucius sighed. He tangled a hand through his hair. "You're turning out to be more than I ever expected. I've told you that, haven't I?"

"Yes, and I still take it as a compliment." I inched off him and sat down, remaining in a crouch.

He pulled himself up and met my stare. "That's how it was meant. Now, tell me what happened at Jonathan's. Why was there blood on your shirt? Why were those two guards dead?"

"I did a little exploring, and those men followed me. They dragged me outside, behind some bushes, hoping to steal my skin and hair."

His ice-blue eyes became hard, steely. "For the gold?"

"Yes."

"And?" he prompted when I said no more.

"And I killed them."

"Were you hurt?" Once again his muscles tensed as he waited for my answer. He reached out and gripped my arm with viselike strength.

"Not even bruised," I assured him. I tossed the blade aside.

Instantly he relaxed. I told him what I'd learned about the solar flares, and he nodded. "That's good stuff. There's more there, I know it. Keep digging."

"You do realize I'm winning, right? I'm truly kicking your ass."

He grinned. "Yes, I realize you're winning. You want to hear what happened after you left Jonathan's or not?"

I tried not to let my eagerness show. "Tell me."

First, he surprised me by tugging me to his side. I didn't protest, but all the while I told myself I wasn't going to have sex with him again. We'd been there, done that. Didn't need the added complication. Again. One of his hands gently caressed my back, the other clasped my palm. "The men were found, but Jonathan assumed they'd simply killed each other.

After we cleaned up the mess, Jonathan pulled me inside his study for a chat. He wouldn't say EenLi's name, but he offered to put me in touch with a man who could help me 'obtain' you."

Excitement pounded through me. This was it. We were so close. Without removing my hand from his, I leaned back and rested my weight on one of my elbows. My hair spilled over my shoulder and onto his stomach, gold against our black clothing. "It won't be long now."

"No. It won't be long."

I nodded as satisfaction blended with my excitement. "I'm glad." EenLi would soon send someone to abduct me. I couldn't wait!

With his free hand Lucius wound long strands of my hair around his palm and tugged my face close to his. "I know having you taken is the plan, but I expect you to be armed. From this moment on, wear your weapons twenty-four/seven."

"I do, anyway."

"You'll also inject the isotope I brought. It bonds to your cells and helps us track you."

I frowned. "For how long?"

"Three months."

"And if the mission is completed in two days?"

"Don't argue." His expression turned hard, unbending. "You understand the reason for it."

"I don't like the fact that anyone who knows about isotopes and computers will have access to my location."

"We're setting you up to become some bastard's

slave, Eden. Hopefully mine, but maybe not. You want to risk being captured and no one knowing where to find you?"

Damn it. I hated it when someone had a good point—a point that annihilated *my* point. He was right. There was a chance I'd be taken underground, hidden away by a stranger. "You're right." I sighed. "I'll inject it."

"Good girl."

"I'll inject it," I added, "on one condition."

"What condition is that?"

"Tell me your real name."

He shook his head. "You still have two guesses, and I'm not telling you a damn thing."

"At least tell me what your first name starts with."

"Why do you even care?" he asked, an edge to his voice, layered by a forced casualness.

"I don't like calling out a fake name during sex, okay?"

"We having sex again?" His lips twitched, and I felt my heart skip a beat. He looked so relaxed just then, so sexy. I loved it when he lost his reserve and simply enjoyed the moment. I don't think he allowed himself to do that very often. Neither did I.

"No?" I said, more a question than a statement. Damn it.

"Liar. Tell me what the F stands for in your name."

Oh, oh, oh. What was this? "I thought you didn't care."

"Maybe, like you, I was lying."

"I'm not telling," I said in a singsong voice. I liked, really liked, that he wanted to know.

His eyes dipped to my mouth, and he ran his bottom lip between his teeth. "I'm not telling, either, so I guess we have ourselves what's called a Mexican standoff."

"Looks that way." I lost my smile. He looked like pure desire just then. Total pleasure. I gulped and hurried to change the subject, to get our minds on the right track. "When I'm taken I want you to kidnap Luc from here and take care of her until I return."

"Consider it done." The teasing light slowly extinguished in his eyes. Before I could protest, he rolled over and pinned me.

I held my breath as he stared down at me. Hell, even the room seemed to hold its breath. A thin beam of moonlight slipped past the curtains over the window, illuminating his bronze skin. A gentle breeze caused those curtains to dance over us, circle us in a wispy, private haven. My pulse leapt.

He braced himself on his hands, and his gaze raked over my clothes. His lips twitched. "Did you really think locking the balcony doors would stop me?"

Stay strong. Don't give in. "Look, we have more to talk about."

"You're right. We've got a lot to talk about." Reaching behind him, he tugged his shirt over his head.

My mouth watered at the sight of his pecs . . . his shredded abs. "Put your shirt back on." I didn't sound convincing, not in the least.

As he stared deeply into my eyes, he *tsked* under his tongue. "Silly girl. You're going to be the death of me. You know that?" He leaned down, placing his mouth within a whisper of mine. His warm, soapy scent enveloped me. "Talk later. Fuck now."

Then he was kissing me, and I was kissing him back. I forgot what I wanted to tell him, forgot everything but this man and his wicked mouth. Without slowing our kiss, he peeled away my clothes and weapons, as if I'd never been stupid enough to don them.

I tore off his pants, wanting—needing—skin-to-skin contact. His hardness to my softness. Nothing else mattered. I might hate myself for it later, but there it was. I knew how he felt buried deep inside me, and I craved that again. I knew how my name sounded on his lips as he found his pleasure.

I *would* have that again.

"You didn't cut into my skin this time," he whispered huskily against my lips. He stood, scooped me up and tossed me on the bed. The mattress bounced with my weight. He was beside me in the next instant. "That's progress."

"Why are you talking?" I tugged him down on top of me. He gave me his full, muscled weight.

I cradled his long, thick erection between my legs

and rubbed against him, already wet, already willing. The friction nearly caused me to go off like a rocket. My honey scent blended with his pine scent, fragrancing the air.

He paused while I nipped at his jawbone, his neck, and he blinked. He pulled back, searching my gaze. Then he slowly grinned. "You smell like honey when you're turned on."

I stilled. I didn't deny it, but I didn't confess, either.

His smile widened. "I may be slow, but I finally figured it out. That day in the gym . . ."

"So what?" I snapped, my cheeks heating.

"Admit it, baby." He laughed with genuine amusement. "I rocked your world then, and I'm rocking your world tonight."

His male superiority irritated me. My eyes narrowed, and I seductively licked my lips. "Just for that," I told him, "you're going to be punished."

Heat flared in his eyes, melting the ice into blue fire. "How? A spanking?"

He sounded so eager, I almost laughed. "Not a spanking." Though I liked the idea of inflicting a bit of innocent pain, then easing away the sting.

"You sure?" A bead of sweat rolled down his temple and dangled at his chin. "I probably deserve a good, hard one."

"You have to make me come three times."

"Three?" He smirked.

"You only managed two last time." I traced my hand between our bodies, letting my fingers graze his erection.

"Damn, you're evil," he said, but there was a layer of anticipation and relish in his tone. "Thankfully I'm up to the task."

He swooped in and gave me another tongue-thrusting, frantic kiss. His hands and fingers worked over my body, plumping my breasts, pinching my nipples, caressing between my legs before darting away.

Within minutes, I was writhing and moaning his name. He licked his way down my body, and my belly quivered. Without pause or breath, he drove his tongue into the heart of me. I had to bite my hand to cut off the screams I couldn't allow, causing sultry, hungry moans of total abandon to emerge. His tongue tormented me, made me ache and claw at his shoulders.

"You taste like you smell," he murmured against me. "Honey and cinnamon."

The moment he worked two fingers inside me, I shattered. I arched and writhed and chanted his name in my head. Still he didn't stop. He worked me with his fingers, rubbing deliciously—without ever entering me—until I climaxed twice more.

"That was three orgasms," I gasped when I was able.

"I'm going to give you an extra one because of the naughty thoughts I'm having."

I would have laughed if I'd had the strength.

"Am I forgiven for teasing you?" he asked, his chin resting on my pubic bone, his breath fanning my stomach.

Yes, yes, a thousand times yes. I nodded.

I thrummed and pulsed from the force of my last orgasm as he climbed up my body and entered me. Hard. Swift. Expertly. I wound my hand around his neck and drew his head to me. Our lips met, our tongues clashed. He tasted hot, like me, like himself. Like pure passion. A taste I already craved like an addiction.

His hands coasted to my hips, gripped them and urged me higher, to take him deeper. His teeth nipped at my lips. I nipped back. We were fierce and growling with our need.

"It shouldn't be this good," he said hoarsely, darkly. As he spoke, one of his hands moved to my breast and pinched the golden nipple between his fingers. His hips began a rotating dance that increased my pleasure.

I came again, squeezing his back, gripping him.

His orgasm quickly followed mine. He bit the cord of my neck to contain his roar. *So good, so good, so good,* my mind chanted as I floated to the stars.

Afterward we lay together, silent. He rolled to my side, keeping me cradled in the strength and torridity of his arms. A sensuous spell wrapped around us. I could have stayed there forever, I think. And that scared me.

Business, remember. I swept my hair from my sweat-beaded face. "Did Jonathan say anything else to you?" I asked, getting back on track.

Lucius didn't speak for several minutes, and the wall clock ticked away. Finally he said, "After he made the offer to help me, he started acting strangely."

"Strangely how?"

"He wouldn't meet my gaze and hurried me out of his office. He's up to something, I'm sure of it. Something more than acquiring you for me."

"Any idea what?"

He pushed out a frustrated breath. "I think something's going down. I think another girl is going to be taken. He got a call and, well, I listened from the two-way. He talked about needing a girl for one of his associates while flipping through a file of pictures. I tried to find out more, but he never brought it up again."

So. Another girl could very well be taken. I couldn't let that happen. Not when there was something I could do. "I can find out what he's doing," I said hesitantly.

Lucius's gaze sharpened on me. "How?"

My next words froze in my throat. I'd kept this part of myself secret for so long. Even Michael didn't know. Telling someone now was difficult. It exposed me, made me vulnerable. Lucius wouldn't hurt me, would fight to protect me. I knew that deep down. I never would have slept with him otherwise. But . . .

"I can spirit-walk," I said, glancing away from him.

His head tilted to the side as he studied my features. "I don't understand."

"My spirit leaves my body and roams free on another plane or dimension. I'm like a ghost. No one can see me, but I see them. No one can hear me, but I hear them. I'll spirit-walk to Jonathan's, watch him, listen to him, and he'll never know."

For a long while, Lucius continued to study me. He stared down at me, his ice-blue gaze unreadable. Then he said, "You've done this to me." His tone was devoid of emotion as well.

I didn't try to deny it. "Yes."

"At Jonathan's."

"Yes," I said again. "How did you know?" I'd suspected then that he'd sensed me, but the thought had been laughable. Then. Not any longer.

"I smelled you. No one smells like you, like rich, warm honey . . ." He paused. "And sex."

I expected him to be angry at what I'd done, but he surprised me by adding, "Smart trick. Can you take your weapons?"

"I take whatever is strapped to my body."

"Does Michael know any of this?"

Looking away, I shook my head.

His expression became pensive. "Why not? What's the downside?"

I hated admitting to weakness of any kind, but he had to know. "If I'm gone too long, my body grows weak. Plus, while I'm gone my body is left completely vulnerable to attack. Someone can hurt me, kill me, and there's nothing I can do about it. No way I can fight."

He paused, tense as my words churned inside his mind. "So if the room your physical body is in catches on fire—"

"I burn with it."

Pause. Then, "Is your *spirit* ever in danger?"

"Only if my body is hurt."

Silence surrounded us as he pondered everything I'd said. Finally, he nodded. "Then do it. We need to know what's going on."

"If someone comes to the door—"

"I know what to do."

Yes, he knew exactly what to do. He'd kill if he had to. He'd create a distraction if he had to. No one would get into this room without his approval. "Where can I find Jonathan?"

Lucius named several places. I nodded, leaned toward him, and placed a soft kiss on his lips. "No worries," I told him. "I know what to do, too."

"You just get back here in one piece. Understand?"

CHAPTER
18

After I dressed, I lay back atop the yellow sheets and closed my eyes. A deliciously naked, but awake Lucius rested beside me. Not even his sultry scent could distract me from my unease.

I was nervous about doing this in front of him. The fact that I felt his intense blue stare boring into me didn't help. *Just do it.*

Deep breath in, deep breath out—more of Lucius's scent. Concentrate. Another deep breath gradually released. Save the girl. *That's* what mattered. Very slowly, my mind faded to black. My body relaxed into the mattress. My energy centered inside my stomach, swirling and pushing for release. My spirit began to rise up, up, and then I was standing beside the bed, looking at myself. And Lucius.

His bare skin glowed in the moonlight. My hair draped over him like a blanket, playing peekaboo with his nipples. The golden hue of my skin complemented the bronze of his. As he lay beside me, his big, hard body could have completely engulfed and overshadowed my smaller, seemingly delicate one. But it didn't. I looked protected by him. Even . . . loved?

I shied away from that thought, though a sense of rightness lingered.

He fingered several strands of my hair between his fingers. "Be careful," he whispered.

The huskiness of his voice sent a shiver through me. I shouldn't have, but I *did* relish his concern for me. Unbidden, I reached out for him, for his heat. I allowed my fingers to caress his chest. Sometimes, with intense concentration, I could actually bring an object into this enigmatic realm with me. Now, however, my fingers simply coasted through him.

He sucked in a breath, and his muscles jerked under my touch.

I forced myself to step away, to leave the house altogether. I had a job to do.

Because I was not bonded to Jonathan in any way, I had to find him on my own, without any invisible tug. When I spied a sedan on the side of a dim road, I slipped inside. The driver, an older male human, tapped his foot impatiently against the floorboards as he waited for the car to finish changing its own flat tire. Soon we were flying down the highway, listening to songs about beer and nasty women and pickup trucks.

When the man swerved down a different exit than I needed, I simply propelled myself through the car door, like mist leaving at morning's first light. I floated to the ground and treaded over two miles through forest before finally reaching my destination. Most of the inside lights were out, making the home appear dark and littered with shadows. Anticipatory, I slipped over the bridge and past the front door. That anticipation dimmed after a thorough search of every room.

Jonathan was not home, nor were any servants up and around, but I did catch a glimpse of his wife. She lay on a lacy bed better suited for a fairy princess, and I watched as the shell of a woman sucked back a mutated form of Onadyn as if it were her favorite candy. As the drug worked its way through her body, her mind flew higher and higher, as if she were being asphyxiated. A few days of that, and she'd be dead.

Shaking my head, I caught a ride to one of the other places Lucius had mentioned, a dim, smoky private bar. Gyrating music blared from every corner. There were about thirty occupants, a dozen or so men interspersed with naked, dancing women. Some of the women were otherworlders. A Mec, like EenLi, with glowing greenish skin that proclaimed her arousal, slid provocatively up and down a pole. She had no breasts, only a flat chest that appeared softer than silk. Strangely enough, the human men couldn't get enough of her. They constantly petted her skin as if they were addicted to her touch.

But I'd finally found my man.

Jonathan sat alone, drinking golden liquid from a crystal glass. He watched the dancing women silently, his expression pensive and drawn. One woman, a Delensean with blue hair, azure skin, and four arms, approached him, a seductive pout to her cerulean lips. He growled and shooed her away with a stiff wave of his hand.

I claimed the seat in front of him and studied him, this enemy of mine. His clothes were wrinkled, and lines of tension bracketed his mouth. Here, he wasn't the smooth, stylish man he'd been at the party.

He remained where he was for the next hour. Why was he here? Was he waiting for someone? He never spoke to anyone, only raised his index finger every so often to signal his need for another drink. After he finished his fourth glass, the wall clock flashed five A.M. A look of determination settled over his features, and he very calmly stood and strode from the building.

I blinked in surprise, but followed him. A car and driver waited for him out front.

"Home," he told the driver, his first word of the night.

He settled in the plush back seat, and I slipped in beside him—just as the door closed on half of my ghostly form. A slight tingle worked through me, my spirit's only reaction.

The car eased into motion. Jonathan stared out

the window the entire drive, and the closer he came to his estate, the deeper the lines of anxiety around his mouth became. What the hell was wrong with him? Damn it, I wanted inside his head.

Once he reached his home, I followed him as he pounded up the stairs and into a bedroom. Not his wife's, I noticed, but his own, a room with masculine decor in dark shades of greens and blues. I hadn't had time to study it the last time I'd been here. The large four-poster bed had bloodred silk sheets, and there were mirrors on the ceiling. A harness hung in the far right corner, and a clear plastic carpet covered the floor below it—to prevent any bodily fluids from staining his pristine floor.

So he liked harsh sexual games. How surprising.

He didn't change clothes, but remained in his striped slacks, tie, and jacket. He strode straight to the phone beside the bed, lifted the receiver, and said, "Wayne."

My heart galloping in my chest, I hurried to his side. "Wayne" was a human name EenLi often used.

I didn't hear the person on the other end answer, but in the next instant Jonathan said, "I changed my mind. Forget the woman you told me about earlier. She won't work."

Silence. I cursed under my breath because I couldn't hear the other voice.

"Just get the Rakan." A pause. Then, "Hunter is willing to pay whatever it costs. Get it done. Soon."

I rubbed my hands together and grinned. He didn't want the other girl. Good. They were planning my abduction for Lucius. Even better. Everything was falling into place.

EenLi said something that made Jonathan chuckle, made his shoulders relax. "No," he said. "Make sure she's unharmed. For every bruise your men put on her, for every tiny scratch, the price for her dwindles."

I didn't doubt that the "no harm" came straight from Lucius.

The men disconnected, but I waited for something more to happen. I watched as Jonathan stripped naked, humming happily under his breath. He wore a smug smile as he climbed into his bed. I hoped the phone would ring, but it didn't. A few minutes later, Jonathan began snoring. I walked to the edge of the bed and gazed down at him. His features were completely relaxed in sleep, giving him a boyish, innocent quality.

How deceptive.

How easy to kill just then.

Unfortunately, we still needed him. I made my way outside. The moon had already begun its descent, giving way to the sun. I quickened my step, focusing my mind's eye on Lucius and my own body. Very soon, I felt my spirit being sucked back, closer and closer. I lost my foundation, saw sparkling white lights.

Soon I caught a quick glimpse of the ambassador's house, an even quicker glance of my bedroom and Lucius pacing around the bed, Luc trailing his every step, before my body and soul collided. *Click.* For a moment, I saw only darkness. Then my eyelids popped open.

Lucius must have sensed my presence because he was suddenly right beside me, glaring down at me. Luc jumped up and propped herself at the foot of the bed, watching our interaction.

"Where. The hell. Have you been?" Lucius gritted out softly, menacingly. "What took you so damn long?"

"He wasn't at home. I had to search for him."

His eyes flashed with furious fire as he lowered his head closer to me, so close our noses touched. "Do you have any idea—any fucking idea—what I've been imagining?"

I returned his glare with one of my own.

"That I was doing the job I told you I'd do?"

"Not quite," he grumbled.

"That I'm a capable woman?"

"Damn it, Eden." His warm breath whipped over my face. "This isn't about your silly need to prove you're as strong and capable as I am."

"Silly!" was all I could get out. "Silly?"

"In case you didn't notice, it's dawn. I expected you an hour ago. At least. You would have worried had I been gone so long, and don't try to deny it." When I remained stubbornly silent, he added, "Wouldn't you?"

"Yes. Are you happy?" I shoved him off and jolted up. "Yes, I would have worried about you."

Satisfied with that, he dropped beside me and pulled me down. "Tell me everything that happened."

"Jonathan called EenLi," I said, relaxing into the curve of his side. "They've set up the abduction for me, and Jonathan canceled the order for the other girl. I don't know why. He just said she wouldn't work."

"When?" His tone became hard as granite. "Where?"

"They didn't discuss details. It was apparent they had spoken about me before."

Lucius rubbed his neck, his expression darkening. "I don't like this."

"Like *what*? This is what we've been waiting for."

"I don't like the plan. Letting them take you."

"Why the hell not? It's a good plan. And right now it's the only way to save the other slaves EenLi has taken. It's the only way to find out how he's using solar flares as portals."

"You could get hurt."

I rolled my eyes. "Aren't you the man who told me he'd kill me if I got in his way? Aren't you the man who cares about no one and nothing?"

"That was before," he mumbled, looking away from me.

I knew the feeling. I shouldn't have had sex with him the first time, and damn well shouldn't have again. But I had, and there was no going back. I couldn't pretend to dislike him anymore. I liked him. Too much.

"Damn it." He jumped to his feet. "We should never have gotten involved, because I can't stop worrying about you. I won't return here," he said. "It's too dangerous." He reached inside his pants pocket and withdrew a small syringe. Sparkling red liquid swirled inside. He handed it to me. "We don't know when they'll strike, and I can't be with you when they do."

"Is this the isotope?"

"Yes. Inject it into your leg. I'd do it, but . . ."

He didn't want to hurt me. I tried not to soften toward him yet another degree. I wrapped my fingers around the vial, jabbed the needle into my thigh—suppressing a wince at the sharp sting—and pushed. Burning warmth spread from my leg, branching throughout the rest of me. I glared up at Lucius as I shoved the empty syringe into his palm. "Done."

"Thank you."

I dropped my head in my hands. "This has all happened much faster than I imagined," I said, and we both knew I meant more than the case. I didn't know how to deal with Lucius right now, though. With us.

"Too fast?" He chuckled, but the sound lacked any hint of humor. "Maybe. But from now on, we think about the case. Nothing else. Your life could depend on it."

CHAPTER
19

Two days passed without a single abduction attempt. Two angst-filled days.

I spent them accompanying the ambassador on her rounds, translating idle chatter and more in-depth conversations about discrimination, while projecting a carefree facade. I'd seen Lucius only once, at a party hosted by one of the ambassador's friends of a friend. He'd remained at a safe distance from me but had watched me the whole evening.

His gaze had been a living entity, reminding me of the way he'd kissed and caressed me, the way he'd brought me to climax so many times. I'd forced myself to ignore him, to think only of the case.

The following day, I received another message from Colin and used the cell unit Lucius brought me to read it to him. The conversation was short and sweet.

"I have a friend working on solar flares, and he told me he's begun experimenting with small, inanimate objects to find out just what type of magnetic device would be most conducive to molecular transference within a solar flare. So far he's had no luck."

His frustration crackled over the line. "I was hoping for more by now."

"I know. But he did mention that a small, molecule-based magnet would work best. It offers photomodulated magnetization, can store data, and offers magnetic shielding and induction. And, unlike metal-based magnets, it can be deposited as a thin, transparent film or even inserted within another object."

"Yeah, but can something so small generate enough power to transport a body astronomically?"

"I'll ask."

"Let me know if you learn anything else."

And that was it, the end of our conversation.

I disconnected and lay in bed, moonlight bathing me. Agent Luc was already asleep in the bathroom. I didn't want to take a chance that she'd be hurt when I was taken. *When* would I be taken? I hated waiting.

A cricket hummed a lazy tune, and a cool, dew-scented breeze wafted through the open windows. I was making it easy for my abductors. I was also prepared. I wore silver sleep pants and a clinging silver top. They allowed easy movement, but were difficult to pull off. Of course, I had two knives strapped to me—one at the small of my back, the other on the inside of my thigh. My hair clips were too aberrant for bed, as was the anklet. Part of me expected Lucius to arrive at any moment, but he stayed true to his word and didn't visit.

I glared up at the domed ceiling. Men! Who understood them? Not me, certainly. Well, that's not true. I'd once thought I understood them. They needed sex, food, and water to survive, and their every action hinged on whichever need took prominence. Lucius was . . . different.

He worked hard, kept his mind on the prize. He did what was necessary for success, despite his own needs and wants. I respected that. I respected *him*. He was the best agent I'd ever come across. A partner I hadn't wanted, but couldn't deny had been the best thing to happen to this case.

Had I not been so lost in my thoughts, I never would have been caught so unaware. A hand whipped out from the darkness and pinched my nose closed. Panic rocked me at first, and I instinctively grasped at the hand to push it away. I even opened my mouth to suck in a breath. The man, whoever he was, dumped a tart liquid down my throat the moment I parted my lips. I tried to spit it out, but he smothered both my nose and mouth, forcing me to swallow.

"There you go," he said, his voice low and soothing. I didn't recognize his voice. "Sleep now," he added gently. "We won't hurt you."

Finally, EenLi's men had arrived.

I almost laughed through my fading panic. "What did you give me? Poison?" I demanded of my attacker, as any sane woman would. I kicked at him and, like a scared little female, scooted toward the headboard.

A black mask concealed his features, but he couldn't hide the strength and size of his frame. Only slighter shorter than Lucius, he filled out his black military fatigues menacingly. "I gave you an opiate to help you sleep," he said. "We don't want to kill you, I promise."

That showed exactly what he knew about Rakans. Not a damn thing. I was impervious to opiates and most other human drugs. He would have had better luck with a nice aged Scotch or rich brandy.

"I'll scream," I said, making my words slur.

He chuckled. "Screaming won't matter, little girl. We drugged everyone else inside the house, too. They're sleeping the night away."

"You . . . bastard." I pretended relaxation, however, and after a few seconds, gave a grade A performance of falling unconscious. Contrary to what Lucius said, my acting did *not* suck, thank you very much.

EenLi's men agreed with me. "That was easy," one of them said.

If the man decided to rape me, I'd have a miraculous awakening, however, and show them just how sweet I could be. There were some things I would *not* do for my job.

Shockingly, he softly kissed my forehead, a gentle, innocent pressing of lips against skin. Perhaps I shouldn't have been surprised. After all, Jonathan had made it very clear I wasn't to be harmed in any way. EenLi had probably sent his sweetest abductors.

What a lovely oxymoron.

"Look at this gold," he whispered.

"Pretty," another man said, awed. I didn't recognize his voice, either. "Do you know how much money we'd make selling her skin?"

"You won't be hurting her. We're to deliver her as we found her. *We'll* be cut into tiny pieces and sold if we harm her."

"I know, I know." He sighed. "But . . . maybe we could cut off some of her hair. Maybe a few strands," he rushed on. "Nothing that would be noticed."

"No."

"Why not? We—"

"No. Now shut up. We're running out of time."

Strong arms slid under me and lifted. I let my head loll, but not before I caught a whiff of expensive, musky cologne. The scent could not have masked dirty flesh or rotting clothes. No, whoever carried me was clean and well groomed, obviously nicely paid and not the cheap labor EenLi usually used.

Cologne pushed out a breath. "Let's get out of here."

I was gently carried to the balcony, the same balcony Lucius had first used to enter my room. Of course, I'd removed the extra pins when I learned my abduction was being planned, making entry into my room easy.

Being an agent, I'd stalked and hunted victims. I'd never been one myself. Letting these men cart me away warred against every instinct I possessed. My mind wanted me to fight, to prevent this from happening. To kill. How could I allow these men to make me a slave?

There was no better way to find and destroy EenLi and save the others he had enslaved. I knew it, and took what comfort I could in the fact that these men hadn't patted me down and didn't know about my blades. Most likely, they hadn't considered that an otherworlder interpreter—and a peace-loving Rakan, at that—would be armed.

The two men took turns holding me as they harnessed themselves to a wire, then I too was strapped in and braced against one of them. Cool night air slithered around me as I was lowered to the ground.

"Careful, careful," said a rough voice from the window.

"I am careful," the man holding me replied.

"You're letting her dangle. Grip her tighter."

Wind kicked up, and my body shook precariously. I, too, almost shouted an order to be held tighter.

"Screw you," he said, his voice hard with rebellion.

"If I hold her any tighter, I'll cut off her air and she'll die." The bastard squeezed my breast (purposefully) as he tightened his hold to make a point.

Feigning a muscle spasm, I slammed my fist into his balls (also purposefully). He howled in pain, a tortured squeak that echoed in my ears.

"Bitch," Smashed Balls growled when he caught his breath.

I think he meant to backhand me, but Expensive Cologne stopped him with a menacing, "Hurt her, and I'll kill you myself."

My captor cursed under his breath. I could hear the wheels turning inside his mind as he decided whether slapping me around would be worth his death. "She busted my nuts."

"She's fucking asleep, you ass-wipe. Let's just get her out of here before you alert security."

"Security is napping."

"With all your howling, they won't sleep much longer." Pause. "Damn it, now you're holding her *too* tightly. She's turning blue."

"Do you hear her complaining?" Smashed Balls snapped.

"She's asleep, asshole." Another burst of wind circled us. "She can't complain. Release your death grip."

"You should have fucking carried her down yourself."

When the ground touched my feet, I put no weight on my legs, instead letting them buckle as if I were slumbering peacefully. My captor had to brace my entire weight.

He grunted. "She's heavier than she looks."

"Or you're weaker than *you* look."

"Get down here and hold her yourself. And I hope like hell she slams a fist into *your* nuts," he added softly.

I heard the click of metal as Expensive Cologne reached the ground. He liberated me, hefting me into his arms. Immediately he began running, causing my neck, arms, and legs to bounce up and down. They were being paid to keep me unharmed, but at this rate they were going to break me in half. Finally, the three of us reached the getaway vehicle. About that time, a shout sounded in the distance. Lights turned on and illuminated the area.

"See what you did?" Cologne growled.

"Fucking hell," Smashed Balls bellowed. "Drive, just drive."

I was chucked unceremoniously into the back seat and left in a heap as the two men jammed themselves beside me. The sound of squealing tires erupted.

I almost sighed. My abduction was a success. For all of us.

CHAPTER
20

The car ride proved to be long and tedious. The men, now three in number because of the driver, talked and laughed about my fate.

"He's going to do her hard," one of them said.

They were talking about Lucius, who was to be my new master. My reaction? Mental eye-roll and gag. The fact that Lucius had already "done" me pretty damn hard didn't factor into the picture.

"Lucky bastard," the driver muttered.

Rough, scratchy fingers began stroking my jawline, and I almost jerked away from the unwanted touch but managed to restrain myself. Those fingers shifted, tugging at my hair. Several strands popped free, and I watched through cracked lids as the man stealthily slipped them inside his pocket. His movements brought a breeze of clashing scents: excitement, fear, and . . . roses? How odd. Why did he smell like roses?

"I'd like to take her for a ride." The driver laughed crudely. "Yeeehaaaw, baby. Yeehaw."

"Who cares about riding her? She's gold and diamonds." Awe dripped from Ball's words. "We could sell her ourselves and split the money. We'd make a shitload more than what we're being paid now."

"Yeah, and we'd also turn up dead in a matter of days." Cologne. "That kind of puts a damper on spending."

Driver: "Exactly. Don't even joke about selling her. Wayne would kill us with his Mec voodoo."

Balls snorted. "I'm not afraid of that otherworlder bastard." The undertone of apprehension in his voice belied his brave claim.

Honestly, I'd be doing the universe a favor if I slit each one of their throats. And I just might do it once I offed EenLi. How long did they expect me to sleep? How long did I have to listen to this crap without reaction? I kept my lashes cracked slightly open, trying to catch glimpses of the landscape outside. First I saw only night sky, but trees soon came into view. Their branches were bare.

Finally the car eased to a stop. Cologne gently lifted me out and carted me into a small, dark building. A residence? A business? I couldn't tell. There were no surrounding houses, no signs. No telltale sounds. Moonlight danced upon the roof, spilling over and dripping onto the dry, brittle grass.

"Get her inside and put her with the others," the driver said.

"I know what to do."

With the others? That meant they hadn't been sold yet. They could be saved. Excitement unfurled inside me.

My captor pushed the front door open with a booted kick, not bothering with an ID box. Great security. Inside, I heard the creak of old wood, then the grate of rusty iron. My arms and legs flopped up and down as Cologne descended a flight of stairs. The air became cold and dank, musky. In the distance, I heard the rattle of chains and female moans.

My excitement fizzled when I realized I, too, would be placed in chains. I, too, would be made a slave. How could I willingly, no matter the reason, allow this to happen? I asked myself again. If something went wrong . . . If Lucius . . .

No. No! I would not panic. This was the plan. I'd willingly—wholeheartedly—agreed to this, knowing what would happen. Lucius wouldn't fail. *I* wouldn't fail. I had my knives, and I knew how to defend myself. I was going to be okay.

This was the only way to find EenLi. This was the only way to find what magnetic device he used for interworld travel. This was the only way to save all the others who had been taken as slaves. I would not back out now.

"How long do you think she'll be here?" Balls asked from behind Cologne.

"Not sure."

"Do you think we could—"

"No."

"You didn't even hear what I—"

"No."

Balls stalked in front of Cologne. Scowling, he inserted a key inside a lock, then pushed open metal doors. The hinges screeched in protest.

"Out of my way, bitch." Balls kicked a woman who huddled on the floor.

More chains rattled together. Feet shuffled; women whimpered. My determination to see this through intensified. I'd failed to save the two humans EenLi and his men had raped inside that warehouse, but I *would* save these women.

"Why can't you leave them alone?" Cologne growled. "You're going to bruise them."

"We're not to harm the Rakans. These bitches don't matter."

"They're to be sold, too. They matter. Maybe I need to talk to Wayne about your attitude."

Balls shuddered. "You do that, and I'll kill you."

I was laid on a cold floor. My wrists were taken in a warm, callused clasp before being clamped in cold shackles. The heavy metal bit into my skin. So much for keeping me unharmed. My wrists would be raw within the hour.

"Let's go," Cologne said. "We've got to call Wayne and let him know she's here."

Balls hesitated. I think he was considering

squeezing my breasts or between my legs, but he thought better of it. The two men left, their bickering voices fading into the distance. I didn't reveal my wakefulness, however. I remained exactly where I was, still and quiet, listening, waiting. I felt curious stares boring into me. How would the women react to me? What would they say? Minutes later, my patience was rewarded.

"I hate that man," a woman spat.

"We all do," several chimed in dispiritedly.

Footsteps slapped against the concrete floor; chains dragged and rattled. The scent of roses drifted to my nostrils just before a warm leg pressed against mine, offering me body heat. Roses. Like Balls. I knew what that meant.

"Poor thing," said the woman who justifiably hated Smashed Balls.

"We're all poor things," another, more embittered female voice retorted.

"Have you ever seen so much gold?"

"They'll cut it off her soon enough," Embittered said. "If they don't screw it off her first."

They sympathized with me, already saw me as one of them. A slave to be raped and sold. That was good. I moaned to let them know I was "waking up." Instantly conversation ceased, and a heavy silence grew. I slowly cracked open my eyes then, and eased to a sitting position. The chains were heavy, weighing down my wrists and ankles. The woman beside me watched my every movement, her big blue eyes widening. She was a pretty little thing with delicate bones and long shiny blond hair.

"Hello," she said warily.

I cast my gaze through the cell—and that's exactly what it was, a ten-by-ten prison cell—cataloging and memorizing every detail. There were five women, no men. They were young, about eighteen to twenty, and human, dressed in costumes usually seen on the streets of Whore's Corner. Like me, they had their wrists and ankles chained. The length of our binds allowed for a stroll around the entire cell. Just not out of it.

A table piled high with meats, bread, and pitchers of water took up one wall. At least the ladies weren't meant to starve. There was even a toilet on the opposite end of the cell, but no screen or door for privacy.

The only heat provided against the cold dank air was a multitude of thick blankets—all of which were taken. Not that I needed one. I'd endured worse things than cold air. My search continued, and I spotted the far wall etched with a multitude of lines. The number of days they'd been here? A wave of anger rocked me, that these girls were so young, so innocent. I hoped like hell the isotope I'd injected was doing its job, helping Lucius track me here.

Did he even know I'd been taken yet?

Hopefully I wouldn't have to wait for my "sale." I wanted to do some killing ASAP.

"Don't be scared," the blonde said, her tone gentle. "Has anyone told you why you're here?"

"We're being sold to otherworlders as slaves," Embittered informed me. She was the only redhead.

"Otherworlders?" I forced myself to gasp—forced myself not to scoot closer in anticipation of her answer. "On other planets?"

The timid one gulped and nodded.

I clasped my throat, as if in fear. "How?"

"It's not painful," she rushed to assure me. "They'll strap a collar around your neck that somehow produces a wind. One minute you'll be on Earth, and the next you won't, but it doesn't hurt. I promise."

A necklace . . . God, a necklace! Excitement rushed through me, more potent than before, and oh, so exhilarating. Romeo had strapped on a necklace before heading for the clearing. It all made sense now. According to Colin, for any type of interworld travel to be possible, a magnetic strip had to be held close to the body. What better way to hide a magnet close to the body than jewelry?

"Do you still have the necklace?" I asked.

"No." She shook her head, dancing pale tendrils of hair around her shoulders. "Why?"

The metal door ground open, and a man stalked inside our cell, saving me from a response. The women immediately hunched toward the wall, cowering. Even the redhead, who had showed the most spirit, backed away in fear. I hadn't seen this man before. He had dark hair, a plain face. He was tall, well muscled, and radiated a menacing air. I arched a regal brow.

He tossed a blanket at me. "Don't get sick," he commanded, "or I'll make you sorry you were ever born."

"Believe me, the smell of your breath is already making me sorry I was born."

Several feminine gasps filled my ears.

His green eyes narrowed. "Better watch how you talk to me, girl. I can make your stay here seem like a trip into hell." He smiled smugly. "Just ask the others."

"Oh yeah?" I didn't like how fearful the women were of him. It made me think he'd done bad things to them, horrible things. It made me want to hurt him. "Well, I can chop off your balls and feed them to you. What do you think of that?"

Growling low in his throat, he moved toward me. Only three steps in, he remembered his boss's orders not to harm me and stopped. He stood in place, fists clenching, emerald eyes sparking with the need to teach me a lesson. To subdue and overpower me. Finally he stormed out of the cell, slamming the door shut behind him.

The women stared at me in silence for a long while.

The blonde finally gasped out, "He could have killed you. Raped you. Beaten you. He . . . likes that," she admitted, a shameful edge to the words. Color brightened her cheeks, so vivid she appeared feverish.

"Yes," I said with a nod, "he could have done all of those things, but he would not have emerged unscathed." I wanted so badly to help them and take away their pain. I couldn't. Not yet. So I did for them what I could. I tried to teach them what to do if the bastard ever came near them again. "Never let a man see you cower. If he knows he's stronger than you, he'll always attack. It's male nature. Fight them. With words, with your fists. Slam your palm into his nose. Poke his eyes. Don't be afraid to hurt him. He isn't afraid to hurt you."

"But . . . but . . ."

"You may lose," I said, "but I swear to you he'll always think twice before he comes after you again."

"Unless he kills you," the redhead added. She sounded wistful.

Whatever was required, I was getting these women out of here.

CHAPTER
21

I didn't have a long wait until my summons.

Within an hour, two men entered the cell to get me. Expensive Cologne and Smashed Balls. How lovely. A reunion.

"Time to go, sweetheart," Cologne said. Curiously eager, he unchained me and tried to help me to my feet.

I slapped his hand away and stood on my own.

He frowned when he spied the puffy red scuff marks on my wrists and ankles.

"You should have told me you have such delicate skin," he scolded.

"When should I have told you? Before you abducted me? While I was sleeping?" *Idiot.*

"There's going to be trouble for this," he muttered.

"Too bad for you."

Frowning, he shook his head. "I liked you better when you were asleep."

"Well, I never liked you." He might be the kindest of all of the guards, but that didn't make him any less of a slaver.

He sighed and waved me over. "Come on."

"Why?" I remained where I was. "Where are you taking me?"

"Shut your mouth!" Smashed Balls shouted. "You don't ask questions. You just follow orders."

Still I remained stubbornly in place.

"We need to get you cleaned up." Cologne motioned with his fingers again. "Come."

"They're taking you to the bathroom to give you a shower," the blonde whispered.

"They like to watch," the redhead added defiantly, her voice loud and echoing.

Balls stomped a menacing step toward her, his intent to slap her evident by the raising of his palm. Eyes narrowed, I jumped in front of him. His arm stilled.

"I'm ready." I straightened my shoulders. "Lead the way."

He flicked the redhead a you'll-pay glare and spun on his heel. I followed him out of the cell, and Cologne took up the rear. They were so confident in their abilities and strengths that they didn't blindfold me or even try to hide their identities. Idiots, I thought again.

Though I remained on alert, I cast my gaze over my surroundings. Without a doubt, we were underground. Water dripped from the ceiling and dirt lined the floors. The only light sprang from thin bulbs that hung from equally thin wires.

My mind raced with strategies. They planned to watch me shower; I planned to thwart them. But how? They could overpower me by sheer numbers. They could even stun me with a pyre-gun, then clean, molest, or rape me without my being able to protest. That raised the question of why they hadn't stunned me already. Why hadn't they stunned me to bring me here?

Time, I realized in the next instant. A stun lasted twenty-four hours. They must need my cooperation for . . . what? My hands clenched at my sides, but I never slowed my step. I lifted my chin, remaining alert as we entered the foyer of the home. Cologne and Smashed Balls stopped to chat with the three men cleaning and vacuuming, preparing the room for . . . a visitor? For Lucius?

Would he arrive soon to purchase me? My knees almost buckled in relief with the possibility. EenLi would be here, too. Having watched him for weeks, I knew he oversaw all transactions personally. This could all be over in a matter of hours. The possibility was so wonderful that it seemed too good to be true. Surreal, even.

Amid the men's chatter about what the women in the cell needed, I finished my study of the room. There was a spacious living area off to the side, complete with couch, a large holoscreen, and several plush velvet chairs. Empty beer bottles littered a rectangular coffee table. Though there were no windows, lace curtains draped a section of the wall, giving the illusion of glass.

Very domestic and cozy.

Strong male hands gently pushed me forward. "Walk," Cologne said, his conversation with the others finished.

I followed Balls down the hall. Plain, dingy yellow walls closed in around me. They were devoid of any decoration, probably so that the slaves wouldn't have access to a makeshift weapon. There were four doors at the end of the hallway. One of them led into a small, cramped bathroom, which was the room we entered. It had brown plaster walls, a splintered floor. An enzyme spray hose slithered from the far wall, and a toilet pushed against the side.

In front of me, Balls stopped, turned, and folded his arms over his chest. He was very thin, and his skin looked dry and flaky. He was also balding. No wonder he had such an attitude problem.

"Strip." He smiled slowly, evilly. "Then shower. And make sure to clean yourself real good, or I'll have to clean you myself."

I heard the rustle of Cologne's shirt as he too crossed his arms over his chest. That really pissed me off. Of all the men I'd encountered in this house, Cologne seemed the most gentle, the most concerned for the women. Yet he too was willing to humiliate me so he could get his rocks off.

Turning to the side, I gave both men my profile. Unconcerned. "I'll strip when both of you leave."

Balls arched his brows in smug amusement. He had wanted me to resist. Wanted to scare me. "Strip. Now. Or I make you do it."

"Leave. Now," I replied. "Or I make you do it."

Cologne sighed, and the sound drifted through the small bathroom. "We're not going to hurt you. Just watch."

"Just violate my privacy, you mean."

"This is your last chance. Strip on your own," Balls said, "or strip with our help."

One, I didn't want them to see my weapons. And two, getting naked most likely meant rape. No, thank you. A cold sweat broke out over my skin. Not good. Unlike humans, my sweat made me more attractive. The beads of moisture made my flesh look like polished, dewy gold. Glittery. Like a fairy. I didn't want to be attractive at this moment. I wanted to appear mean and ugly, capable of any evil deed.

Knowing the other women had endured this, yet had had no way to prevent it, turned my fear to protectiveness. "If you help me undress," I said slowly, carefully, "there will be a fight. A to-the-death fight. Understand?"

"Rakan, you're a woman." Wearing an expression that begged me to understand, Cologne stepped toward me. "You can't hurt us."

Balls moved toward me as well. They were trying to close me in, to threaten and intimidate me with their strength.

"But I'll get hurt, and that will make me damaged goods. See, I talked to the girls. I know why we're here. We're being sold as slaves. Your boss wants top dollar for me, doesn't he?"

Silence reigned as they considered my words. I didn't know how long or often I could get by with that particular threat, but I'd use it as long as I could.

Thankfully, it worked.

"You win," Cologne said on a resigned sigh.

"What!" Balls shouted.

"There are no windows here. The only exit is the door. We will be here, waiting, and if you try to escape, we will punish you. Whether it decreases your value or not. Do you understand?"

"Coward!" Balls slammed his fist into his open palm. "We're not walking away. Hold her, and I'll cut those fucking clothes off her body."

Anticipating an attack from him, I bent my knees slightly and centered my energy. He never moved toward me, however. Cologne grabbed him by the arm and flung him outside the bathroom. The smaller man crashed into the wall and slithered into a heap on the rotting wood floor.

"You will not always get your way," he said to me. "It will be best for you if you realize that quickly." With narrowed eyes, he strode from the room and shut the door behind him. "You have fifteen minutes. Get clean and put on the clothes resting on the toilet lid."

I glanced at the toilet. A sheer pink sheath draped the lid. I lifted the material between pinched fingers. Pantaloons and a halter top. They were dressing me like a harem slut. Wonderful.

Frowning, I turned on the shower by punching the labeled buttons. Hot spray instantly misted the porcelain tub. I didn't climb inside, however. I spent most of my fifteen minutes watching the door and finding ways to hide my blades under the new sheer outfit.

Only once did someone try to sneak inside. As the knob turned, I said, "Do it and die." The door remained firmly shut after that, not opening until I knocked and said, "All done."

In the end, I only managed to conceal one knife. I wrapped it around the back shoulder strap of the top's internal bra. The other, well, I had to chuck it between slabs of wood on the floor.

I would have liked to study my reflection in the mirror. I'm sure I appeared dainty and fragile, a sex slave desperate for her master's attentions. The low-riding bottoms started at the flare of my hips, and my shirt—if it could be called that—ended just under my breasts.

My two guards were frowning when they opened the door, but their eyes widened and their mouths dropped when they spied me. Balls even reached out to trace his finger over my collarbone, but I gripped the offending appendage and twisted. He yelped and used his other hand to slap me.

I felt a sharp sting, and my head snapped to the side. Slowly, I faced him with narrowed eyes and wiped at my now throbbing lip. Warm wetness greeted my fingers.

A gleam of horror entered his brown eyes. "You tell anyone I did that," he said quietly, menacingly, "and I'll kill you."

Oh, how I wanted to slit his throat just then, but I did nothing. I nodded as if I cared about the warning. He backed off, pivoted on his heel, and strode away.

"You okay?" Cologne asked, his concern unwanted and unneeded.

"I'm fine."

"Time to go, then." He nudged my shoulder, a demand to move. My gaze bored into Balls's back as I followed him into the living room the guards had been cleaning earlier. The moment I stepped inside and saw what awaited me, I froze. My abrupt stop caused Cologne to ram into my back, shoving me forward. He tried to help me regain my balance, but I slapped his hands away.

When I steadied my feet, my pulse leapt and my blood alternately heated and chilled. This was it. My sale. The cleaning crew was gone, and in their place was Jonathan Parker, Lucius, and another man, an otherworlder I didn't recognize.

My gaze locked with Lucius's. I was beyond happy to see him. He gave an almost imperceptible nod of his head before his eyes narrowed on the bruise on my lip.

Fighting a smile, I forced my attention elsewhere. The otherworlder seated next to him was a Targon, the most feared race of warriors ever to come to Earth. Our government would do anything to have a few of them fighting for us. They were a tall, built race, to be sure, but that wasn't their main worth. Their telekinetic abilities surpassed even the Arcadians'.

This one was handsome, as muscled as any man I'd ever seen. He had dark hair, eerie amber eyes. Light, light skin. He was wearing a gold necklace with a dull, ugly stone in the center. My gaze narrowed on it. Was it used for interworld travel?

When would EenLi arrive? A wave of impatience crashed through me, and I wasn't sure how I would react when I saw the bastard.

"I'm so glad everyone could make it," a heavily accented voice suddenly proclaimed.

EenLi.

Heart drumming erratically, I quickly scanned the room. Where was he? I didn't see—I sucked in a breath. There, on the large holoscreen above the couch, was EenLi's smug, smiling, ugly face. He glowed bright pink. He was very happy with himself.

Disappointment nearly felled me, nearly dropped me to my knees. I'd expected him here, to see to the details of this sale in person. Damn. Damn!

His bald head gleamed brightly in the fluorescent lighting. That same lighting made his large, pupil-less white eyes and pink skin appear translucent. Very eerie. And completely at odds with his cowboy shirt and the red bandana tied around his neck.

I desperately wanted this bastard dead. He was evil incarnate, and he deserved to die. I felt as if I'd been waiting forever, and now it seemed I had to wait even longer. Technology allowed for many things, but we still couldn't assassinate a man through a television. Damn this, and damn me!

Lucius and I were now at a major disadvantage. If either of us acted, we wouldn't get EenLi and we'd blow our covers and most likely be killed in the ensuing crossfire. And there *would* be crossfire. Guards were posted all through the house; the moment they heard gunshots or screaming, they'd rush inside this room. If Lucius and I were killed, the women below would be sentenced to a life of rape, humiliation, and servitude. I couldn't let that happen.

I exhaled a breath, fighting past my disappointment, not knowing what to do at this point.

I cast my gaze at the men sitting on the couch, noticing little details I'd missed before. Each man held a cigar and a glass of Scotch. How quaint. A real bonding moment for them.

"You," I said to Lucius, trying to act shocked and horrified when the image of him gave me my only sense of peace. If EenLi knew I was an agent, I didn't want him to suspect who I was really working with. I leveled a faux pleading gaze on Parker, even tried to rush to him before Balls grabbed my arm and stopped me. "Jonathan, you have to help me. I've been abducted, and—"

"I know, darling." He sipped at his Scotch as cigar smoke curled in front of his face. "You shouldn't have been such a naughty girl."

I uttered an I'm-so-scared gasp while I mentally pictured his demise. *Rot in hell, you son of a bitch.*

"Touch my property again," Lucius ground out, his dark, slitted gaze shooting blazes of fire at Cologne and Balls, "and I'll cut off your hands." He slammed his glass and cigar onto the table, causing a loud *boom.*

Both guards instantly jumped away from me. I really, *really* liked it when Lucius went all commando.

From the screen, EenLi laughed. The sound of his voice echoed from nearby speakers. "Patience, human," he said. His skin pinkened further. "She's not yours yet." With a simple wave of his fingers, he commanded the guards to return to me. "Keep her still."

Hesitantly, the men gripped my forearms and held me in place. As I stood there, those on the couch surveyed me. "I want to know who struck her," Lucius demanded. "She was to be brought here unharmed."

Beside me, Balls trembled. There was only silence.

"Who struck you?" Lucius repeated, an edge of danger in his tone I'd never heard before.

"We did ask that she be unharmed," Jonathan re-iterated with a frown.

"I demand reparation." Lucius.

EenLi lost his grin. "Answer us, girl. Who struck you?"

I motioned to Balls with an accusing tilt of my chin. "He did."

"Bitch!" Balls screeched, nearly jerking my arm from its socket. He gazed imploringly at EenLi. "She's lying. I swear she's lying."

"She speaks the truth," Cologne interjected firmly.

"No, no, I didn't touch her. I—"

"I saw him do it." Cologne again.

Realizing he could not continue to refute the charges, Balls changed his tactics. "I'm so sorry, Wayne." He released me and dropped to his knees. Tears streamed down his eyes. "I didn't mean to hurt her, I swear. She tripped and ran into my hand. That's all that happened. Please don't hurt me. Give me another chance."

Unconcerned, EenLi nodded to Cologne. Amid Balls's cries for mercy, my guard withdrew an electro-gun from the back waist of his slacks. Shock thundered inside me as I realized what I was looking at. My mouth dropped open. The body of the gun was clear, making the flashes of electricity visible inside. This type of gun was not on the market yet because Michael, who was its creator, had yet to perfect it.

Even I had yet to use one.

Was there a traitor in our midst? The idea turned my blood to ice because it raised another, more terrible question. Did EenLi know Lucius was an agent? No, I assured myself. However he'd gotten the electro-gun, I didn't think he knew who Lucius was. He would have killed my partner immediately.

Balls began sobbing. Eyes bright with resignation, Cologne unhesitatingly placed the barrel at the other man's temple and pulled the trigger. To us, it appeared nothing happened. No flash of light. No emission of sound. Balls's body shook and shuddered as electricity poured through him. His nostrils soon rimmed with black, and steam rose from his ears. Then he collapsed face-first on the carpet.

Cologne holstered the gun. EenLi and Jonathan nodded in satisfaction. Lucius's expression was blank as he crossed his arms over his chest, discreetly putting his fingers within reaching distance of his weapons.

What the hell had we gotten ourselves into?

CHAPTER
22

No one bothered to move the body.

The scent of charred human flesh blended with the odor of cigar smoke and expensive Scotch as the meeting continued. Cologne took up residence behind me and gripped my shoulders to once more hold me in place. I didn't protest.

I was ready to get this "purchase" over with.

"Jonathan, Hunter, Devyn," EenLi said with another evil grin. "Let the bidding begin."

At his words, I didn't panic. So they were having a bidding war for me. Lucius and I had suspected that might happen. My gaze traveled to his. Yes, he was supposed to buy me, then purchase our way to another planet for "legal" reasons. Once we had that information, we were to kill EenLi. Now, there was a very good chance someone else would purchase me.

Lucius appeared relaxed, totally calm, as if he knew

exactly what to do. Good. I knew he'd do everything in his power to win me, and if he didn't, he'd do what needed to be done. As would I. I trusted him. Fully and completely, I realized. And I was pretty sure he trusted me.

"Turn around," EenLi commanded me in an imperious tone.

My cheeks reddened at being treated like one of his "cattle." Every man present was watching me, studying me, looking for flaws. The Targon rubbed his jaw, his expression blank, as his gaze raked over me.

Cologne's grip on me tightened. "Do it."

If I didn't turn for them, I would be forced. And there would be no more reprieves for me under the guise of keeping me unbruised. I saw that knowledge in EenLi's now glowing red eyes. *You want to get the sale over with, remember?*

I lifted my chin and turned. Slowly. Giving them all a chance to look their fill at my sheer, pink-clad curves. I felt the heat of their gazes touching me everywhere, stripping me.

How many times had the other women endured this? How many times had they been forced to display their bodies for men they despised? My hands shook with the force of my humiliation. And beneath it all, a new sense of respect and admiration for the five women locked below grew within me. They were survivors.

Yes, I *would* save them; my determination increased all the more. No matter what was required of me.

When I faced the men again, EenLi was smiling happily from the screen, his ugly face stretched into a toothy monstrosity. Red faded to pink. "I'm almost tempted to keep the little agent for myself," he said. "She's powerful under all that delicacy."

So. He *did* know that I was an agent. It was probably why he was here on the holoscreen and not in person. I was only surprised he wasn't gloating about capturing me.

"Whatever your price," Lucius said, his rough, gravelly voice claiming me, "I'll pay."

"And I'll double that." Jonathan.

Lucius hissed in a breath. "What did you say?"

"You heard me." Jonathan became defensive. "I want her, too. You didn't think I helped you out of the goodness of my heart, did you?" He tapped his cigar ashes on Lucius's expensive Italian loafers. "Please tell me you aren't that stupid."

My partner snarled low in his throat—and I didn't think it was mere pretense. "I can't believe you're going through with this. She's mine. You knew I wanted her."

"We'll see about that, won't we?" Jonathan arched his brows, his expression haughty.

Deadly silence filled the room, slithering along the walls like a snake ready to strike. *Come on, boys. Just buy me already.*

Leaning forward, Lucius said darkly, "Are you sure you want to take me on?"

Jonathan laughed nervously and assumed a feigned casual pose, legs stretched, hands linked over the lapels of his dark blue jacket. "You can have her when I'm done with her."

"Neither of you will have her." The Targon had remained silent until that point, and now his deep timbre echoed off the walls. As he studied me, he caressed the gold band he wore around his neck, his fingers circling the ugly brown stone in the middle. "I'll take her," he said, as if that settled the entire matter.

"Numbers, gentlemen." EenLi rubbed his hands together like a greedy child. "I need actual figures."

"One million." Jonathan.

"Two." The Targon.

"Five." Lucius. He relaxed in his seat, growing more assured of his victory. Whatever monetary capital was needed, he would pay. Or pretend to pay, I should say.

The Targon countered. "Five million Earth dollars, plus two Targon warriors."

"Done." Grinning, EenLi clapped his hands. "The woman is yours."

"No." In a dark, fluid motion, Lucius jumped to his feet.

EenLi's eyes narrowed to tiny slits. "I will find you another Rakan, Hunter."

"I want *this* one." He pointed to me. "She's mine. She was promised to me. Find *him* another."

"Actually, she was promised to me." Jonathan gripped his cigar so tightly it snapped in half.

"Please tell me you were not foolish enough to think I'd save her for you, Jonathan," EenLi said, repeating the man's earlier words to Lucius. "I already own your soul. What need have I to keep you happy?" To Lucius he said, "I respected your father, and I will be happy to work with you in the future to secure you another Rakan. As for this one, a better offer came along."

"She's mine, goddamn you," Lucius growled. "This is bad for business. What will your other clients say when they realize you aren't a man of your word?"

Another silence erupted, this one heavier than the last.

EenLi's skin pulsed a dark crimson. "Do not make me your enemy." His lips pressed together, providing only a tight slit for his words.

Lucius stalked toward the screen. "Let's talk about this."

"No."

As I listened, I realized EenLi had always meant to sell me to the Targon. What better way to gain an alliance with such invincible warriors? After losing Mris-ste and discovering he himself was a government target for elimination, EenLi probably saw this as his opportunity to acquire an impenetrable shield. Or two.

"I want to talk," Lucius insisted. "Man to man. Face to face."

"Ha. You're angry enough to try and kill me right now."

I knew what he was doing, trying to draw EenLi out, and I approved. However, I didn't want to be taken from this building until the women below were safe. I'd have to put up some kind of fight, perhaps race down there. Then . . . what? I guess we'd find out. I stealthily inched my fingers toward the small blade strapped to my back.

The Targon eased to his feet, his eyes watching my every move. I'd never seen eyes like his. Like molten flames of gold, glowing hotly, almost hypnotically. His clean-cut features were lit with amusement.

"Come to me," he said, even his voice layered with a hypnotic quality.

Oddly, I was compelled to obey. Something deep inside me heard and responded to his voice, wanting to do everything in my power to please him. The rest of the room faded until I saw only the Targon. My thoughts scattered, realigning around his beautiful image.

"Come," he said again.

Focus, Eden. Focus. Do not listen to his voice. Think only of what you need to do. Fight. Yes, I needed to fight, to save the women. With that thought, I snapped out of his spell. Where was he vulnerable? His neck? His chest? I'd never killed a Targon before.

"Come," he said for the third time.

I moved toward him, sliding my blade out of its

strap. I used my wrist and arm to shield it from his view.

Lucius jumped in front of me and faced the Targon. "Since Wayne is refusing to meet with me, I'll deal with you. Let me buy her from you. I'll pay you whatever you want."

"She is no longer for sale," the otherworlder said with a hint of irritation.

"You're not taking her off this planet."

I touched my fingers to Lucius's back, silently letting him know I knew what I had to do and *would* do it. He didn't step aside. I knew he'd felt my touch, however, because his muscles clenched at first contact.

The Targon raised his brows. "If you plan to stop me, human, I suggest you not even try. People tend to get hurt when they annoy me."

"Now that our business is concluded," EenLi interjected, as someone approached his image from behind, "I will leave you alone to collect your prize. I expect those Targon warriors on my doorstep tomorrow morning, Devyn."

The holoscreen went blank.

Jonathan reached toward Lucius, but Lucius grabbed his arm and twisted, snapping the bone. Jonathan howled in pain and dropped to his knees. Then Lucius sprang at the Targon. Without ever moving an inch, the otherworlder somehow forced Lucius to the ground beside Jonathan.

I too sprang forward, my knife raised and ready

for insertion. But in the next instant, my feet froze in place and the knife dropped from my hand. I couldn't move. Could barely breathe.

"Do not panic, little Rakan." The Targon sent me a gentle smile. "I'll release you from the paralysis soon enough."

The bastard was controlling me with his mind. Panic coiled inside me, but I fought against it, trying to erect some sort of shield against him. His power proved too strong, however.

Still grinning, he flung a gold torque at me. Like a snake, the band wrapped itself at the base of my throat, not tight enough to choke, just tight enough to ensure it stayed in place. I flicked a horrified gaze down; an amber gem stone winked up at me. I wanted so badly to tear at the band, but couldn't. I returned my gaze to Lucius, staring helplessly at him, just as horrified.

Since hitting the carpet, he'd had yet to move.

"What did you do to him?" I demanded.

"He merely sleeps," the Targon said.

Proving the otherworlder's words, Lucius moaned. His eyes opened, and he weakly raised his head. When he spied me, he attempted to crawl to me, to protect me.

"I think he needs to sleep permanently," Jonathan said, whipping out an old gun. I couldn't do anything but scream, locked in place as I was, as he fired. A bullet lodged itself just below Lucius's left shoulder, causing his entire body to spasm. In his heart?

Cold rage slashed inside me. The Targon removed his focus from me and frowned down at the now-bleeding Lucius. His inattention released me from paralysis. I immediately picked up my blade and, without a second's thought, hurtled it at Jonathan. The sharp metal sliced into his throat. His eyes widened, and he gurgled as his knees gave out and he sank to the ground. I leaped forward and was just reaching for the blade when a dark cloud covered my mind. Sinking . . . sinking . . . I fought past it, cutting with mental claws.

Unexpectedly, the fog lifted. "What's happening?" I asked, dazed.

The Targon blinked in surprise. "You have mental shields, though they are not very strong." He sighed, and I froze in place once again. He withdrew a small vial from his pocket, pushed my hair out of my face, and forced the contents down my throat. I choked it back, but it was too late to spit out the bitter liquid. I knew the moment the taste of it hit my tongue that it wasn't an opiate like Cologne had given me.

This man had done his homework on Rakans. He knew the human medicine called antihistamine, when mixed with alcohol, knocked us out every time. When lethargy hit me, it hit swiftly and full force. The last picture to drift through my mind was of Lucius, covered in his own blood.

CHAPTER
23

The image of Lucius's strong vibrant body, bloody and lifeless, slammed past a black fog of lethargy and into my mind. "Lucius!" I screamed. The sound of his name echoed all around me.

"Welcome to Targon," whispered through my mind.

Targon. No. No! My eyelids popped open. My breath was coming in short, erratic pants, like I'd just run a marathon uphill. I searched for another person, but saw no one. Had I been dreaming . . . a nightmare, perhaps? No. I bit my bottom lip, creating a sharp sting and a bead of blood. Lucius had really been shot. I remembered the auction for me and the booming sound of Jonathan's gun being fired, remembered the metallic smell of human blood.

Lucius, I thought, a wave of panic overtaking me. I had to get to him. He was now injured and defenseless in a house full of EenLi's guards, and no one knew he was there but me. I would *not* allow myself to think of him as . . . No, I wouldn't.

The women, too, were helpless. I had to save them.

I jerked upright, taking the soft white comforter draping my body with me. My gaze shot throughout the room. Unfamiliar. Wide and open. White gauze billowed from the many windows and doors. I was seated on a white pallet of velvetlike cushions. There were no guards posted that I could see.

Where the hell was I?

Targon . . .

I wasn't sure if the isotope I'd ingested had tracked me here, and there wasn't time to find out. An other-world rescue seemed impossible, anyway, since we did not have all the facts about solar flares. No, I'd have to free myself. Quickly.

I needed to get home.

I shoved my way out from the covers and stood. My legs were shaky, making me wonder just how long I'd been asleep. At least the Targon hadn't stripped me. He'd left me in the pink harem costume. I reached up, but the necklace he'd thrown at me was gone. I needed it to pass through a solar flare. Where was it?

Breathing a deep inhalation of sweet, flowery air, I scanned the spacious room again. Would he have hidden the necklace in a fruit bowl? No. Empty. A drawer . . . maybe he had tucked it inside. I bounded forward, but skidded to a stop when I heard him speak.

"I am so happy you are, at last, awake," his rich, sensual voice said from behind me.

I spun around. The Targon leaned against one of the large entryways, white lace dancing from the windows and over his bare legs. His eyes swirled with a life all their own; his dark hair flowed around his shoulders, the sides hooked behind his ears. I could see that his ears were pointy, like the magical Fae in children's stories. He wore some type of black Scottish-looking kilt and no shirt.

"Give me the necklace and take me back," I demanded.

He *tsked* under his tongue. "We haven't been properly introduced. You are Eden Black, otherworlder interpreter and government agent. I am Devyn Cambrii, king of this land."

King. The freaking king. I knew a little about Targon history. A king was appointed not by birth but by telekinetic strength. A thousand tiny knots twisted my stomach. I was weaponless, and my opponent had the power to freeze me in place. How the hell could I fight him?

"Please," I said, the word escaping through scowling lips. "Take me back."

"It has taken EenLi over a year to find me a Rakan," he replied. "I'm sorry, sweet angel, but the only place I will be taking you is my bed."

My fists clenched at my sides. "And if I refuse?"

His lips twitched, and amusement twinkled in his too-amber eyes. "Your refusal will not be a problem."

No, it wouldn't, I thought darkly. He'd already proven his ability quite nicely. If he decided to freeze me and rape me, there would be nothing I could do to stop him from doing so. I refused to show him an outward reaction to that comment, however. If he thrived on female fear, he might become aroused.

"Why a Rakan?" I asked, to keep him talking. I lifted my chin. "There's nothing special about my race."

"Oh, I beg to differ."

"Because of the gold?"

He chuckled richly. "I am not human. Gold means nothing to me."

"Then why?"

"I've never tasted a Rakan. There are so few of you on Earth because those silly humans are greedy. And outsiders are not allowed on the planet Raka. Which is a shame, really. I could have feasted for months had I been allowed entry." His voice lowered one octave. "I've wanted to taste a Rakan for a long, long time."

I arched a brow, feigning nonchalance. "Tasted in passion? Or as dinner?"

He laughed again, his features softening. The woman in me appreciated his masculine beauty, his male sensuality. But he wasn't Lucius. I would have no man but Lucius. In our short time together, I'd learned to respect and like him. I'd desired him constantly. He meant something to me. What, I didn't know. I just knew that he *did* matter.

"Passion, of course," the Targon said. "I've sampled women from across the galaxies. I'm in need of something different. Something unique." He straightened and slowly moved toward me.

"Stop," I shouted, bending my knees and preparing for battle.

Surprisingly, he did. He remained a safe distance away as his gaze traveled the length of me. "I only wish to know if you are as soft to my touch as you look. Surely you will not deny me a simple touch."

"I deny you the right to even breathe in my direction."

"Your resistance is adorable, so I will grant your request and not touch you. For now."

"Thank you," I said, my tone dry.

"You are welcome." He grinned at me. "I am glad to add you to my collection."

"Your collection?"

"Oh, yes. I love women, you see. I love their softness, their complexities, their scents, and have decided to sample a woman of every color, race, and size."

"And it doesn't matter to you that some of these women might not desire you?"

"They may not desire me . . . at first." His grin widened. "I always change their minds."

"I don't want you," I gnashed out. "I want another."

The Targon merely shrugged. "You, too, will change your mind." He sounded so confident, so completely certain of my capitulation. Watching me through those too-amber, amused eyes, he renewed his path toward me. "I could begin changing your mind right now," he said, but he switched directions and stopped at a bureau. He lifted the white stone fruit bowl. Having searched it, I knew only small, azure spheres were inside.

I didn't move when he closed the distance between us, though my every instinct demanded I attack. He merely brushed past me. Our bare shoulders met, skin to skin, his surprisingly cool, mine hot with desperation to leave. He eased atop the mound of pillows. The scent of exotic spices followed him and lingered in the air. He leaned back, assuming a lazy, seductive pose, and patted the seat beside him.

"Is this part of changing my mind?"

"So suspicious, little Rakan." He popped a fruit into his mouth and chewed. "Alas no, this is a getting-to-know-you moment. If you prefer, we can jump ahead. I am not picky. Come to me."

I considered refusing his demand. I didn't want to get to know him better; I didn't want to sit next to him and play his silly game of seduction. The need to get to Lucius and the women intensified with every second that passed. Damn it! I'd never felt more helpless.

"Come," Devyn said, his tone firmer and harder

than before. The amused sparkle faded from his eyes, going flat with expectation.

I approached him and sank onto the pillows beside him.

"That's better," he said, reaching into the bowl and withdrawing a sphere. His stark white teeth sank into it, consuming half. "You will eat." When he attempted to slip the rest past my lips, I ripped it out of his hands and tossed it across the room.

I grabbed a piece of fruit without Targon germs and shoved it into my mouth. The sweet, sweet flavor made each of my taste buds shoot to life. I found myself reaching out for another.

He sighed, pieces of his amusement having returned. "We will have to work on your stubbornness. It is an honor to eat with the king, you know."

"I have to go back to Earth, Devyn."

"*This* is to be your home."

I leaned forward, beseeching with my eyes, my voice. "Please. Give me the necklace and take me back. I have a man, a mission, and I *must* get back."

Devyn reached out and sifted my hair through his fingers. The gold strands were beautiful draped over his pale skin. "The man who was shot. Hunter, I think was his name. He is your man, yes?"

"Yes." I clenched the pillows, wadding the material between my fists. "How did you know?"

His huge shoulders lifted in a shrug. "The way you looked at him; the way he looked at you. I'm curious, though. If he is your man, why was he there to buy you?"

I ignored the question. "He's hurt. You saw Jonathan shoot him. I have to help him, get him medical care."

"He is not hurt, angel. He's dead."

Everything inside me frosted with ice. Cold, hard ice. Strong, vital Lucius was not dead. I would have known it, felt it. We were connected in a way that I didn't understand, but now accepted—and was grateful for. I could not, would not, believe he was dead. He possessed too much life, too much strength. He was indestructible. *Please let him be indestructible.*

"How do you know that?" I said softly, my jawbone so tight it could snap at any moment.

"I saw the blood just as you did. He is human, and humans cannot lose so much blood."

"Humans can survive with blood transfusions. That's why I have to get to him."

"If there was any life left inside him, EenLi would patch him up and sell him as a slave. This I promise you."

Yes, I thought, hope melting the ice. Ever the businessman, EenLi would not let a prime specimen like Lucius die when he could be bringing in a profit. "I cannot let him become a slave. Nor can I allow the other women who were imprisoned in that house to become slaves. I have to go back. I'll do anything you ask if you'll just take me back."

"What does this man give you that is so special,

so *different* from what I can give you?" Devyn's tone was hard.

"He's . . . mine." It was the only answer I had at the moment.

Hands fisted, he shoved angrily to his feet. He glared down at me. "I will not send you back, because I am not willing to give you up. I have had enough talk of dead men and enslaved women."

We'd see about that. He might be telekinetic, but perhaps if I worked quickly enough, I could defeat him. I kicked out my leg and connected with his ankles. He toppled backward, dropping the fruit bowl with a clang. Blue spheres scattered across the floor as I sprang on top of him, using my weight to cut off his air, my knee in his windpipe.

"I'll kill you if I remain here," I vowed.

Far from being intimidated, he grinned. "I see I will have to bring my guards back. I had hoped you would appreciate the privacy."

I fought a wave of defeat. "You aren't even winded, are you?"

"No." A wicked gleam flittered over his amused expression. "I can put you to sleep with only a blink of my eyes, and then I can do whatever I want to you."

I jerked back my elbow, making a fist along the way. As my hand flew closer to his face, his grin only grew wider . . . and the muscles in my arm stiffened completely, holding me in place before I ever reached his nose.

"I like your spirit," he said, the words laden with excitement. "You will be my finest possession."

I grated my teeth together so forcefully, I could have made powder. "Let me tell you something, Targon. I will never willingly give myself to you, and if you try and force me, I will carve you into little pieces and feed you to your people."

His lips dipped into a pout. "It will not be force. You are my slave—"

"It *will* be force. Hunter is the only lover I desire."

That angry spark lit once more in Devyn's tawny gaze. "You are my property, and I will not allow you to think of another man."

"I'll think of him and desire him and long for him for the rest of my life," I said, pricking his male pride. "Every time you touch me, I'll pretend it's *him*. That *he's* the one giving me pleasure."

Growling low in his throat, he shoved me off him and jumped to his feet. I jumped up, as well, my arm muscles released from his spell. We faced off.

"You are more than you seem, Rakan," he bit out, "and I admit I was beginning to like that. You have the courage of a warrior, but you are as foolish as every other woman, and *that* I do not like. I am king here, and you will learn not to fan the flames of my anger."

"Please," I said then, desperate. How could I make him do what I wanted?

"Please what? Please touch you? Please be merciful?"

"Please send me home."

A heavy pause erupted, our breathing the only sound. Then he grabbed my hand and tugged me down a wide, open hallway, as white and pure and mocking as a virgin's bedsheets. At the far end was a bedroom, as open as the rest of the house and just as white. Pillows littered the floor, and a pool occupied the far end.

He tossed me onto the pillows. When my back hit, air whooshed from my lungs. I hopped up immediately, panting for breath.

"I told you not to ask to be returned again. And so, your training will begin now." He crossed his arms over his chest.

"Training to do what?"

"Pleasure me, of course."

CHAPTER

24

Devyn's gaze remained locked with mine as he stripped out of his only clothing, the black kiltlike skirt. He posed before me wearing nothing more than a smug smile. His skin was pale. His dark hair hung around his shoulders in disarray. He made a striking picture, handsome and strong.

I wanted no part of him.

Unfortunately, he was determined to have every part of me.

My blood boiled at his arrogance and intentions, at his sheer selfishness, and I forced my energy to center. I would have to attack him; surprise would be my only avenue against this Targon. I drew in a deep, cleansing breath. Hold . . . hold . . . His attention deviated from me.

I was just about to pounce on him when I noticed the two naked alien women entering through the side doorway, one with thick, silky blue skin, the other with white skin—and five arms.

What was going on?

Devyn waved them over. "Come, ladies."

The first, the pretty, pale-skinned blonde with too many arms, clapped and giggled. The second, the exotic azure one, licked her lips. Both possessed lean bodies and sculpted muscles.

"Watch us," Devyn told me. "And learn."

My mouth almost dropped in shock. He didn't mean to rape me, but merely wanted me to watch how others pleased him? I shook my head, unsure I had heard him correctly.

"Do not think to leave, either, while I am distracted," he said, admonishment ripe in his tone.

In the next instant, my knees buckled of their own accord and I fell onto the pillows. My muscles froze in place. I tried to fight against the paralysis, to no avail. Damn him.

The two women reached him, eagerly scratching their hands over his body and leaving amber welts in their path. The five-armed woman was able to cover a lot of ground. Not even trying to be gentle, they nipped at his chest with their teeth, drawing little beads of gold blood. They pinched his nipples and tightly squeezed and pumped his erection.

The Targon groaned with rapture. His eyes closed.

This is it, I thought. *My only chance.* I couldn't move my body, but I could still move my spirit. I concentrated on a spot just beyond his shoulder, focusing my energy inward. I had to risk leaving my body vulnerable. This might be my only chance to find the necklace he'd used to send me here.

Soon my spirit broke from my body, leaving it cold, forgotten, and I was looking down at myself. My eyes were open, and I appeared to be watching the straining, writhing trio. Good. The only thing that gave me away was my blank, unmoving expression, but I doubted Professor Sex and his apprentices would notice.

There was no furniture in the room, nothing to search, so I abandoned it. I didn't know how long Targon sex lasted, so I quickened my step. Thankfully, there were no closed doorways.

Devyn hadn't lied when he claimed he'd dismissed his guards. There were no males of any kind—that I could see—inside. There were only women, a handful of humans ranging in size and color, and all of them were naked.

Inside another bedroom, I searched a vanity. Found nothing. I came to a wooden chest. Searched and found nothing but sex toys. Every piece of furniture, every knickknack I stumbled upon, I searched. And found nothing. My frustration grew with every second that passed.

Finally, however, I came to a hallway that appeared different than the rest of the house. It was narrow and closed. At each section of the wall was an armed guard. This was it. I knew it. Felt it. The weapon-heavy men (also in kilts) stood sentry to whatever lay beyond the far door. In my spirit form, doors proved no obstacle. I brushed past the scantily clad man in front of the steel-like entrance. Where our bodies intertwined, I tingled. He must have felt it too, because he jumped.

"What was that?" he demanded, gripping his long, sharp blade. His narrowed gaze darted left and right.

"What?" the man next to him asked, stiffening.

Silence, then, "My mistake."

"Bracken," someone muttered. English translation: idiot.

I slipped through the door . . . and gasped. Inside the new room was what looked to be a doorway straight into the heavens. Black velvet sky, brilliant pinpricks of stars. It swirled. Beckoned. Was it some type of portal? Did the Targons not need to wait for solar flares? I wanted so badly to touch the liquid, but resisted the temptation. For now, at least. I couldn't risk world travel without my physical body.

Besides, if it *was* a portal, I could end up on a worse planet than Targon. I needed that necklace!

I looked around. Towering columns stretched to the domed ceiling, and white stone glistened all around me, leading up, up, up a staircase. At the top rested twelve pedestals. Curious and anxious, but most of all hopeful, I climbed the stairs. When I saw what lay inside each display case, I laughed. The necklace was here! I'd found it. Actually, I'd found eleven others as well.

Each necklace boasted a different stone, though all were roughly the same size. Did the stone matter? I wondered. What if the stone held the magnetic force? What if the stone decided which planet to carry its wearer?

Which stone would take me to Earth?

I studied each. Blue, red, violet, green, amber. I paused, a memory surfacing. The amber stone had brought me here, which meant amber represented Targon. Nodding, I continued my search. Brown, gray . . . My attention abruptly returned to the brown, drinking in every detail. It was dull, a bit jagged, flat in color.

Devyn had worn it during the auction. Nearly jumping up and down with my exhilaration, I concentrated a mass of energy between my hands. The air soon swirled and sizzled, growing heavier, denser. My spirit, too, began to burn. Burn, burn. I grimaced, but didn't stop. When the air held sufficient weight, I used the clustered molecules to lift the necklace from its perch and hover between my hands.

Instantly alarms erupted.

I quickly guided the energy and necklace high above me, and prayed no one looked up. A legion of guards stormed the chamber. They raised spears and blades, and their gazes shot throughout the room. Thankfully, they couldn't see me.

I cast a longing glance to the dappled pool and raced out the open door, taking the path I'd traveled to get here. All the while, the necklace hovered above me. Along the way I must have navigated a wrong turn, because I didn't enter the room that held my body. Damn it! I raced onward, rushing into every room I found, rushing past the guards headed toward the necklace room.

Finally—thank God—I found my body. The king and women were gone, but my body was just where I'd left it. I entered quickly and discovered that my muscles were still frozen. The necklace fell from the air and landed on the pillow beside me. If I could move, I could escape amid the confusion. I could hide the necklace.

I just had to move!

I struggled and fought for what seemed an hour, all the while remaining immobile. The king at last remembered my presence and strode back into the room. His amber eyes were narrowed as he knelt in front of me.

"How did you do it?" he asked, the words stilted, halting.

Even my lips refused to move.

"Answer me," he growled.

I glared up at him and flicked my gaze to my mouth. Realizing I couldn't speak, he finally released me from the paralysis.

"Do what?" I scooted away from him. The action sent a sharp ache all the way through me.

"How did you steal the torque? My Earth torque is missing, woman, and only you have an interest in it."

"I've been right here." Hoping I appeared nonchalant, I covered the necklace with my butt. "You saw to that. How could I have stolen anything?"

He reached out, intending to search me. I kicked his chest, and he stumbled backward a few feet. A mere second later, I found my arms and lower body frozen again. Dark fury exploded through my veins. I hated how easily he subdued me.

His hands roved over my every curve and hollow, but he found nothing. His frown deepening, he scooped me up and set me aside. That's when he saw the gold band. Scowling, he lifted it and shoved it in my face. "How did you get this?" When I remained silent, he added, "I didn't immobilize your mouth this time. Answer me."

A wave of helplessness joined my fury, swirling together in an escalating tempest. How could I win against such powerful telekinesis?

The answer hit me with the force of pyre-fire.

I couldn't fight him like this, but I could fight him another way. Vulnerability be damned. My lips twisted in an evil smile. "Why don't I show you?"

I centered quickly, and my spirit sprang from my body. In seconds, I was behind him. I focused energy between my hands, then shoved it at him, nailing him in the head. He crashed sideways, but fluidly jumped to his feet. Scowling, he spun away from my body and toward my spirit.

When he failed to see what had hit him, his eyes widened. "What's going on?"

Next I shot a burst of energy dead center between his legs, hitting his precious penis with enough force to drop him to his knees, groaning in pain. He looked back at my body, then whipped back to search the center of the room.

"How are you doing this?" he demanded.

Now that my emotions had been released, I couldn't hold back. I gathered clusters of energy and continued to toss them at him. Over and over, with all the fury and helplessness raging inside me. He fell, and I used the thickened air to gather his knife. The sharp blade hovered in the air. As his eyes widened, I inched it closer to his neck.

He stilled, not daring to breathe.

"How does it feel to be helpless against another's powers?" I taunted. The words were a whisper of wind, but he understood.

He opened his mouth to yell for help.

"Call your guards," I said, pressing the knife even closer, "and it will be the last sound you ever make."

His voice gurgled to quiet.

"That's better." Keeping the knife steady with one hand, I used my other to gather enough energy and tug off the gold band anchored at his neck.

"The moment you release me, I'll be able to kill your body. A spirit cannot live without a host."

"That's true," I admitted.

"How long do you think you can hold me like this?"

"As long as it takes. Are you an honorable man, Devyn?"

From the corner of my eyes, I saw him reaching up, intending to grab the knife and throw it away from him.

"Uh, uh, uh," I said, and pushed more energy toward him, digging the tip a little deeper into his neck. A drop of amber-colored blood formed.

A growl of frustration parted his mouth, but his hands stilled.

"Are you an honorable man?" I asked again.

"Yes, damn you."

"Then vow to me here and now to send me home at the next solar flare, and I will let you live."

"No."

"No? I can kill you now, reenter my body, and escape this place."

"You would never make it past my guards. They were chosen for their telekinetic abilities as well as their sadistic natures. When they spot you, and they will, they will make you regret the decision to leave me."

"I bet you thought I'd never be able to hold a blade at your throat, either."

Silence.

"You're not going to kill me," he finally said. Sweat dripped from his temples. "You're a woman and a Rakan. Your people might be rare, but I know you are peaceful. Sensual. Violence is used only by the ruling class."

"Maybe I'm part of the ruling class, because you see, Devyn, I'm more than a government agent. I'm an assassin. I've killed countless people, and killing you will be no hardship. Why do you think I let EenLi capture me? Why do you think my man was trying to 'buy' me? So I could kill EenLi and destroy his slave ring."

The Targon stiffened.

"I'm willing to let you live, however." The moment I'd met those women in the cell, my goal had ceased to be proving my own worth or being known as the best. My goal had changed to one of savior. The women, Lucius. And I'd make a deal with the devil himself to do so. "What do you say, Targon? Your life for a ticket home."

"Do I get to bed you for my troubles?"

"No. I will let you kiss my feet, though."

He snorted. One of his hands tangled roughly in his hair as he considered my offer. Obviously, no one had ever gotten the best of him, and he didn't know what to make of me—a true threat or a novel amusement. Had I been here on vacation, I might have enjoyed the king's antics.

"What do you say?" I demanded. "I'm growing impatient."

"I paid good money for you," he whined.

"So I'll pay you back."

"You cannot pay me back the two warriors I gave up for you."

"What if I promise not to cut off your penis? Will that help alleviate your sense of loss?"

He gulped. "We have ourselves a deal, Rakan."

CHAPTER
25

Though I remained on alert, I released my energy-hold on the knife and necklace and they clanged to the floor. I quickly reentered my body and popped to my feet. Devyn stayed true to his word and didn't call for his men, nor did he try to kill me. He merely pushed to his feet, then dusted off his kilt (or whatever the hell that skirt thing was called). All the while, a dark expression tightened his handsome features.

I gathered the fallen items and faced him directly. "You got something to say?"

"I am very angry about this."

"You'll get over it. How long until the next solar flare?"

At first, he didn't answer. He shoved a hand through his hair and stared up at the ceiling, before finally expelling a long breath. "A solar flare isn't needed. Come," he said, the single word whipping out with the force of a bullet. He spun on his heel.

I followed after him, still not dropping my guard. "What do you mean, one is not needed?"

"Solar flares are only needed to travel from Earth, not Targon. Here we use the Skyway."

The gel-like pool, I realized. I tucked that information away, knowing I'd have to give a full report to Michael.

When Devyn and I strode into the narrow hallway that led into the white stone room where I'd found the necklaces, the guards posted at the walls stood at perfect attention. I was so agitated, so ready to be home, my limbs were shaking.

"Open," Devyn said.

Two of the men immediately complied, prying the doors apart. Devyn and I slipped inside. As the doors closed behind us, Devyn said, "This human of yours." His tone displayed a complete lack of interest, but I knew better. He didn't turn to look at me. "What makes him so special? And do not tell me he is yours. There is a reason, something that sets him apart."

I leapt up the stairs two at a time, the king right on my heels. This man was taking me to Lucius and the enslaved women, so I was feeling generous toward him. "He stirs something inside me," I answered. "He fires my blood in a way I don't understand."

"I could do the same. I promise you."

"Perhaps. Perhaps not."

A pause. Then, "What if I am taking you back to Earth simply to kill your human and get him out of my way? If he's not already dead," he added. He took the necklace I still held and wrapped it around his neck.

"He's not, and you know I'll kill you if you hurt him." I had placed a lot of trust in this one self-centered man. But I *was* prepared to kill him at any time—if he didn't kill me first. I was willing to take the chance, though.

"I want you for my own," he said. "I haven't tried to hide that fact."

"You do have some pride, don't you?"

"Not really." A wicked twinkle entered his eyes, and he grabbed my hand, jerking me to a stop. Light from the Skyway caressed his face, illuminating his pale skin. His dark hair wisped over his forehead. "Why don't we strike another bargain, you and I, hmm? I'll give you my royal oath to help you save your man if you'll give me a single night with you."

I flipped my hair over my shoulder with a flick of my wrist. "We made a bargain already. I didn't knife you, and now you're taking me home."

"Ah, but I can do more than simply take you home. I can save your man . . . and take you to EenLi."

He was deadly serious, no hint of teasing in his expression. The wicked twinkle was gone. I stood, watching him, bathed in indecision. Trust him. Not trust him. Either way, he'd just offered me something I couldn't turn down, no matter the price.

"Deal," I said, the word a hard knot in my throat.

He nodded. "The deal must be sealed in blood." He kneeled, dragging me down with him, and unsheathed a blade from his side. I tensed, but didn't move as he sliced the silver tip down his bare chest. Amber blood dripped down his rippled muscles. "Give me your arm."

Tentative, I stretched my arm toward him. He clasped my wrist and slipped the blade over the skin, cutting. Not deep, just enough to draw blood. He lifted my wrist and meshed it against the wound in his chest. I could feel his heartbeat, a rapid *bump, bump.*

"You have my vow of aid, Eden Black. Your man and your enemy will be mine to give you." He motioned to me with a tilt of his chin. "Now you."

"You have my vow, Devyn," I said, shaking inside. If there were any other way, I'd take it. But there wasn't, and I knew it. "One night with me."

After the words were spoken, the air around us thickened, became as dappled as the Skyway. A living force. I blinked and gazed around in shock. I even reached out, sliding my fingertips over the jellylike air. It was as cool and ephemeral as a dream.

"To break either vow means death," he said, standing. He pulled me up beside him. He watched me for a long while, then nodded. "The bargain is now struck. Come."

We zigzagged through several more hallways and

finally hit the top of the stairs. My arm burned, but I ignored the slight pain. Devyn grabbed my hand and tugged me toward the pool.

"I need a necklace, too," I said, dragging my feet to slow him.

"Just hold on to me, and you will be fine." He flicked me an unreadable glance. "There is still time to change your mind."

"No."

"Very well," he sighed.

"What happens if—" I wanted to know what would happen if we became separated, but he pulled me inside the oddly dry jelly before I could finish my sentence. I was sucked into a vacuum. My feet lost their solid anchor, and my heartbeat quickened, nearly exploding inside my chest. Screams erupted, winding around me like ivy leaves reaching for the sun. Too-bright stars buzzed past my head.

A terrible wind kicked up, shoving me from every angle. I had to fight to remain upright, and clutched desperately at Devyn's hand. Round and round we began to spin, stars winking and flashing at me.

The wind became so violent, the Targon was ripped from my grip. "No!" I screamed. "Devyn!" He wore the necklace. I needed him to reach Earth. Didn't I? Without him . . . Blindly I groped the air with both hands, searching for him. For any type of anchor.

Instead of finding him, I felt everything still. The screams ceased abruptly. The lights faded. My feet hit a solid foundation. I swayed. My pulse continued to hammer, but I regained my equilibrium. I opened my eyes. And gasped.

I stood in an open forest of tall, green trees. Cool air enveloped me, not dry but humid. Crickets chirped a lazy tune, and moonlight dripped hazy rays on the grass. I sucked in a breath, inhaling familiar scents of pine and dirt. Of Earth.

Golden tendrils of hair were glued to my temples, and I pushed them back with shaky fingers. I'd made it. I'd truly returned. I scanned the area for the Targon.

He wasn't here.

I couldn't concern myself with him right now. I had to find a phone. Had to call Michael. I sprinted through the trees, my determination giving me swift wings. Gnarled limbs whipped at my face, and stones and twigs attempted to trip my feet. I ran for over an hour, toward the buildings I saw towering on the horizon. Breath burned my throat and lungs, but I never slowed.

When I reached the first building, I realized they were homes. Only one glowed with internal lights. I ran to the front door and slammed my fists against the thick oak entrance. When no one answered, I banged harder.

"Stop that racket," someone shouted from above. "I'm trying to sleep."

My gaze followed the sound, and I found myself staring up at a silver-headed man with a wrinkled, irritated face. "I need to use your phone."

"You need to learn how to shut up. I'm tired."

Scowling, I grabbed a rock from the colorful, blooming garden and broke the window. I didn't have time to pick the lock or mess with the ID box. Their security system erupted in a series of high-pitched beeps. I reached through the shattered glass, cringed when a sharp piece sliced my skin, adding another wound, and ripped the lock system from the side wall. The door opened of its own accord.

I shoved my way inside.

The silver-headed man was racing down the steps, and now he had a civilian pyre-gun in hand. "I'm armed," he shouted, "and I *will* shoot to kill."

I moved swiftly, met him halfway, and tripped him down the stairs. He squeezed off a shot, but the stream of fire whizzed past my shoulder. As he fell, I wrenched the gun from his hands. By the time he reached the bottom, I had the barrel pointed at his heart.

"Where's your phone?" I demanded, my aim steady and sure.

"Don't hurt me," he cried.

"Just tell me where your phone is, and you'll be fine."

Tears streamed down his cheeks as he pointed

a shaky finger to a nearby table. I hated that I had terrified the human, but I didn't have time for niceties.

"You move and you die. Understand?"

A sob racked him, but he nodded.

Keeping the pyre-gun directed on him, I walked backward to the table. With one hand, I punched Michael's number into the unit. The silver-headed man never moved a muscle.

"This is Black," my boss soon answered.

How wonderful it was to hear his voice. "Michael, Lucius has been shot."

"Eden?" Shock and happiness and relief mingled in his tone. "Please, Eden, tell me it's you. You've been gone three days without a word. We lost your signal, and I thought—"

"I'm fine, but I don't have a lot of time." Three days had passed, yet only one had passed on Targon. "Have you spoken to Lucius? Has he checked in?"

"Last he checked in, he told me you had been abducted as planned and he was going in to buy you. After that, we never heard from him again. We've been searching for him but haven't caught a trace. We had your location locked, and even checked there. Nothing. What's going on?"

"Jonathan Parker shot him."

"Is he de—"

"No!" I shouted. I still wasn't ready to consider the possibility. "I think EenLi has him now and means to sell him as a slave. There are five women, too, meant to be put up for sale. Has EenLi been spotted at all?"

"No, but Jonathan Parker was found dead."

"I know. I killed him. Michael," I said, my voice shaky. "I need you."

"Where the hell are you, sweetie? I'll be there as fast as I can."

"Where am I?" I demanded of the man at the foot of the stairs. My urgency made me sound fierce, lethal.

His already pale face went white at my renewed attention, and he gaggled out a few unintelligible sounds.

"Tell me where I am," I said gently. "Please. I'm not going to hurt you."

My gentleness lifted him out of his terror-filled shock. "New Mon-montana," he stuttered.

"New Montana," I told Michael. "Can you get my signal now?"

"Let's see." A moment passed, the sound of his breathing and the clicking of computer keys the only sound. "Got you now," he said with satisfaction. "We'll get you home, baby, we'll get you home."

"No. I need you to take me back to New Dallas. Back to the house they kept me in. EenLi is still here, I know it, and that means Lucius is here, too. They might still be inside. We've got to save him, Michael. The others, too."

"We will," he said, hearing my panic. "We will. I promise you."

The sound of police sirens penetrated the background. Their blue and red lights soon followed. "Just get here as fast as you can," I said and left the house the same way I'd come.

CHAPTER
26

Y ou enlisted the aid of a Targon?" Michael
growled.

His familiar voice boomed from the headphones
covering my ears and was like a soothing spell from
a voodoo priest. I gazed out the experimental hovercraft's window, drinking in the dark, almost velvet sky
and diamond-glistening stars. The vehicle's engine
was small and quiet, emitting only a slight hum as the
twenty-three-million-dollar machine soared through
the air.

I'd already explained to him how the solar flare
worked, and about the necklace. I told him about
EenLi's man having an electro-gun. He had listened in
stony silence. I wasn't sure how I felt that the first thing
he'd reacted to was my involvement with the Targon.

"Do you realize," he continued, speaking into his
small black mouthpiece, "that the Targon king, what-

ever the hell his name is, could right now be warning EenLi about you? Your cover could be completely blown."

My cover *was* blown, but I didn't point that out. "Saving Lucius matters. Saving the women matters. Nothing else." And after Devyn's vow, I didn't think he'd betray me. That vow had seemed so . . . official. So life-threatening, just as he'd claimed. "Maybe Devyn has told EenLi I'm here and after him, maybe he hasn't. Either way, I'm hunting him down."

Michael expelled a frustrated breath through his teeth. "All right," he said. "I'll let you go to the building, but you're taking Ren and Marko with you. They'll—"

"No. I go alone." I was willing to use the Targon. He had powers that could work to my advantage. I wouldn't be taking humans—especially not Michael's agents. After seeing EenLi with that electro-gun, I knew there was a very real possibility Michael had a leak. I couldn't risk EenLi going underground again.

I explained this to Michael, but he shook his head. "EenLi and I worked on that gun together. There isn't a leak. You're taking my men, and that's final."

Maybe there wasn't a leak. I still wasn't willing to risk it. "I guess that means I quit." At last I turned and faced him. His expression was hard, resolute. I think he had more gray hair than the last time I'd seen him. "Now try and give orders."

Something cold and hard glistened in his eyes—a

glint that had never been directed at me before. "You're willing to give up your place within the agency, to give up everything you and I have worked toward, just to save Lucius on your own?"

"That's right," I answered without hesitation. "It's safest that way."

"Well, guess what? The man you so desperately want to save, the government didn't pay him to be your partner. *I* paid him to keep you safe. Me personally. And he failed."

"Excuse me?"

"*He* was to keep you from EenLi and kill him himself. *He* was to protect you and bring you home unscathed. He did none of those things. He failed."

My stomach clenched as his words sunk in and brought a memory to the forefront of my mind. Once, when I'd first met Lucius, he'd said something about being paid by Michael. At the time, I'd thought nothing of it, that it had been a slip of the tongue. A mix of shock and anger poured through me.

Lucius should have told me. He'd had plenty of opportunities while we were in bed together. I didn't like that he'd lied to me. Still, that didn't change how I felt about him. I'd punish him for lying, of course, but first I'd save his life.

"You want me to be mad at him, and I am. But I'm also mad at you. You paid him, Michael. Do you really trust me so little?" My voice was quiet. Hurt. "Do you really see me as so incapable?"

When he realized the darkest heat of my anger wasn't directed at Lucius, but at him, he experienced his own wave of shock. "I love you. I'll do whatever I have to do to keep you safe. Please. Take a few of my men with you."

That was it. That was all he had to say to me. Sadness beat through me. "I know you love me, Michael, but I see now that you'll never see me the way I want—need—you to. As a woman of strength and courage—a woman who can successfully complete any task. The way Lucius sees me," I said, and realized it was true. He'd told me he was proud of me, that I'd done a good job. *He'd* released me into the lion's den, so to speak, and trusted me to find my way out.

"My resignation stands," I said. "I go alone."

His nostrils flared and his cheeks flushed, obvious signs he was angry at my lack of capitulation. "If you're no longer an agent, you have no business going after Lucius. I'll take you home. You need the rest, anyway."

"Take me to New Dallas," I snapped, "or I swear I'll join EenLi and become his right-hand woman." I'd do it, too. I'd do whatever was necessary for Lucius and the women. "When I was a little girl, you used to count to three when I refused to do your bidding. And if you made it to three and I didn't act, I'd be punished. Not that you'd ever see the punishment through."

"Don't be this way, Eden."

"One."

"Please. Just let it go."

"Two."

"Why are you doing this?"

"Thre—"

"Fine." Michael's lips thinned, but he nodded stiffly. "I'll take you to New Dallas. I'll send you straight into the heart of danger alone." He knew I never made empty threats. "Just don't cry foul when I send my guys after you. You've been warned." Motions stiff, he punched a button on the side of his headset, switching his communication link to the pilot.

When he returned the link to me, I said, "Give me the map to the house where I was held."

He did, and a little while later we landed in New Dallas. I hurriedly changed into the standard agent attire Michael had brought me—black pants, shirt, boots, and weapons, lots and lots of weapons—then stole a black duffel bag loaded with even more weapons and necessities from the hovercraft.

I left the private airstrip on foot without another word to or from Michael. The moment I was out of hearing distance, I knew he commanded two of his men to dog my steps. To *protect* me, I thought, scowling.

When it came to EenLi, they'd do more harm than good. Alert him, perhaps. Frighten him away.

Feigning nonchalance, I drew the men into a

darkened alley. Unfortunately, the pyre-gun in my bag only stunned and immobilized otherworlders. Fortunately, the bag also held a new prototype for a human pyre-gun. I'd practiced using the weapon only once before, and now prayed I didn't accidentally fry up Michael's men like a Fourth of July barbecue.

When they sneaked their way into the alley, I aimed and fired. A thin red beam erupted, freezing the first man in place. The second drew his gun, but I'd already shifted my aim. I squeezed the trigger, emitting another thin red beam. It hit him dead center in the chest.

"Sorry, boys," I said, pushing their frozen bodies into the shadows. I turned on their cell units so Michael could track them when they didn't check in.

Alone now, I entered a busy street lined with cars. I picked the most expensive and heavily secured because I knew how to reprogram it. Luck was on my side. The black luxury sedan was covered in shadows. Kneeling down, I opened my duffel bag. After withdrawing the proper tools, I used a mini wire cutter to rearrange the ID pad, then inserted a new control chip. Standard issue. The driver's-side door opened automatically. I then reprogrammed the command unit to my specifications, and the car roared to life.

Quick. Easy.

I followed the map Michael had given me and

drove within a mile of the house, unwilling to risk hidden cameras and security by stopping too close. I parked the car in a thicket of trees and emerged. I didn't bother with the duffel bag. Everything I needed was strapped to me.

Weighed down as I was with weapons, I had to move slowly through the forest. Slivers of moonlight guided me. Too bad the air was warm and dry.

Finally, the old house came into view. It appeared like an average home—well kept, gray stone. Not too big. A rush of emotions overtook me: fury, hope, dread. For an instant, I flashed back to the first mission that had brought me to EenLi. I'd gone in alone then, too. I'd also failed. But I wouldn't fail now. Too much was at stake.

Though the lights were out, making the isolated residence appear empty, I didn't relax my guard. My gaze constantly soaked in the details of my surroundings. It wouldn't do to trip a wire or motion detector and alert the inhabitants of my approach.

Pyre-gun in one hand, blade in the other, I entered the house. No alarm sounded. I moved through the shadows, searching every room, every corner—even the dungeon. The sentinels were gone; the women were gone.

Lucius was gone.

"Damn it," I snarled. I leaned against a corner wall in the living room—the very place my auction had been held—staring down at the blood dried on the carpet. Lucius's blood. There was a large pool of it that blended with Jonathan's, making the air reek with a metallic tang.

Where was Lucius? Where had the women been taken?

Think, Eden, think. Where would EenLi have gone from here? Most likely the same place he'd been hiding all these many weeks—a place we had been unable to discover.

A board creaked.

My hands clenched around my weapons. Instinctively I sank deeper into the shadows and slowly turned to find the source of the noise.

"Eden," a familiar male voice said. "I know you're there. I can smell your woman's scent."

My mouth pulled in a scowl. I didn't relax my hold on the gun. "How did you get here so quickly, Targon? I had to take a hovercraft."

"I knew where to land." He entered the living room completely. Moonlight flooded through the far window and bathed him in light. "You won't find anyone here."

"I know." I, too, abandoned the shadows as I reholstered the pyre-gun. "Do you know where EenLi is?"

He grinned, a familiar expression of smugness. "Of course I know where he is. I am his best customer."

I stepped toward him. "You swore to help me,

and I'm holding you to your word. Take me to him."

His grin widened, stretching across his entire face. So handsome. So in need of a beating. "You also promised me one night. We failed to work out a few details, though. Like who would get their reward first."

So, he wanted to rebargain. I pretended to soften, to sink into his body. His arms instantly wrapped around me. I let my blade slide past my wrist cuff until my fingers circled the handle, and then I inched the sharp edge toward his penis. "By all means, let's rebargain."

"Ah, Eden, you are so predictable. If you'll notice, I'm wearing a metal shield this time."

I scowled as I sheathed the knife. Intimidation wouldn't work with this man, this sex fiend. "Will you help me for a kiss?"

"Just one?"

"With tongue," I snapped.

"Now?"

"Now." I stood on my tiptoes, but let him come to me.

"Deal." Slowly, so slowly, he lowered his head. Our lips met, soft and gentle. He didn't give me his tongue. No, he made me give him mine. I cupped his cheeks and angled his head, then swept my tongue into his mouth.

His arms locked around my waist, holding me

captive in his embrace. He tasted hot and virile. He was strong; he was all man. But he wasn't Lucius, and he didn't make me burn for more.

He pulled from me with regret and trailed his fingertip over the seam of my lips. "I must be losing my touch."

"EenLi," I prompted.

"He is at his warehouse, and if your human is alive he will be at the warehouse, too, soon to be sold as a slave."

Frowning, I shook my head. "They are not at the warehouse. We have control of it."

"Yes, I heard about that. Too bad you didn't seize his other one."

Breath whooshed out of my lungs. I'd never thought, not once, that EenLi might have another warehouse. I felt stupid; I wanted to scream. And dance. This was it; I was at last on the right course. "Where is it?" My voice was raw, hoarse with emotion.

Devyn sighed, and his warm breath fanned my cheek. "Why, next door to the first. Isn't that the way of it? Hide under your enemies' nose, and they'll never find you? There's a big sale tonight, a sale I originally planned to attend."

Yes, this was it. I practically hummed with the force of my fervor. "I need you to take me to that sale."

"And I need you to promise me another kiss."

I didn't hesitate. "Done."

"I love bargaining with you, sweet." He leaned down until his lips brushed my ear. "But you know what? I would have taken you to the sale," he said, drawing out the words and giving them a proper Texas accent, "for free."

CHAPTER
27

Devyn kept a car in this world, so I left the one I'd stolen and climbed into his—a sleek red Jaguar parked in back of the home. As we drove to EenLi's second warehouse, my stomach tightened and my blood heated. Soft classical music poured from the speakers, which surprised me. I'd expected Devyn to like gyrating rock, fast and hard, the way he wanted his sex.

Minutes dragged by as we sped down the highway.

More minutes dragged by.

Even more passed without a word.

"What did you think of my kiss?" he asked me. I think he asked just to cut through the silence. Maybe to relieve my tension.

"It was . . . good."

"Good? Good!" His amber eyes gleamed with affront. "I expect to hear words like *magnificent. Wondrous. Unequaled.* Not *good.*"

"It was missing something, okay? Don't be a baby."

"It was missing nothing."

I pinched the bridge of my nose. "Mind if I give you a piece of advice, Devyn?"

"Yes." He still sounded offended. "I do mind."

"Don't force your way into a woman's life. The kiss would have been a whole lot better if I'd wanted to give it to you."

"There would not have been a kiss if I hadn't pushed you for it." He shifted in his seat. "You will not think I am missing something when we have our night together."

I gave no reply. I didn't know what to say, really. I'd give him his night because I'd promised it to him. That didn't mean I'd enjoy it or be an eager participant.

At last we reached our destination. We slowed, then stopped altogether. There was a long, long line of cars ahead of us, awaiting the valet, I supposed. Facing the window, I cast my gaze to the dusty, spacious warehouse. A crowd of people, otherworlder and human combined, ambled inside, nearly busting the building at its seams.

"We have the other warehouse under surveillance. Why aren't agents all over this place?"

"Your surveillance cameras are easily rigged. Isn't that the reason they were outlawed without license?"

My lips dipped in a frown, and I tangled a hand through my hair. "All right. This is what we're going to do," I told Devyn on a sigh. "When we get inside, I want you to pretend to be eager to take part in the auction. I also want you to pretend to be my master."

"Pretend?" He caressed his thick fingers over the program box and grinned at me.

"Yes, damn it. Pretend," I said, purposefully mistaking his meaning. "You can act, can't you?" The car eased forward a bit.

"Oh, I know I can. But can you? You will have to act the part of my slave."

His enjoyment irritated me. "I will." I hated to rely on him so much, but it couldn't be helped. I couldn't do this without him, and we both knew it. Not successfully, at least. First Lucius, now Devyn. I'd always been a woman who prided myself on getting the job done right all on my own. Admitting I needed help left a bitter taste in my mouth. Right now I was too concerned with saving the man I loved to give a shit.

Loved?

I almost groaned. I did, I realized. I loved him. Somehow, during this mission, he'd become everything to me. He was smart, resourceful. Intense. Sarcastic. He was everything I'd needed in my life, but hadn't known until just now.

The car moved another inch. "Once Lucius and the others are safe, I'll need you to get me close to EenLi. He will be here tonight, won't he?"

"He has attended every auction in the past, so I expect him to be at this one. Are you going to kill him?"

"Yes," I answered without hesitation, relish dripping from my tone.

Devyn's head tilted to the side as he considered my words. "I do not think I want him dead."

"Why the hell not? He's evil."

"Yes, but he supplies my women."

I rolled my eyes. "Why do you enslave women like that? You're a handsome man. Females of every race would willingly come to you if you only asked."

One of his brows arched. "You wouldn't. You *didn't*."

Good point. "I'm an exception to the rule."

"Not for long," he said cockily. As he spoke, he reached over and traced a fingertip over my thigh. His skin was callused and surprisingly cool, a sweet contrast to the heat outside.

"Get your hand off me before you don't have a hand to remove. Your night hasn't started yet."

His mouth stretched wide in a grin, but he did as I'd asked and removed his hand. "Touchy, touchy. You should be rejoicing, little Rakan. One day soon, if not this very night, you're going to be lying in my arms. Where is your joy? Your words of thanks?"

"Your other women got to scratch you and draw your blood. That's the only thought giving me joy right now."

"Silly woman." His grin slowly faded. His expression became deadly serious. Gone was the man of easy humor, and in his place was the king of Targon. I didn't know what had brought about the change, but I could guess. He'd actually begun to enjoy the intrigue and danger of this mission, and he wanted to win.

"When we get inside," he said, his tone as cool as his touch had been, "you need to walk two steps behind me. You will sit at my feet when I take a chair." His gaze flickered over my black pants and shirt. "You'll need something sexier to wear. I would never bring my slave out in public like that. What happened to your pink clothing?"

"I trashed it. And I have nothing else to wear."

"Then strip," he said, as if it was a perfectly natural thing to demand of me.

Scowling, I ripped off my shirt and threw the material in the back seat, leaving me in my bra. It was black, not particularly sexy, but it did showcase my golden skin in a nice way. Several blade handles poked above the waist of my pants. Without the shirt, my guns were also visible. I had to remove most of them.

"Take off the pants," Devyn ordered.

"Go to hell," I said, but withdrew my knife and cut the legs off the pants until I wore the tiniest scrap of material—barely covering the curve of my ass.

"Much better. Now release your hair from confinement."

I ripped the band from my hair, and the silky strands instantly fell over my shoulders, down my back.

"I cannot wait to have you," he said on a breath of desire.

Well, he was just going to have to.

Our car finally moved to the front of the line and stopped. A cowboy-clad human opened my door, and I emerged. The midnight air boasted the scent of hay and car fumes. The human's eyes drank me in, his expression lighting with awe. I don't think he even realized he was reaching out to me, to caress a hand down my bare stomach. I stepped aside, not wanting his fingers anywhere on me.

Devyn came around the car and moved in front of me, looking sexy as hell in his moss green kilt and white shirt. His glossy brown hair was pulled back in a ponytail. His amber eyes were alive. Without a word, he began walking, expecting me to follow. I did. The crowd parted automatically for him as we entered the building. I felt many stares but I didn't acknowledge them.

My boots bit into the dirt floor. Devyn stopped several times to speak with an acquaintance, and I used the time to search for EenLi. He was nowhere that I could see, and that caused shards of frustration to cut through me. What if he did not attend?

I was soon led to a group of folding chairs lined up in front of a scaffold. My heart thundered in my chest. Atop the scaffold were the "slaves." Their hands were tied over their heads and anchored to a wooden beam. They wore gauzy white robes, easily parted and removable for viewing.

I saw the five women from the cell, and my knees almost buckled in relief. Their expressions were pale with fear, but they were alive. There were six other women as well, but I didn't recognize them. Nor did I recognize the strong, muscled men bound beside them. My gaze darted to the others, the ones in back, but I couldn't see them all. *Lucius, Lucius,* my mind chanted as I searched for him, praying he was here. My muscles kept a viselike grip on my bones.

The Targon king claimed a seat on the first row. Recalling his words to me, I stiffly sank down at his feet. God, I didn't want to. I wanted to stand, to scream, to act. *Patience,* I reminded myself. *Patience.*

He patted my head. "Good girl," he said, obviously enjoying himself.

My new position did not change my actions. I continued to scan the slaves. The one at the end of the scaffold was partially hidden by shadows and the two men who were inspecting him. The slave's legs were extended, his robe parted, and I could see his bronzed skin. For a minute, my lungs refused to draw in a breath.

I gulped, willing the men to move out of my line of vision. Sweat beaded on my forehead. My shaky hands clutched at the dirt beneath me. *Move,* my mind screamed. Patience proved too elusive, so I gave up the effort to find it.

Finally the men ambled off the scaffold, giving me a clear view of the slave.

My lungs jolted into motion, and at last I sucked in a breath. I nearly jumped to my feet and raced up those wooden stairs. He was here. Lucius was here. And he was alive. Relief and joy pounded through me so potently, I could have wept. His features were blank and pale; his fake scar was gone, and I was willing to bet his contacts had been removed. His robe covered his shoulder and chest, so I couldn't see his wound. His clothes weren't bloody, so that meant he'd been bandaged up.

"I told you he would be here," Devyn said.

A woman approached Lucius, parted his robe, and gazed at his nakedness. Her large frame blocked my own viewing. Lucius passively accepted her perusal, which wasn't like him. What was wrong with him?

I didn't want to, but I switched my attention to Devyn. "See the woman at the end of the scaffold?"

Without looking down at me, he nodded.

"Get her to move. Please."

In the next instant, the woman yelped and tumbled off the edge as if she'd been propelled by a great gust of wind. I jolted to my feet, hoping to gain Lucius's attention.

His gaze was moving listlessly over the crowd, then . . . our eyes locked.

Relief, hope, joy, fury, all washed over his face—all the emotions I felt—and he snapped out of his passive haze. He jerked against the ties at his wrists, shaking the entire scaffold.

"Take me to him," I whispered, looking down at Devyn. "Please."

"Of course. A favor for a favor," he said. He stood, eyes straight ahead. "You will follow me on your knees, slave."

I bent down and crawled after him. Sand and rocks dug into my skin. I even crawled up the splintery steps. I endured it without comment, knowing where it was leading me.

When we reached Lucius, Devyn stopped and grinned over at him. "We're going to buy you," he said. "You will belong to us."

Lucius had eyes only for me. "Is she—"

"She is fine."

I nodded to let him know it was true.

"She has bargained much to get you free. I hope you appreciate her."

Lucius's brow wrinkled in curiosity, but Devyn didn't explain. He walked away, back to his chair, and I had to follow him. I wanted to run back to Lucius, almost did in fact. Devyn sensed it and locked me in place with his mental shield. As my heart thumped and my blood rushed, I tried to tell Lucius with my eyes that everything really was going to be okay.

"Eden," the Targon said suddenly, "my calves are

aching from those stairs. Massage the muscles for me."

I leveled him my deadliest glare. He gave an almost imperceptible nod to Lucius and released me from the frozen stun. Free to move, I began kneading my fingers into his calves. I used so much force, he hissed in a breath of pain that he tried to cover with a cough. "This isn't a game," I growled quietly.

Lucius looked at Devyn, then at me, and a light of understanding dawned in his eyes. Furious, he bucked against his chains, causing a trickle of blood to run down his arms.

"Put him to sleep," I beseeched, stopping my massage and giving the Targon my full attention. "Please, put him to sleep like you did before. The guards will subdue him if this continues."

With another stiff nod, he gazed over at Lucius, and within seconds Lucius's muscles were relaxing. His head lolled forward as he sank into a deep slumber.

"Thank you," I whispered. "Thank you."

"Do you see? I'm not such a bad man, Eden."

"Do I owe you another kiss?" I couldn't keep the aggravation from my voice.

He frowned. "I *am* capable of giving free gifts."

Just then, the murmurs of the crowd quieted. The people began to part, and whispers of "EenLi" surfaced. My head whipped up, and I scanned the building. My eyes narrowed as deep-seated loathing filled me.

EenLi had just entered the warehouse.

CHAPTER
28

Everyone hurriedly claimed their seats while EenLi climbed the stairs and meandered his way to center stage. As he walked, he waved and winked at the crowd as if he were a superstar and everyone here was his devoted fan. Full cowboy regalia covered his thin Mec body. Cowboy hat, vest, chaps. He looked ridiculous. Smiling, he held up his hands in a gesture for utter silence.

My hatred grew and festered, bubbled over and spewed. I could throw my dagger at his throat, but I didn't want a long-distance kill this time. I wanted up close and personal, so there would be no doubt of his death, no mistake.

"Can you put everyone to sleep?" I quietly asked Devyn. If the crowd, guards, and EenLi passed out cold, I would blithely walk onto the stage and stab EenLi in the heart. Not that he had one.

Devyn thought about it for a moment. "One at a time, but yes, I could do it."

"Do it," I said, the words lashing from me. "Now. Please."

"No."

"Please."

"Where is the fun in that? I came all this way, wasted money and two warriors, and I expect a show guaranteed to amuse me."

I bit my tongue until blood seeped down my throat.

"Welcome," EenLi said, hushing our conversation. "Welcome, everyone. AIR thought they could close us down, but here we are."

Cheers erupted.

After a sufficient length of time, EenLi waved again for silence. "I am honored to have everyone here, especially such honored guests as the king of Morevv and the king of Targon." His gaze paused on Devyn. "I see you brought your new slave, Devyn."

The Targon nodded regally, his fingers stroking my hair. "That I did, but one can never have enough servants."

"I hadn't expected you to tame this one so quickly."

"Who said she was tame?" Devyn winked.

The crowd laughed. I glared up at EenLi, not even trying to dampen the disgust and loathing in my eyes. His skin glowed a bright shade of blue and pink—he was enjoying himself.

"Ladies and gentlemen," he said, returning his attention to the crowd. "You have a wide variety to choose from today. Are you ready to begin?"

Another round of cheers.

"Then so we shall." EenLi stepped to the side as one of his new Targon guards brought forth the first victim, a young, pretty girl of no more than fifteen. Her body trembled, causing locks of her carmine hair to spill forward. Tears streamed down her cheeks, and she bit back a sob when EenLi parted her robe, revealing her still-developing nakedness to the onlookers. She didn't fight. I doubted any of them would. They'd probably been threatened by unimaginable horrors if they so much as uttered a single protest.

"A virgin to tempt any man," EenLi boasted.

And so the bidding began.

One by one, men and women were sold to the highest bidder. I wanted Devyn to buy them all, but he only bought the virgin as well as the women who had been locked inside the cell with me. Perhaps because I'd squeezed his thigh until he'd hissed out a price.

Then, finally, Lucius's turn arrived. He still slept peacefully.

"Look at this prime piece," EenLi said. "He will be good for manual labor as well as bedroom labor."

"Buy him for me," I whispered up to Devyn.

"I believe I've done quite enough for you," he said, prim now.

"I'll give you two nights instead of one, plus the two kisses I owe you."

The king's eyes swirled vivid amber, and he immediately placed his first bid. Someone else, a white-headed Arcadian female, countered. On and on they bickered. EenLi's gaze remained narrowed on Devyn, as if he couldn't quite figure out what was going on.

In the end, Devyn won the battle. He put the Arcadian to sleep, effectively ending her bidding. And so, the auction was over.

"Thank you for coming," EenLi told everyone. "If you didn't win or didn't find what you were looking for, please contact me. I usually hold private auctions, but because of a recent upheaval we had to do things a little differently this time around."

The people around me stood. "If you put everyone to sleep, I'll give you three nights," I said, desperate to keep anyone from leaving. I didn't want a single "slave" to be dragged out that door. I would set them free—or die trying.

"I might be tired of you after two nights." Devyn uttered a breezy yawn. "The heat in here is stifling. Should we collect your humans and leave?"

"You vowed to take me to my enemy."

"And so I have. You see him, do you not?"

"What is it you want from me?" I asked, more desperate now than before.

"The same devotion you give your human. Your vow to eagerly accept me when I take you."

"Done," I said, though we both knew I lied.

His gaze darted to the warehouse's only door. "No one seems to be leaving yet. They're lingering."

"So? Put them to sleep before they decide to *stop* lingering."

"First I want to thank our host for a wonderful evening."

Yes, I thought darkly. Let's thank him properly, shall we? I should have protested, should have insisted Devyn do my bidding, yet the thought of finally, at long last, coming face-to-face with EenLi proved too intoxicating.

Devyn rose. When he moved past me, I followed behind him like a good little slave. We climbed the steps, me on my knees. My gaze lingered on Lucius's sleeping form until I rammed into a large piece of splintered wood.

EenLi was in deep conversation with another Mec. When he noticed Devyn, he waved the Mec away. "I made quite a profit from you this evening," he said with a grin.

"That you did," Devyn responded.

I reached behind my back to slide my knife from the waist of my pants . . . only to realize my knife was gone. My blood ran like ice in my veins. How Devyn had removed it, I didn't know. Bastard. He knew I'd been planning to kill EenLi, here and now.

Why had he stopped me? Did he mean to betray me? No, I thought. Devyn wanted his nights with me; he wanted me willing. He'd given me his vow.

That meant . . . what?

"Eden, rest your head on my leg like a good little girl."

I did so without hesitation, and he sifted his fingers through my hair.

"How did you train her so quickly?" EenLi's white gaze raked over me, lingering on my breasts, between my legs. "She's a delectable little morsel, isn't she? Perhaps I should have kept her for myself. I just didn't expect her to be so docile so quickly."

"I have the most . . . persuasive training techniques."

The two men shared a hearty laugh.

"Thank you for the warriors," EenLi said, all business now. "They are proving to be very useful already."

"Excellent." He paused. "There's something I need to speak with you about. In private."

"Now is not the time, I'm afraid."

"Make the time." Devyn's tone was hard, promising retribution if his request wasn't met.

EenLi's skin glowed a light red, meaning he was only mildly perturbed. His white eyes narrowed. "Very well. Shall we adjourn to my office?"

"That won't be necessary." One by one, the people inside the warehouse began dropping to the dirt.

Snores soon abounded. I jumped up, unable to hold myself back a moment longer.

This ended now. Knife or no knife.

"What's going on?" EenLi demanded, a look of confusion flittering over his face. His red skin turned to a dark, molten yellow.

"I believe you have unfinished business with my slave," the Targon answered and stepped back.

"Not a slave," I said, moving forward. "Assassin. You see, I plan to do to you what I did to your partner, Mris-ste."

The Mec's color changed again, once again glowing that deep, dark red. "So it was you. I suspected Michael, not his daughter." He backed a step away from me, one of his hands slowly slipping inside his pockets.

"Give me the knife," I demanded of Devyn without ever turning my attention.

"No," was his reply.

I stomped my foot.

"I'm doing you another favor, Eden. I once had an enemy I despised with the same intensity you have for EenLi. I know that if you kill him too quickly, you will always regret it. Fight him. Beat him. Make him pay."

In the next instant, EenLi whipped out a gun. Devyn *tsked* under his tongue and mentally swept the weapon across the room. It hit the floor with a thump. EenLi gasped, and I slowly stalked toward him. With every step I tried to center my energy, but that proved impossible. Too many hot emotions clamored for release.

"Targon," he said, casting the king a nervous glance. "Help me, and I will—"

"This is between you and the Rakan," Devyn said. He grinned. "Enjoy, both of you. I know I will. Is there any popcorn? I love Earth popcorn." He continued to mutter about the popcorn as he hopped off the stage and sat in a chair.

I sprang. EenLi leapt to the side, but I managed to kick his shoulder. As he stumbled, he growled low in his throat. We circled each other. His white eyes continually darted toward the door, and I knew he planned to run.

Realizing he could go nowhere without me following, he tried another tactic. "Do you think I knew nothing about you, Eden?" There was an evilness to his tone, a darkness that made me shudder. "I know more than you think."

I didn't respond. I just edged closer.

"I took great pleasure in enslaving you," he gloated. "You, a trained assassin. You, Michael Black's beloved daughter."

Closer. Closer. Like a tiger moving in for the kill, I circled him.

"I'd hoped the Targon could control you," he said. "And I liked that Michael would never see you again, that he would always wonder what happened to you."

I went low and kicked his ankles. Contact. He fell with a whoosh, but sprang up quickly. He pulsed with the barest hint of blue. "Why do you want to kill me so desperately, hmm?"

"For the pleasure of it."

"You should want to destroy the one who killed your parents. Why do you think Michael took you in? He'd been assigned to kill your father. But your mother got in the way, so he killed her, too."

Fury boiled inside me, hotter, hotter. I sprinted toward him and jumped, spinning midair, crunching the heel of my boot into his nose. It snapped, and black-hued blood sprayed across the platform. "Liar," I lashed out.

EenLi stumbled to his feet, blood and spittle trickling down his face, onto his lips. He struggled for air as his skin turned a mottled hue of purple. "I used to work for him. Did he tell you that?"

I knew what EenLi was doing. Offering a truth to make his lie appear believable. "I don't believe trash like you, EenLi, so save your breath." I hopped from foot to foot, and I moved toward him. No more playing.

He ran to one of the sleeping guards and grabbed a weapon. His eyes gleamed with victory as he aimed the pyre-gun, but I was already on him. I kicked the gun from his hand, and it flew across the room.

I punted him in the chest. He swung at me as he tumbled down. His fist connected with my jaw, and my head whipped to the side.

He was up and on me before I could blink, pushing me down and trying to choke me. I rocked back and wound my legs around his neck. With one hard jerk, he was sailing backward. I used the momentum to gain my footing and leapt to an upright position. I lunged for him as he, too, jolted to his feet. My head butted into his stomach, causing him to double over as his breath whooshed from his mouth.

Straightening, I beat my fists into his face like I was a machine, over and over, again and again. He fell onto the wood. I fell with him, never pausing. Blood flew left and right with every blow.

Devyn called from below, "Here." His words reached my haze of destruction. "I'm getting bored. Finish it," and he tossed me a knife.

I caught the hilt midair. EenLi gurgled something, perhaps, "No, please," and tried to crawl away. I grabbed his head and positioned my knife. Then I slit his throat the way I'd wanted to from the beginning.

When his eyes glazed, I dropped his head with a thud. It wasn't enough, though. Devyn had been right. It wasn't enough. I wanted EenLi to suffer longer. I wanted him to suffer for eternity.

"Nicely done," the Targon said.

"Give me your phone," I commanded, wiping the Mec's black blood onto my pants.

He did so without another comment. As I strode to Lucius's slumped, sleeping form, I dialed Michael. When he answered, I told him where I was.

"I know where you are," he barked. "I tracked you with the isotope. You'll notice I trusted you enough not to send my men in."

"Bring a van and medical supplies."

A pause. A hiss of breath. "Are you hurt? What's—"

"I'm fine, Lucius isn't. Hurry." I hung up on him. I'd never done that before, but I didn't know what else to say to him right now.

I tossed the phone back to Devyn and knelt beside the only man who had ever made me feel complete. I caressed my hands over his heartbeat. My shoulders slumped with relief when I felt a steady, even thumping. He would live.

EenLi was dead, the slaves were free. We had won. So why did I feel so lost? A lone tear slithered its way down my cheek.

CHAPTER
29

I didn't allow Devyn to awaken Lucius.

I used my lover's slumber to my advantage and parted his robe, checking his body for more injuries. His left shoulder sported a thick white bandage, and he had an assortment of bruises across his chest. Other than that, he appeared fine.

Winding one arm around his waist, I used the other to cut the bonds at his wrists. His weight immediately hit me, and I eased him to the ground as gently as I could.

I'd missed him so much I ached. I traced a fingertip over his stubbled jaw. This man had believed in me when my own father hadn't. He might have lied to me about his reasons for becoming my partner, but in the end he had believed enough in me to let me work without trying to shield me or keep me safe at home.

Without any prompting from me, Devyn cut down the rest of the sleeping slaves. When he reached a curvy blonde, he glanced over at me. "We bought this one, didn't we?"

"You can't keep her," I replied on a strangled laugh.

"You're keeping that one," he said, motioning to Lucius with his chin.

"Yeah, but he's willing to be kept."

He looked at the blonde, then back at me. "This one might be willing, too. I just need five minutes alone with her."

I shook my head. "You can ask her if she wants to spend five minutes with you, but you can't force her."

He pouted.

Michael and ten other agents burst into the warehouse moments later, pyre-guns drawn. When they realized everyone was sleeping, they lowered their weapons but remained on alert.

"Over here," I called. Two agents reached me before Michael. "Take this man to a medic, then to my apartment." I gave them the address, and they nodded.

Together, they lifted Lucius into their arms. He moaned, the sound one of pain.

"Careful," I snapped. "He's injured."

"Take him to my house," Michael interjected. "I'll have our doctors patch him up there."

"Take him to a medic, then to my apartment, or I'll introduce both of you to my knife."

They looked fearfully to Michael, because they knew I'd do it. He gave an abrupt nod. "Do what she says."

As the men tromped off with Lucius, I faced my father. Our gazes met, locked. We still had business to settle. "Everyone on the scaffold was kidnapped by EenLi to be sold as slaves. There are a few on the ground as well."

"And EenLi?" he asked.

I stood, shrugged. "Dead. By my hand."

His shoulders relaxed, and he ran a hand over his ragged features. "Then it's over."

"Yes."

"I'm proud of you, Eden." He reached out and squeezed my shoulder. "I don't tell you that enough."

"You're proud, yes, but do you finally believe in me?"

"I've always believed in you."

I brushed away his hold. "You paid men to look out for me, Michael. You never trusted me to do it on my own."

"I was scared for you. There's a difference." He rubbed his temples. "Let's get you home. You can write me up a full report in the morning. We'll have breakfast and then you can get started on your next job. I've already got one lined up—"

"I told you I don't work for you anymore."

"We both know you didn't mean it." When I didn't say anything, he kicked sand with the tip of his shoe. "Fine, if you don't want to work for me, you don't have to. Claudia Chow has been worried about you and has been calling me for two days. You can always go back to her and continue being her interpreter."

I wasn't going to do that, either. I didn't know what I was going to do, actually. Biting my lip, I stared down at my boots and tried to prepare myself for the conversation I was about to start. Bringing it up was harder than killing a target but if I didn't do it now, I wouldn't. *Just say it.* "EenLi mentioned something about my parents. You and I never talk about them, but I need to know if you ever found out who killed them."

He didn't say anything. And as the moments ticked by, guilt washed over his still handsome features.

I blinked over at him. "Michael?"

"Eden," he began before cutting himself off. "I'm so sorry. So sorry. I've wanted to beg your forgiveness for so long, but I couldn't bring it up. I just couldn't."

In that moment, I realized it was true. EenLi hadn't lied. Deep down, I think I'd expected Michael to tell me EenLi had done it. But no, Michael had actually dealt the death blows. A sharp pain lanced through my chest, and I almost moaned. He'd never told me; he'd kept it secret all these years. Hadn't trusted me to love him anyway. To forgive.

With the realization, something inside me snapped, released. Anger and impotence for all the years I hadn't talked about my parents because I'd assumed Michael didn't want the reminder that he wasn't my biological father.

I backhanded him. His head whipped to the side. Slowly he faced me, rubbing his now-bleeding lip.

"I deserved that," he said calmly.

I stared into his face, the face I loved and had worshiped for so long. "Tell me why."

"They were a job, sweetie. Only a job. They might have loved you, protected you, and treated you as a precious treasure, but they still sold drugs. Drugs that killed humans. I did what I had to do, what I was paid to do. How many parents have you killed?" he asked quietly, darkly. Pointedly.

Low blow. So low. My knees almost buckled as his words slammed into my mind, echoing over and over. The truth was, I didn't know the answer to that question. The most likely answer was many. *Many.* I didn't know how many parents, brothers, sisters, aunts, and uncles I'd killed over the years. Perhaps I hadn't let myself consider the possibility. I'd always embraced my job—just as Michael did.

"Eden, I—" He reached for my hand.

I slapped his wrist. "Save it. I can't talk to you right now. I'll forgive you, yes, and I even understand, but I just can't talk to you right now."

I turned away from him then and helped the other agents separate EenLi's men from the slaves and auctiongoers. The guards would be kept alive for another day or two and questioned, just in case there were any other humans stashed away. Then they would be killed. I didn't know what would happen to the auction bidders. At this point, I just didn't care.

Michael worked alongside me, silent and brooding. He loved me. I knew he did. And that made the torment inside me even worse.

Devyn worked with me, too. Michael ignored him, most likely still upset that I'd enlisted the king's help instead of his. Lord, I felt so raw. I needed Lucius. His strength. His comforting arms.

When we finished clearing out the warehouse, I pulled Devyn aside. "Will you drive me home?"

He wrapped an arm around my waist and gave me a comforting, brotherly squeeze. "Of course."

I walked out of the building without a backward glance. I felt Michael's gaze boring into my back.

Dawn would arrive soon. At last the air was cool, but it smelled of loneliness and despair. Or perhaps that was me. I was shutting down. This was all too much. My legs felt tied down, my shoulders too heavy. My neck protested the weight of my head. I had to force one foot in front of the other until I reached Devyn's Jag. I plopped inside ungracefully as he settled into the driver's seat.

"Do not worry about the nights you owe me," he said. "I will come back when you are better rested."

I leaned back and closed my eyes. "I'll give you your nights, Devyn. You more than earned them. But you know what? I don't think you'll claim them. You're a man of honor, and you know I love another man."

Silence.

Silence that lasted a long, long time.

"Damn you," he finally muttered.

I was close to breaking completely, and I didn't want it to be here, with this man. I wanted Lucius.

Devyn drove me to my apartment building. Finally. Home. When he reached the building, I trudged out of the car, and the door shut with a snap. The air was cooler than it had been all week—more fragrant, less dry.

The window eased down with a quiet whoosh. "Eden," Devyn called.

I don't know what he planned to say, but I spun around and reentered his car. I owed Devyn everything, yet he was getting nothing in return. He truly did possess too much honor to hold on to me. Without a word, I leaned into him and brushed my lips against his. Softly at first, then I increased the pressure. When his mouth parted, I swept my tongue inside. Again I tasted his warmth, his masculinity.

It didn't last long, only a few seconds before I pulled away. I watched Devyn lick his lips, savoring my taste. "Thank you for everything."

"I hope we meet again," he said, his amber eyes glowing. "And I hope your human is worthy of you."

"He is," I said. I knew this one thing for sure. "He is."

CHAPTER
30

Bandaged and medicated, Lucius was sleeping soundly in my bed. I showered, the dry spray washing away the horrors of the night. Clean at last, I curled into bed beside him. His warmth seeped into me. A tear rolled down my cheek, followed quickly by another. Down, down the golden droplets fell until I was sobbing, shaking, convulsing. I sobbed until my eyes swelled shut, sobbed for the family I had lost, both my parents and Michael, sobbed for the things I had done.

While I had probably destroyed families, I had also rid the world of evil. People slept peacefully because of the kills I had made. I had to be content with that knowledge. And know that Michael had done the same.

Finally, I drifted off to sleep.

When I awoke, the surroundings were unfamiliar

to me at first. It seemed like an eternity since I had gazed at this room, and it took me a minute to recall that I was inside my new apartment. The canopied bed, the coffee-colored walls. Lucius was still asleep, was still beside me.

I lumbered off the mattress and stumbled into the kitchen, where I fixed myself a glass of sugar water. I drank deeply. I was just refilling my glass, with every intention of dumping the contents in Lucius's face to wake him up, when he raced into the kitchen, a wild glaze in his ice-blue eyes. He stilled when he spied me.

"I now own you," were the first words out of my mouth. "You're bought and paid for."

"Hell, Eden. I nearly killed myself with worry about you."

"I know the feeling."

He stalked toward me, and his hard expression was the most beautiful thing I'd ever seen. Something I couldn't read glowed in those electric eyes of his. My heart thumped in my chest as he jerked me into his embrace.

"I thought I'd lost you," he said roughly. Rawly. He pushed me to arm's length. "Where the hell have you been? What happened?"

"I—"

His gaze went to my mouth. "Explain later. I've missed you too much." Then he was kissing me.

We didn't make it to the bed. We just pulled off

each other's clothes and went at it on the self-warming kitchen tile. I couldn't touch him enough. My hands were all over him, and his were all over me.

We strained and moved together, and when he entered me, I screamed with the force of my climax. His soon followed mine. And this time, we let the walls reverberate with the sounds of our pleasure.

In the aftermath, we lay together, panting. I explained what had happened to me after the sale. I even told him about Michael killing my parents.

His arms tightened around me. "I didn't know," he said. "I'm so sorry, baby."

"That's *cookie* to you." I brushed aside the pain inside me and smiled playfully. "And I'll get over it. I need time, that's all. Michael's a good man, and he loves me."

"He loves you a hell of a lot. Maybe not as much as I do, but he loves you all the same."

I jolted up and spun to face him. He'd offered the words so casually, I was afraid I'd misunderstood. "What did you say?"

His gaze bored deeply into mine. He didn't pretend to misunderstand. "I love you. I have for a while."

A weight lifted off my shoulders, and I suddenly felt lighter than air. I felt my mouth curl into a wide grin. "Well, I love you, too."

"Maybe now you can stop trying to prove yourself all the time." He cupped my face in his hands. "I know how great you are. There's no one better."

His words touched me, *freed* me somehow. I had his love. I'd closed this case and killed my target. I *had* proved myself. I *was* a success. "You're pretty amazing yourself, you know that?"

With a gentle tug, he urged me on top of him. "What did the Targon mean, that you'd made a bargain with him to free me?"

"I kissed him," I said. "Twice. And I'm not sorry. I would have given him everything to save you."

"Hell, I would kiss him too if it meant saving your life. Just make sure it doesn't happen again. You're mine."

I loved hearing those words. *You're mine.* "I'd believe you," I said, biting my lower lip and forcing an expression of desolation. "Except . . ."

"What?" he asked, frowning. "Except what?"

"I don't know your real name." I stroked his abdomen . . . then his cock. "Tell me, and I'll let you come." I squeezed him. Tight.

"Phineas Gaylord Hargrove," he said on a moan. "Now what the hell does the *F* stand for?"

"Wait." My hold on him loosened. "Did you say Phineas? Phineas Gaylord? You're kidding me, right? Trying to get me to tell you my deepest secret?"

"It's the truth," he growled. "That's my name, so put your hand back where it was."

I laughed until my side hurt. Now I knew why he'd guarded his name so zealously.

He sat up and tapped his fingers against the tile.

"I believe you have something to tell me, and I'm tired of waiting."

"Fine. I'll tell you. I bedeviled Michael so relentlessly, he added a middle name when he adopted me, making my name Eden Fucking Black."

Lucius gave a husky bark of laughter. "You're shitting me."

"I wish I were, *Phineas*."

He tried to level me with a glare, but his eyes were sparkling too much. We both burst into another round of laughter. But once the amusement subsided, we sank into a heavy silence. There was still something nagging and dragging between us, but I was loath to bring it up.

"Where's Agent Luc?" I finally asked, staying on safe ground by avoiding what we really needed to discuss.

"Safe. We can go get her, later. First, I have a confession to make." Lucius did what I'd been unable to do; he brought our troubles out into the open. "Michael paid me to guard you. He—"

"I know," I said, relieved that he'd finally told me.

"Don't be mad," he rushed on. "I realized early in the case that you could take care of yourself."

"I'm not mad." I intertwined our fingers and squeezed. "I'm grateful."

He stared at me for a long while. "Okay. Where's the Eden Black I know and love? I expected another knife at my throat."

I snorted.

"Maybe I should be mad at *you*. I wanted a piece of EenLi myself."

"Maybe I'll give you the next one. No, wait." I nestled my head into the hollow of his neck. My hair spread over his chest like a golden curtain. "I left the agency. As of now, I'm unemployed."

His fingers caressed the length of my spine, making me shiver. "Maybe we should start our own company."

"Maybe."

"Definitely. Tell me again about the Targon. I didn't like the way he looked at you during your auction, and I still don't like that he actually had his lips on you. I'm thinking he'll be our first target."

I laughed. I just couldn't help myself. I might be jobless, but right now, in Lucius's arms, life had never seemed more ripe with promise.

UP CLOSE AND PERSONAL
WITH THE AUTHOR

You called your parents "ass kissers" in the dedication of *Awaken Me Darkly*. Did you mean to do that?

First, I'm sorry, Mom and Dad! No, that was a total accident—although my mom tells me it must have been a Freudian slip. Thankfully, they found my mistake amusing. I had no idea I'd done it until my friend and fellow author Jill Monroe called me and mentioned it. Talk about being horrified! I'd meant to call my parents "ass kickers." KICKERS. K-I-C-K-E-R-S. And no, I'll never live this down.

How come Mia Snow didn't make an appearance in this book?

Have no fears, I do plan to bring Mia Snow back into play. In fact, she and Kyrin make an appearance in the third Alien Huntress book, *Savor Me Slowly*. Let's just say Mia and the star of that book do not get along. Eden Black and her man will be there, too.

Tell us more about this next book. Please, please, please . . .

Miska Le'ace, a woman whose DNA has been spliced and honed by scientists, making her an empath and gifting her with superhuman strength, is recruited by Alien Investigation and Removal agents to find and stop the alien wreaking havoc in near future New Chicago. Also, Jaxon can't resist her. . . .

Why don't you write these Alien Huntress books faster?

I also write paranormal romances, contemporary romances, and young adult books, so I promise you that I'm writing all the time, as fast as I can. I've even forgotten what *spare time* and *vacation* mean.

What do you like best about writing the Alien Huntress books?

Creating this world where the good guys aren't always good and are sometimes worse than the bad guys. It's exciting, thrilling, and I'm never bored. There's something absolutely wondrous about weaving the right words together and breathing life into a story, into people.

Who are some of your favorite authors?

I love a plethora of authors. Jill Monroe, Kresley Cole, Roxanne St. Claire, Louisa Edwards, Kristen Painters, Deirdre Knight, Nalini Singh, P. C. Cast, Karen Marie Moning, Katie McGarry, and Rinda Elliott. I could go on and on. Books—not just my own—are my passion. Reading is one of my favorite things to do.

Have you ever been abducted by an otherworlder?

No. But if there truly were an otherworlder, like Devyn, I might voluntarily go. However, I've been told by a certain friend (who shall remain nameless for now—oh, what the hell: *Kelli*) that Devyn is her property and I'm to keep my hands off.

Where do you get your ideas?

If I told the truth—from the voices inside my head (they're characters, so it's okay—I promise!)—I'd be committed, so I'll stick with my standard answer: everywhere. No conversation around me is safe, no action is exempt. God, I love my job!